Shades of Innocence

Shades
of
Innocence

Kurt Koss

ꝺP

Aventine Press LLC

Published by Aventine Press, LLC
2208 Cabo Bahia
Chula Vista, CA 91914, USA

www.aventinepress.com

ISBN: 1-59330-089-1
Printed in the United States of America

To my wife, Sandy, who may not be my ideal reader, but suffered through writes and rewrites and supplied timely encouragement.

one

Smoke hugged the tin ceiling of the obscure barroom stirred slowly by the clank-clank of overhead fans. Locals lined the bar boasting, laughing, complaining about their day at work. The Sand Dollar Bar, a prevailing haven for picking up women, was the third attempt for a successful establishment at that same location on the historic main street of Beaufort, South Carolina. Bulky pine tables surrounded a rectangular bar situated in the middle of the space. Outside, the picturesque inter-coastal waterway drifted lazily past the back porch reflecting the lights from the drawbridge a mile down the river.

Returning home with a willing woman became my sole objective for visiting the Sand Dollar. Flunking miserably as an accomplished drinker, potential lovers frequently surpassed my guzzling abilities resulting in many solitary nights. However, I was still in decent physical shape; no beer-belly, few age lines around the eyes, only a little balding on top.

As the Beaufort natives grumbled about their jobs, my blood boiled. Gainfully employed continuously since 16 had not prepared me for the humility of the layoff. After achieving 25 years of dedicated service with the same company, they locked the doors, leaving 200 others similarly disadvantaged.

With a keen eye, I scanned for potential female prospects. A fortyish attractive brunette poured into black jeans and matching colored T-shirt, sat silently by herself at the bar. Closely cropped pitch-black hair produced a mysterious, Mediterranean look, which became a definite turn-on for me. I recognized all of the other losers roosting at the bar except this stranger. She refused to look up as I gracefully moved onto the empty stool next to her and ordered a Heineken.

Slouched over the bar, the stranger leaned on her folded arms holding her head slightly above her shoulders. Her drink sloshed in the glass as she drained one after another. I observed her without staring. She had obviously been drinking most of that afternoon.

Although not a massive woman, it was evident by the toned arms and absence of any fat, she worked out often. Having no recollection of her presence in the Sand Dollar before that evening, I could not help wondering where I might have seen her otherwise familiar face. Similar to other lapse in memory as I grew older, I would not be satisfied until I could figure it out.

I could not help notice her head sluggishly sinking to meet her folded arms on the bar. Mindy the bartender witnessed her actions, or lack of, for a minute and then escaped into the kitchen. This was great luck for me, I imagined, finally finding fresh meat and she was half passed out.

The Sand Dollar requested William the cook, a 250-pound black ex-marine, to perform the traditional bouncer functions from time to time. Most of the time, he would suggest that a person leave the bar, and upon witnessing his size, they would vacate the bar without confrontation. However, William did not mind confrontation. In fact, he rather enjoyed it.

William circled behind me and approached the souse from behind. He solidly placed his massive hand on the woman's shoulder.

"Hey, Pal!" William commanded expecting a groggy drunk to slowly raise her head.

In one swift movement, the stranger rotated her upper torso, raised her left arm and planted her elbow squarely against William's face, spewing blood out of his nose and onto my khaki-colored pressed Dockers. Without taking a step, the stranger locked her leg around William's and slammed the 250-pound man to the deck scattering the wooden stool in pieces across the barroom floor.

The boisterous crowd quieted to a whisper and all eyes were on the action next to me.

I sat paralyzed on my stool contemplating a quick exit from the tense situation unfolding inside the bar. I had been in bars before when the bouncer threw out a drunk, but never before had I seen the drunk get the upper hand, and never before had it been a woman. William was a large ex-marine that was well trained and in excellent shape. I had never seen anyone kick his ass. This stranger was obviously a professional, to be able to snap out of a drunken controless state to defend herself without any wasted motion.

With her left-hand firmly cupped around William's throat and her knee placed powerfully against his groin, the stranger's fist coiled, ready to produce a knockout blow.

William lay motionless. He could already be dead for all I knew. "Stop!" I cried out sliding myself backward off my stool, surprised at what I had blurted, but preparing myself for a quick getaway.

The stranger stared at me with an intense yet drunken piercing stare that was difficult to describe. Surprised she had heard my cry for passivity, I was fearful that she would very likely kick my ass as well.

"You'd better get out of here. The black man that you just took down has a lot of friends around here," I continued my attempts to distract her long enough to slow her apparent rage.

The stranger looked back at William and seeing no movement, slowly released her unyielding grip from around his throat. Without saying a word, she staggered out the front door and out on to Bay Street. While several others went to William's aid, I trailed her out the front door. I am not completely sure why I followed my instincts, but I had a strong desire to confirm a conceivably earlier encounter with this stranger.

The inebriated woman turned onto the alley between the old block buildings and stumbled towards Riverfront Park. I pursued cautiously. Young couples occupied most of the good seats on the wall overlooking the Beaufort River. In the shadows cast by the massive live oaks, the outsider settled against a tree neighboring several couples. She supported her head in her hands looking extremely pathetic. After surveying the situation for several minutes, my curiosity got the better of me and I decided to approach.

"Hey. What was that in there?" I asked, keeping a little distance between us and hoping that I could outrun her if need be.

"What?" She afforded me that same stare as previously in the Sand Dollar.

"You all right?"

"Get lost."

"Look lady, this is a small town. I'm just trying to help you out."

"I don't need your help. I don't need anyone's help." She dropped her head back into her hands.

"You in the service or something?" I asked, persistent as hell.

"Why?"

"Cause there are a lot of soldiers around here, that's all," I answered.

"Do I look like I am in the service?"

"Well, yes you do. You look like you take care of yourself."

"Yea."

"Yea!" I moved a few steps closer as we had attracted the glances of one of the couples seated nearby.

"Yea, well, I was in the service. You could say that I . . . um . . . retired."

"You look kind of young. When did you retire?"

"Yesterday!"

"Really! Marines?" I asked, thinking specifically of the Marine Corps Air Station a few miles north of downtown.

"No!" she gave me a disgusted glare as if she had no respect for Marines.

"Navy?"

"You could say that."

"Seals?"

"Yea, I was a Seal for awhile."

"What else is there?" I asked.

"There are other programs."

"What other programs?"

"I really can't say," she answered protecting herself.

"Why not?"

"Cause I swore I wouldn't."

"You can tell me," I quickly replied.

"I don't even know you," she stared back up at me.

"I'm just trying to be a friend." I could not understand my unusual concern for this woman. I still could not place where I had seen her before, but something about her made me want to help her, even though she seemed to be resistant.

"I don't need any friends."

"Where you staying?" I asked.

"In town," the stranger answered.

"Where at?"

"I'd rather not say."

"Why not?" I asked, knowing that she was tiring of my questions.

"There may be some people looking for me."

"Who's that?"

"I don't know exactly."

"Are you in some kind of trouble?" I asked.

"Nothing I can't handle," she answered quickly.

"You got that right."

"You know that black guy in the bar?" she started asking the questions.

"Yea, he's the cook. I don't think he was looking for you. When he wakes up though, he might try to find you."

"Damn. I cannot handle whiskey anymore. What's your name?"

"Ben. Ben White."

"Ben, thanks for stopping me back at the bar. I guess I owe you one. I need to go and sleep this one off."

"Maybe, I'll see you around town," I said.

"I doubt it," the stranger said, "but thanks for your help back there."

"Here's my address," I handed her a generic business card I made while interviewing for jobs. "It's a small servant's house buried in the historic district. Maybe you'll need a place to disappear for awhile."

It had quickly occurred to me that I might get lucky after all and have some companionship for a change. I had been lucky a few nights since my wife and family moved out several months back, but no one quite as fit and attractive as this stranger.

"I'll be all right," the stranger said as she struggled to her feet.

"What's your name?" I asked.

"It might be better for you, if you didn't know."

"You're probably right."

The stranger headed west out of the park while I continued east towards the house I was renting. That would be the last time that I did not try to follow her.

two

Harsh light from the computer screen washed the living room walls as I opened the door of my historic servant's residence. Using the personal computer at all hours of the day or night, I became accustomed to the constant bluish light in the front room.

Because of my recent separation, I needed a cheap place to live. This cozy historic servant's quarters fell right into my hands when, at a bar, I overheard the previous tenant announce that he was leaving Beaufort. The owner of the main house resided in New York City and traveled to Beaufort only on occasion. To live in the servant's quarters I paid $100 per month and was responsible for maintaining the yard and handling basic maintenance on the main house. Still unemployed, with significant time available for keeping up the grounds, I knew I had a favorable deal.

Taking my customary seat in front of the computer, I clicked on the Internet icon. After e-mailing resumes to four companies earlier that morning, I optimistically checked for responses from those companies. When the computer screen came back to me, I clicked on the e-mail button.

NO MESSAGES.

How could that be? With so many resumes out to hundreds of companies, there must be someone out there that would hire me. After six tedious months of the same thing day after day, I became irreversibly depressed.

After my honorable discharge from the Navy, I was an optimistic twenty-two year old ready to set the world on fire. When I discovered an opening at a manufacturing plant, I quickly applied, and the company hired me the following day. I continue to remember the words of encouragement that my father gave to me the day I started working.

"Son. This is a great company to work for. You just need to get in and you can eventually retire there. You really have to screw up to be fired."

My father's words haunt me every time I think of the past 25 years. Each day I try to forget and move on, but I cannot.

Switching quickly to my favorite search engine, I searched the Internet for NUDE BEACHES, which was considerably less depressing. Thirty links quickly came up on the screen. I clicked on the one for Sandy Beach in Florida. I anxiously scanned all of the pictures looking for nude pictures of women. At the bottom of the web page, there was a link for INTRODUCTION TO NUDISM. A click of the button connected me to a website with no pictures. In the middle of this page was an advertisement for NUDISM IN EUROPE.

Following that link, a very colorful ad appeared with many unattractive nude women and men of all sizes on the opening screen. In the middle of this screen were links to other pages on the same site described as PREVIEW JOIN MEMBERS. I clicked on the JOIN button. A screen popped up immediately describing how to charge the $19.95 per month to view all of the pictures and videos on the site. Clicking on the cancel button, I jotted down the name of the web site in case I wanted to return to it some day.

Disconnecting from the Internet, I locked the front door, and went to bed.

#

Pressure on my bladder woke me from a restful sleep. Knowing very well my middle age limitations, I knew that I would not get back to sleep until I took care of the problem. With eyes half open, I shuffled out of the bedroom to the bathroom. Finishing in the bathroom, I moved towards the little kitchenette to chug from the tomato juice bottle.

"Don't you normally flush your toilet?" a woman's voice echoed from the couch breaking the silence and frightening me like never before.

"Jesus Christ! Who is there?" I cried out, startled.

"It is just me," the voice replied as if she had known me all of her life.

"Just who?" I asked, trying to make out the figure sitting in the dark.

The woman reached over and clicked on the lamp next to her. It was the ex-Navy Seal from the previous night at the bar. "You were sleeping so comfortably, I didn't want to wake you."

Still wearing the black jeans and black T-shirt, she was now in sufficient light to examine her face and body. She had a great build: slim at the waist, muscular upper body, and after a night of drinking appeared tired and worn.

"How did you get in here?" My blood pressure returned to normal.

"There are a lot of ways to get into places even when people don't want you to. This was fairly simple."

"What are you doing here? I asked, a little more relaxed.

"You invited me. Remember?"

"I . . . I guess so."

"Well, as it turns out, I could use a place to hang out for a few days until I decide what I'm going to do."

"Who you hiding from?" I asked.

"I don't know, exactly."

"The police?"

"That's precisely what I need to find out."

"How are you going to do that?" I asked, moving methodically to the chair across from her, combing my thinning hair with my fingers.

"Well, I see that you have a computer here. Do you have Internet access?"

"Yea, but how are you going to . ."

"There are many ways to find information, even if people don't want you to," she interrupted.

"But . ."

"I'll show you some things tomorrow. Is it all right if I crash here on the couch for tonight?"

"Yea, sure," I answered, still confused from the break in my routine.

"Thanks."

Shaking my head in disbelief, I retreated to the bedroom, and then turned as I got to the door. "If you're going to stay here, I need to know a name."

"Karen," she answered as if she had just made up the name.

"All right. Karen. Good night." Returning to the bathroom, I flushed the toilet.

Apparently confident that I would not take advantage of her, my new houseguest sunk quickly onto the couch and assumed the fetal position. Retrieving a wool blanket from the closet, I spread it over her as she lay safely in my living room. With an obviously forced smile, Karen shut her eyes and groaned pleasantly.

As I lay in bed, I wondered why I had not offered her my bed as I could have taken the couch. On the other hand, I could have suggested that she share the bed with me, even though, I still felt slightly intimidated by her presence. Time would help me overcome that problem.

#

Opening my eyes, I squinted at the clock next to the bed. Five thirty became a habit that I could not break from the many years of getting up and going to work early. The peculiar occurrences from the previous night crept into my head, as I lay motionless staring precariously at the ceiling.

Heading for the bathroom, I expected to witness my new roommate fast asleep on the couch. Instead, she sat in front of the computer screen punching away at the keyboard like a computer champion.

"Morning!" she said without turning around.

"Don't you need to know my password?" I asked.

"Not necessary."

"No, I mean my Internet password," I insisted.

"I already have it," she turned with a grin.

"How did you do that?"

"Remember, I told you last night that there are many ways to find out information, even if people don't want you to. Anyhow, I'm doing just fine."

"Oh."

"Don't let me stop you from going to work. I'll be just fine here," she said.

"I don't exactly go to work. I've been laid off," I replied pitifully.

"So . . . then . . . what do you do all day?"

"I look for jobs on the computer."

"All day?"

"Well, most of the day. Sometimes I just play around on the computer, waiting for some company to call me."

"Well, in that case, I'll get off in a few minutes."

"Take your time. I'm going to take a shower," I explained.

Karen continued to punch the keys after I returned from the shower. "What's this?" she asked, holding up the piece of paper with the web address for the NUDISM IN EUROPE site.

"It's nothing." Embarrassed from her finding the piece of paper, I hoped that she would not press the issue.

"It looks like something to me. Let's go there and see what we've got."

"It's not worth the trouble."

"Whoa. This is a great site. Have you gotten into it yet?" Seemingly, she was not at all shocked about the contents.

"No, I don't have a password and I am not going to pay for it," I answered reluctantly.

"Maybe we can find a password for you. Come on over here and sit down."

"How are you going to do that?"

"Hacking, man! Welcome to my Computer Hacking 101 Class."

"All right," I said, guiltily willing to give up my responsibility to search for a new job, and secretly enticed by the thought of seeing some gorgeous nude bodies. "I'm not doing very well at getting any other work anyhow."

"First. The easiest way to hack into a site that is password protected is to find out if others have already hacked into it. Let's go back to your search engine and type in HACKED PASSWORDS." The screen went blank and then came up with two links. "We'll choose this one, ARNOLD'S PASSES."

The screen switched immediately to the Arnold's Passes' site where there was a list of hundreds of adult web sites with login ID and password identified next to them.

"Whoa, I didn't know that this existed," I said.

"Let's see if we can find your site?" Karen quickly scanned down the list, faster than I could follow. She scrolled down past the section of recent passwords, to the next section of new passwords. "Right here." She stopped at the Nudism in Europe web site. "Let's click on this." The screen went black and soon came up to a screen that read WELCOME TO THE MEMBERS SECTION. "There you go. You are in. Make sure that write down the login and password, so you can get in next time."

"That was too easy. How did Arnold's Passes get this information?"

"People send in their passwords after they have paid the $19.95 or they have hackers that have discovered the web designers password or have found a backdoor into the site."

"What if you are trying to hack into a site that is not an adult site?"

"Well, you can still search the Internet for someone who may have hacked the site you are looking for, but if all else fails, hack it yourself."

"That sounds like it is beyond my capability."

"Most web site designers are so proud of what they create, they will print their name on the bottom of the site. They will also create an administrative login and password so they can get into the site while they are working on it. Sometimes, you can guess the web designer's login and password because they use their own name or their birth date or social security number or wife's first name."

"How would you know any of that information?"

"Well, if you know their name, you can use that to find the other information. There is a lot of information to be found on the Internet."

"I'm beginning to see that."

"Sometimes the web designer uses words like TEST or ADMIN or LOGIN. You just have to be persistent. However, if all of that fails, I do have a piece of software that will get to a good login and password. It works almost every time, buts takes a while to run."

"Where did you learn all of this?"

"OJT," she answered.

"What's that?"

"On the job training."

"What was the job?" I asked, knowing that she would probably not share that information with me.

"Let's just say that it was my job to find people that no one else could find."

"That's it?"

"That's not all, but I made it a point that no one could find me."

"And you made good money at that?" I asked.

"Good enough."

"So why did you retire?"

"I got a little careless, that's all," she answered reluctantly.

"You got caught?"

"Let's just say that they know who I am now, but they just don't know exactly where I am."

"Who are they?" I asked.

"Well, after checking some things out this morning, I'd say it's the FBI."

"The FBI? Jesus Christ Karen, am I in trouble?" I asked, shocked that I would actually know someone who was wanted and actively sought by the best investigators in the world.

"Nah. I'll be out of here before that happens."

"Where will you go?" I developed a knot in my stomach as I contemplated myself in the same position. And, what about being an accomplice? Regardless what Karen said, I was worried.

"Somewhere warm. I have to go get some money first."

"A bank?" I asked, not knowing whether she would make a withdrawal or hold up the place.

"No, never a bank, especially a domestic bank. That would be too easy to trace. I have hidden my money in different places."

"Where?"

"You ask a lot of questions," she complained. "Look Ben, I'm a lot like you are right now. I don't have a job. I don't know what I am going to do. I have dangerous people looking for me. I worked for a boss who will never again recognize me as being an employee. The last thing I need is to answer a lot of questions."

"I'm sorry. You're right. I am very pissed myself. I lost my job, my marriage, and at 48, I can't get anyone to hire me."

"You want me to logoff?" she asked, turning back towards the screen.

"No, that's not necessary. I am going to run out and get some groceries. Do you want anything from the store?"

"Yes. Please get me a box of blond hair color. I don't care which brand."

"Sure," I answered, wondering if this action was grounds for prosecution as an accomplice.

#

Returning from the store, I heard the faint sounds of the shower. After placing the groceries in the kitchen, I carried the box of blonde hair coloring to the bathroom. With the bathroom door slightly ajar, I paused outside deciding what to do. I could wait until she was finished, go into the bathroom and put the box on the sink, or I could go into the bathroom take off my clothes and get into the shower with her.

As I opened the door very quietly, unhappy for having an opaque shower curtain, I placed the box on the bathroom sink.

"I hope that's you Ben," Karen yelled over the sound of the shower.

"Yep. I just put the hair coloring on the sink."

"Thanks Ben."

"You're welcome."

"Oh, Ben? Check the machine. Someone left you a message. This might be your lucky day."

"I doubt it," I complained. Returning to the living room, I pushed the play button on my five-year-old answering machine.

"Ben, this is Tom Davis from Carolina Manufacturing Technologies. We spoke on the phone last week. I would like to get you up here in Charlotte for an interview. Please give me a call and we can get that scheduled. My number here is 704-555-3439. Look forward to hearing from you."

A brief sense of excitement returned as I reached for the phone to dial his number. After four rings, his voice mail picked up. Phone tag had become a way of life for me. Many of the recruiters or human resource managers would never answer their phone directly. Since this was for an interview, I decided to leave a message.

"Mr. Davis. This is Ben White returning your call. I would be pleased to come to Charlotte for an interview. I am available anytime for that trip and I will stay close to the phone awaiting your return call."

With all of my previous rejections, I forced myself to be respectful and anxious, but not too anxious. Tom Davis and I had not met other than the promising phone interview that we conducted the previous week. Mr. Davis' voice seemed much younger than mine. I normally would have no problem working for someone younger than myself except that the junior, recently educated managers always thought that they knew everything, when in fact, they knew very little about how to lead people.

Almost as quick as I hung up the phone, it rang again.

"Ben, this is Tom Davis again. I must have just missed you. When would it be convenient for you to come and visit us?"

"Any time that is convenient for you," I answered quickly.

"How about tomorrow?"

"Tomorrow is fine," I answered, trying to be as accommodating as possible.

"Would you be able to drive up here?"

"Of course."

"If you leave by 7:00 am, you should be here by noon. We'll go out to lunch and only keep you for a couple of hours. Does that sound all right?"

"Not a problem. Can you give me directions to your plant?"

"I'll send them to your e-mail address. Call me if you don't get them. I'll look forward to seeing you tomorrow."

"Thanks a lot."

Karen stood in the doorway of the bathroom wrapped in a towel eavesdropping on my conversation. "Well, does it sound promising?"

"They all do, at first. Then I have the interview and either I don't have the specific experience that they are looking for, the position has changed from what they had advertised, or they are only offering half of the money that I was previously making."

"Hopefully, you don't take that attitude with you to the interview."

"No, I'm a good actor. But I'm old enough to know now that if it smells like shit, and it tastes like shit, it probably is shit."

"Wow! You got it bad."

"Got what bad?"

"The blues, man. You need to go there tomorrow and knock their socks off," she sounded like my mother.

"Been there. Done that."

"Maybe you'll be surprised at this one," Karen added as she escaped back into the bathroom.

Returning from the bathroom, she wore the same jeans and T-shirt, but her hair was now a light blond. Karen was quite attractive as a blond as she had been as a brunette. She carried a perfect smile exposing luring white teeth surrounded by cheerful delicate lips that begged kissing.

At five foot nine inches, my recent houseguest could not have topped the scales over 120 pounds. I assessed Karen to be about 35 years old, but because she took such good care of herself, she could have been older. I enjoyed looking at her. Moreover, I was equally fond of her quick wit. She certainly did not fit the blond stereotype, as I sensed a sophisticated intellectual mind.

"Not bad, huh?" she boasted, seeking acceptance of her new look.

"You look great."

"Better?"

"I've always been a sucker for blondes," was my favorite line when meeting a blond for the first time. Of course, I also used the line for redheads and brunettes as well.

"You gonna be all right here by yourself tomorrow?" I asked.

"I'll leave when you leave tomorrow morning."

"Do you need a ride somewhere?"

"You could drive me as far as Charleston, if that wouldn't be out of the way for you."

"Can I ask you a question?"

"I think you've already asked me a lot of questions," Karen smiled.

"How did you get to Beaufort?"

"I drove."

"Where is your car?"

"It's not really my car. It's a rental."

"Don't you have to turn it back in?"

"No, they'll find it," she answered immediately without an apparent concern.

"Won't they charge you for it?"

"No, they'll be looking for a Carol Schwartz from 125 Fletcher Street in Newark, New Jersey. There is no such person."

"I'll be leaving early in the morning," I said, shaking my head.

"I rarely get much sleep anyhow," she admitted.

three

The alarm rang at 5:00am and I initiated a routine that I was very accustomed. Rising from my bed, I laid out my brown Glenplaid suit and took a long hot shower.

While I shaved that morning, I noticed the hair-coloring box in the wastebasket, and wondered whether I should color my hair. The graying began a few years earlier around the temples, but now had spread to where most of my hair was gray. For the first time I recognized my age. I would definitely remedy this situation before the next interview, if there were one.

Getting dressed, I left my tie loose around my neck and carried my suit coat. When I reached the living room, Karen, dressed in a new outfit, sat quietly on the couch. A small suitcase and backpack lay on the floor near the door.

"Mornin'," I said puzzled.

"Wow, don't you look professional."

"Thanks. Where did the bags come from?" I motioned towards the door.

"I went and got them from the hotel room last night."

"Any trouble?"

"Not at all," she answered quickly.

"Are you ready?" I asked.

"Let's go."

Throwing Karen's bags in the back of my Nissan pickup, I laid my suit coat over the back of the seat. The early morning allowed a very quiet ride past the old historic homes, live oak trees draped with Spanish moss, and the expansive tidal marsh that surrounded Beaufort. I hated to leave. Although this was just an interview, I feared my eventual move from Beaufort.

Karen laid her head back and closed her eyes. I stole a glance at her hundreds of times on the trip north. I sensed that she trusted me.

Arriving in Charleston at about 7:45am, I stopped on King Street per her specific instructions. The old brick and block multi-colored storefronts lined the street and it occurred to me that she did not want me, or anyone else, to know exactly where she was going. Sad to see her leave, this was the first time in a long time that I had the opportunity to really help someone.

"Good luck to you," I said.

"You've really gone out of your way to help. Thanks, Ben. Maybe I can repay the favor sometime. Good luck on the interview. And, if you don't get this one, I know that there is the perfect job out there for you."

"Bye," I said as she leaned over and softly kissed my cheek.

"You're a nice man," she ended it and slammed the door.

After she retrieved her bags from the back of the pickup truck, I observed Karen for as long as I could in the rear view mirror. I turned towards I-26 and my interview in Charlotte.

#

Palmetto palms lined the entrance to the Carolina Manufacturing Technologies plant. I eased the Nissan up the drive and parked in an open visitor's spot. It was 11:55am. I was seldom late for appointments. Actually, I was never late.

The manufacturing plant was clean and well landscaped, unlike some that I had recently visited in my pursuit of employment. Manufacturing awards adorned the walls in the lobby from customers I did not recognize. Gleaning as much as possible about the company, their products, and their customers before the interview, I studied all of the information provided in the lobby.

Walking up to the receptionist smiling, I signed in, then asked for Tom Davis. She punched in four numbers on her phone. You could always tell how big the company was by the number of digits in the phone extension. Four digits – medium size company.

"Mr. Davis? There is a gentleman in the lobby here to see you. Yes sir. A Mr. Ben White. Yes sir."

She turned back to me. "Mr. Davis will be right up."

"Thanks," I answered politely.

Avoiding any of the chairs, I strolled around the lobby reading the awards, mission statement, and EOE statement. After witnessing many lobbies at many manufacturing plants, I concluded that this one was no different. I observed the activities of the receptionist and other assistants through the window. They did not know how well they had it. At least they had a job and could look out at the rest of us poor suckers who did not. They had all of the power and I had none. With my tie now pushed up tight against my neck, I took a deep breath hoping I would have the answers that this company was seeking.

A youthful buck strolled up behind the receptionist, whispered something in her ear causing her to laugh. Dress pants and a black sport shirt with the company logo must be the culture around here, I thought. I was disappointed.

"Ben. Tom Davis. Nice to meet you." A firm handshake with a squeeze to announce the fact that he probably had the time to work out at a gym.

"Nice to meet you," I repeated.

He had to be all of 30 years old. I almost said sir to him but caught myself just in time.

"Are you ready for some lunch?"

"Sure."

"Did you have a good trip?" he asked as we made our way to his Lexus parked right by the front door.

"Yea, it wasn't bad." Then I remembered to say yes instead of yea.

"What kinds of food do you like?"

"All kinds, actually."

"I should have told you to dress casually for this interview."

"Well, I'm a bit of a dinosaur when it comes to office fashion. I like to dress professionally." I sincerely hoped that that comment would not come back to haunt me.

"This position that you are interviewing for will have a lot of involvement on the shop floor, so you will have to dress accordingly."

"I understand." I was again disappointed at the level of the open position.

We arrived at the restaurant and I ordered a small sandwich and ate only half of it. I had experience with eating a large meal and then interviewing. It did not work. We sat and talked about my Master's degree, my experience, and my objectives for a job. I asked what I thought to be relevant questions about the company and he asked questions about my management style.

We left the restaurant at 2:00pm and returned to the plant. I shook hands with a few of the management staff and took a tour of the manufacturing plant. It all seemed so repetitious. We returned to his office.

"Well, what do you think?" Tom asked.

"I think that I can handle the job and I would be successful here. I would like the job."

"That's great. We do have to interview a few more candidates, but I will call you and let you know what we decide."

"When do you think that you will be making a decision?" I had learned which questions to ask based on my many past experiences.

"Probably one or two more weeks," he answered, which probably meant one or two more months.

"Thanks for coming up," he escorted me to the lobby door. "I'll call you."

He will not call me. I will have to call him starting in two weeks, and will call every week after that until he finally tells me that they have selected someone else or they have decided not to fill the position.

Walking out to the truck, I removed my suit coat, and loosened my tie. I headed for the nearest McDonalds to finish my lunch before leaving Charlotte. Based on my assessment, I thought that the interview went very well. Then, I thought that all of the last 10 interviews went very well. Nine long hours of driving just for the opportunity to again receive rejection.

The sun was setting over a vast marshland as I drove over the final bridge to get onto the island where Beaufort is situated. The high tide and low sun reflected the palm trees from the banks. With the windows rolled down, the low country funk from the last low tide was a welcome smell. I really loved this area of the country and the history that surrounded it.

Re-hanging my suit in the closet, I wondered when I might be retrieving it again. Changing into shorts and a T-shirt, I placed a frozen dinner into the microwave and sat down in front of the computer. Per my normal routine, I clicked on the icon for the Internet and then on my e-mail. One message from Karen was waiting for me. The time listed on the e-mail was 2:00pm, so she must have found a computer in Charleston or maybe she had a place there.

Ben,

Thanks again for your help. I hope that your interview went well. Have you always been so thoughtful and ethical? Now that you have an e-mail address for me, stay in touch. Do not worry; no one can trace this e-mail account.

Oh, by the way, I copied that hacking program onto your computer. You will find it in your PERSONAL folder.

Good luck and I hope to be able to repay you sometime.

Karen

Removing the business card for Tom Davis from my briefcase, I wrote a quick e-mail to thank him for the interview. Searching my PERSONAL folder, I quickly found the new hacking program that Karen had placed there. EasyHack.exe was the file name. I double clicked on it to load it.

A simple white skull and crossbones against a black background filled the initial screen. The top of the screen displayed the words EASY HACK using an old English font. A single button on the bottom of the screen labeled LET'S PLAY was the only selection.

Clicking on the button, the screen went black, then logged on to the Internet, and a screen came up prompting the web address to be hacked. Not quite ready for this, I searched for the piece of paper that had the NUDISM IN EUROPE web address. Typing it into the box provided, I then hit enter.

The screen again went black until the figure of a pirate with his arms folded appeared and the words I AM WORKING ON IT flashed on and off. Remembering what Karen commented on the slow process, I went to the kitchen and removed my dinner from the microwave. It was still warm.

After 15 minutes, the computer beeped and a login ID and password displayed in large yellow letters. After locating the paper that I had written on the day before, the login and password on the screen matched exactly.

After accessing the Internet again, I followed a few links to other sites that were password protected, and then used the EasyHack software to determine the login ID and password. Although the software took longer than I cared to wait, it always came up with the right answer.

Searching for jobs on the Internet employment sites, I found the same jobs I had previously sent resumes to, so I decided to stop. Leaning back in my chair, I put my feet up on the desk. Frustrated, I attempted to envisage other businesses that I could develop instead of working for someone else. All of my deliberations concluded with some obstacle preventing further considerations.

I decided to return to the Sand Dollar to celebrate my successful interview. A few regulars were there and Mindy was again tending bar.

"I'll have a Heineken."

"There's a big surprise," Mindy replied.

"Hey, have you seen any more of that woman from the other night?" she asked while opening the green Heineken bottle.

"What woman?"

"The kung fu lady," she added.

"Oh, yea. No I haven't seen her," I answered, hoping to quickly change the subject and cover up any connection I had with Karen.

"Well, the FBI was in here asking about her."

"No kidding. What do they want her for?"

"They wouldn't say exactly. Some kind of investigation."

"How's William?"

"Broken nose, black eye."

"Is he pissed?"

"Yea, big time. He says 'if she ever come here gin, I gon pop a cap in her'."

"I believe he could."

"Any luck on the job search?"

"Nah. I had an interview in Charlotte today. It probably won't amount to anything."

"Too bad, I heard that Charlotte is a party town," Mindy smiled, knowing that I would identify with the comment.

After finishing the beer and spotting no new prospects, I decided to retreat home.

#

The next morning I awoke without the alarm. After a quick shower, I checked e-mails. My new landlord, owner of the big 1830's main house situated 50 feet across the yard, sent me an e-mail. He and his wife were coming down for a long weekend and wanted to make sure that everything was okay. Normally, that meant to have everything looking spotless. I replied to the e-mail assuring everything was great, looking forward to seeing him again.

Aware that I needed to work in the yard for the next few days, I changed into work clothes and at 7:30am headed for the garden shed. The sprinkler system kept the yard green but meant that the grass needed a trim twice a week. I retrieved the garden cart and wheeled it around the yard while I picked up twigs, branches, and Spanish moss that had dropped from the many massive live oak trees that covered the grounds.

Although working in the yard was very rewarding to me, I understood if I was working there, I was not out looking for a job. After taking a break for lunch, I drudged back to the yard to finish. By 4:00pm, I fell exhausted into one of the wrought iron yard benches and admired my accomplishments. I labored back to my servant's quarters, took a shower, then called to schedule a cleaning service to dust and clean the floors in the main house.

The telephone interrupted a well-deserved nap.

"Hello, Mother. How are you?"

"Well, I could be better," she answered with the standard complaints.

"What's wrong?"

"Well, I have been in a lot of pain."

"Did you go to the doctor?" I asked.

"Yes, and they are running some tests, but they don't know what they are doing."

"Mother, you have to trust someone."

"I know, but I don't think that he believes that I am in pain."

"Change doctors!" I suggested firmly.

"Oh, I can't do that."

"Why not?"

"Cause I have been with Dr. Gray for 20 years now."

"Maybe he is getting too old, Mother," I said.

"Any luck on a job?" she asked, changing the subject.

"No, not yet."

"Maybe you want too much money."

"That's not it," I said.

"Have you thought of managing a store of some kind?"

"Yes, Mother. And they all want specific experience managing a store just like theirs."

"Do you have any of your severance money left?"

"About a $1,000."

"That's it?"

"That's it."

"You know that I can't help you with money anymore, I barely have enough to live on," she said.

"I know that. I haven't asked, have I?"

"Have you seen your family lately?" she asked.

"Not for a month."

"Does that bother you?"

"Of course it bothers me. I really don't have anything to offer them right now."

"Do you think that money is the only thing that they need?" she asked.

"No. However, it is certainly a big part of it. Look, Mom, I have to go. I'll call you next week."

"All right. Bye now."

Hanging up the phone, I returned to my favorite pastime. Logging on again to the Internet, I checked my e-mail. One new message, again from my landlord.

Ben,

Mrs. Columbo and I will arrive at the house late on Friday night.

*Could you please leave the lights on for us? Could you also please
see me Saturday morning at the house at about 10:00am?*
   Thank you,
   Angelo
This was traditional for his sojourn to Beaufort. He desired
an account of what was happening in Beaufort and within the
neighborhood. He would also inquire about my recommendations
for any needed maintenance on the house or grounds.

Angelo Columbo was the stereotypical Italian with olive skin and
rich black hair. Never prying into just how he made his money, he
appeared very wealthy. Kathryn, his wife, easily 30 years his junior,
was strikingly attractive. I hardly ever saw her.

Daydreaming more about my newly acquired ability to hack into
password protected web sites, I contemplated various situations,
wondering how I could use this ingenuity to create a job for myself.
Too exhausted to think, I heated up some soup and then went to bed.

four

At 10:00am on Friday morning, after unlocking the door to the main house, I allowed the cleaning crew to dust and spruce up the place. While they wiped down about 6 weeks of dust inside, I swept the wrap around porches on both the first and second floors. Occasionally, I paused to scrutinize the Hispanic cleaning ladies through the windows. Only one of the two was halfway attractive, and she caught me watching her, so I stopped.

I had a standing appointment every six weeks with the Beaufort Unemployment Office to make sure that I was trying to get a job. Arriving at the office, on time as usual, I notified the receptionist of my presence and she instructed me to take a seat. After a five-minute wait, a frumpy looking man, early forties, short sleeve wrinkled white shirt and 20-year-old tie rescued me from the lobby of vagrants, homeless, and otherwise unmotivated losers.

The agent, looking as if he himself needed a job, asked a standard set of questions without looking up from the computer screen. I brought in a four-page list of companies that I had sent resumes during the month with indication of follow-up listing names and dates. The agent could have cared less and it soon became obvious that the only benefit that he could provide was an unemployment check for $190 a week for only a few more weeks. Associating with the likes of the unemployed was not only depressing, but became very embarrassing for me.

Friday evening, walking down to the Low Country Bookstore, I purchased a Beaufort Gazette. Mr. Columbo enjoyed reading the local news when he traveled to Beaufort and expected a recent paper to be at the house when he arrived.

Walking back to the main house, I noticed a front-page article about the new medical services building by Paris Island and another article about annexing the Marine Corps Air Station to the city. The Associated Press wrote one article, spread across the bottom of the front page, about Jonathon Stone, the rock singer from the 60's. The article reported on his life in the 60's, his songs and his addiction to heroin and alcohol. Unlike other rock legends from that era, he had invested his money well, and by the time his singing career ended, he had acquired significant wealth. Two side-by-side pictures depicted him both in the late 60's and from a few months earlier.

Jonathon Stone had a dilemma. Through years of alcoholism and drug addiction, his liver stopped functioning. Within two weeks of placement on the organ recipient list for a new liver, Jonathon Stone received one from a car accident fatality in Houston, Texas. Jennifer Jackson, a twenty-five-year old emergency room nurse, who previously registered to donate her organs in case of death, was involved in a head-on collision with a pickup truck. The EMTs were successful in keeping her alive until she reached the hospital, but she died from head injuries shortly thereafter.

The article went on to say that the demand for organs was at an all time high and that more and more citizens were registering their organs when they renewed their driver's licenses.

After placing the newspaper on the table next to Mr. Columbo's favorite chair in the den, I turned on the hall light, the porch light, and locked the front door behind me.

#

Awake at about 6:00am on Saturday morning, I looked out of the front window to check if the main house porch lights had been turned off. They had. At 9:55am, after walking to town for breakfast, I climbed the steps to the main house.

Kathryn opened the door and escorted me to the den where Angelo was watching TV. "Mr. White is here to see you," she said in a very proper English but hanging with the New York intonation.

"Ah. Come on in, Ben. Did you see this?" He was referring to a news program on TV about Jonathon Stone.

"That asshole. He thinks he can screw up his life and then buy his way out of trouble. He deserved to die. Now he will probably screw up someone else's liver. They should have given it to someone who deserved it. How in the hell do they decide who gets these organs? Stupido!"

"I don't know sir."

"Nah, I wasn't asking you. Come on in and sit down," Angelo commanded as he clicked off the TV.

Just as expected, he asked me about the local news in Beaufort and in the neighborhood. He wanted to know if any of the owners of the large homes in town were selling and how much they sold for if they did.

Angelo looked over his shoulder for Kathryn, and not seeing her he spoke quietly, "Mrs. Columbo will be going home alone on Monday and I will be at this number next week in case you need me for anything."

After handing me his business card with a phone number on it, I slipped it into my shirt pocket without examining. Understanding that our conversation was over, I drifted back to the servant's quarters, threw the card next to phone, and again placed myself in front of the computer. This was another first for my landlord. Never had he confided in me with a telephone number to contact him. It was almost as if these instructions were not pre-planned, but put together at the spur of the moment. The previous spring, when the sprinkler system failed was the only occasion I ever called him, and then I had only spoken with his secretary.

I quickly logged on the Internet and checked my e-mail. Upon receiving two automatic responses for receipt of my resume, I could almost recite these responses without seeing them.

Dear Mr. White,

Thank you for showing interest in employment at -----. We have submitted your resume to hiring managers at our company. If your qualifications match those requested for open positions within our company, we will contact you immediately. We will retain your resume in our files for one year.

Sincerely,

Do not call us, we will call you.

Per habit, I quickly deleted the two e-mails and leaned back in my chair. Glancing down at the card that Angelo presented me a few minutes earlier; I noticed that the phone number included a 305 area code. I went to a web site that identified area codes and entered 305 in the box provided.

A window popped up and identified Miami, Florida as the correct area code. A banner below the area code information advertised a telephone number lookup web site. Clicking almost automatically on the banner, I entered the full telephone number in the place provided.

The screen changed immediately and identified Bennett's Personal Vacations, with an address in Miami, Florida. Returning to the search engine, I typed in "Bennett's Personal Vacations". The first listing appeared to be exactly what I was looking for. I clicked on the name.

Palm trees and attractive Latin girls filled the home page of this web site. Across the top of the screen displayed in bold letters was "Erotic vacations for the affluent business client". The phone number at the bottom of the screen matched the number that Angelo Columbo had given me.

Scanning down the left side of the web page, I clicked on the DESCRIPTIONS button. The page that followed described vacations for men in either Costa Rica or Venezuela.

The page read, "When you arrive in country, you will be greeted by a representative and taken to a hotel room, where you can choose from many girls with which you will spend your entire vacation."

Clicking on the BACK button, I then selected the PICTURES OF THE GIRLS button. Pictures of topless girls with biographies describing height, weight, age, measurements, and specialties were crowded on the screen. I quickly clicked on the FAVORITES button so that I could save this web site.

Jealous that Angelo possessed the money to buy this brand of happiness, I wondered how often he took these vacations and further wondered if Kathryn knew anything about it. At that moment, it occurred to me; I had some dirt on Angelo and I should tuck it into my Cover My Ass file.

Clicking back to my search web site, something on the front page caught my eye: another article on Jonathon Stone. Selecting the article took me to a page and a half of text about the rock star's life and his recent medical problems. The bottom of the article led me to a link for the Gift of Life Foundation. Selecting this button, re-directed me to yet another conglomeration of superfluous information.

The Gift of Life Foundation, a non-profit organization, provided information on organ donation with statistics about donors and recipients. A sample downloadable donor card was also available to sign and return to the Foundation. Near the bottom of the screen was yet another link to the Texas State Organ Donation Program. Curious on the extent of detailed information I could find on this topic, I clicked on this icon as well.

The link transported me to the State of Texas Department of Public Safety web site, where I followed the link for the Organ Donation Program. Not designed as professionally as the other sites, the government site provided the same level of information. Another option on the page allowed the download of a donor card into a word processing document. Following the instructions, I printed out the card on my printer.

This site displayed, rather inconspicuously on the bottom of the screen, another link labeled "Participating Hospital Representatives". Clicking on this icon as well, a window popped up immediately requesting a logon ID and password. Not willing to admit defeat on my information gathering session, I decided to attempt to hack it. I wrote down the web address and then loaded my EASYHACK software.

Following the prompts, the program went off to do what it has done successfully many times before. Retreating to the kitchen, I grabbed a can of coke from the refrigerator, sat back down at the PC, and then gazed at the screen. After 15 minutes of inactivity and squandering of my available time, I sensed how unprolific my behavior had become and reached for the escape key. Just before I pressed it, the screen came back with an ID and password.

"ADMIN and ADMIN" showed on the screen and it reminded me again of Karen and her education on hacking.

Returning to the State of Texas Department of Safety web site, I clicked on the "Participating Hospital Representatives" button for the second time, but this time entered the ID and password that I had just hacked.

A new screen appeared, welcoming hospital administrators and doctors to the site. Several blue buttons down the left side of the screen provided options for the users. Clicking on each button to understand the information available, I focused the most attention the bottom-most button labeled "List of Active Donors". I clicked on it.

The subsequent screen displayed an inventory of names, addresses, phone numbers, blood types, and potential organs available in case of death. The list only cataloged Texas residents. Buttons along the top of the screen allowed the user to view the register sorted by name, by city, or by organ.

The name of the young Houston woman who perished in the car accident that I previous read about in the newspaper, somehow escaped me. Remembering Angelo Columbo retained the newspaper I had read, I put on my sandals and returned downtown to the bookstore.

Margaret Smalls, the elderly owner of the Low Country Bookstore, always confronted her customers as they walked in the front door.

"Twice in one week, Ben?"

"Yea, I guess so." Sauntering to where the newspapers were precisely stacked on the floor, I was pleased to again be working towards something. "Yesterday's paper sold out?" I assumed her negative response.

"The Gazette picks up the old ones when they deliver the new paper."

"Crap!"

"I thought you already bought a paper this morning." Margaret placed her frail clenched fists on her hips.

"That paper was for Mr. Columbo," I said.

"Oh yea, is he back in town?"

"Just for the weekend."

"Do you remember the article about Jonathon Stone, the 60's rocker?" I asked, hoping that she would remember the young woman's name.

"I remember. I really feel sorry for the girl that died in the car accident. I can't say that I feel very sorry for Mr. Stone."

"Do you remember her name?"

"No, why?"

"Oh, my Mother thought that she knew her Mother," I lied.

"Where would I have my best chance at finding a paper?"

"Is that all you want it for?"

"Yea," I answered.

"Well, I suppose that we could look it up in my paper here," Miss Smalls explained as she pulled a folded newspaper from under the front counter. Sifting through the folded bundle, she placed her reading glasses on her nose and scanned the article. "Jennifer Jackson."

"Can I see how that is spelled?"

"Why would you care how it is spelled?"

"Cause my Mother will want to know," I lied again.

"Thanks a lot." I made it to the front door before she glanced up from the paper.

"Hmm," she grunted as the bell on the door jingled.

Back at my computer screen, I scanned down the list of donors, sorted by the donor's last name. When I reached the letter J, I quickly found Jennifer Jackson, 20494 Cypress Lane, Houston, TX, 281-555-5259, Heart, Kidneys, Liver, Tissue, Blood Type O Negative, DOB 10/2/76.

Impressed with my recently acquired Internet abilities, I sensed a slight increase of self-esteem creeping back into my otherwise depleted psyche. I admitted pleasure, finding information that others could not. Wishing I could make money utilizing these new skills, I saved the thought for future reference.

Reminiscing about Karen and her latest visit, I relived the moments we were together and chastised myself for not taking advantage of the situation. She probably expected some advances, but I had to play it like a gentleman. Just one of my many mistakes, I thought, to supplement a growing list.

Saving the address for the Texas organ donor web site, I logged onto my e-mail. No new messages. Returning to the message that Karen had previously sent me, I clicked on reply and wrote:

Dear Karen,

Was thinking about you. Hope that things are going better for you now. The bartender at The Sand Dollar said that the FBI was in there looking for you. Still no luck on the job search for me. I have been practicing on hacking into web sites. It is kind of fun finding out information on people when they probably would rather keep it confidential.

Anyhow, I know that you were only here for a little while, but I miss you. Drop me a line sometime.

Ben

After clicking on the send button, I logged off the Internet, turned on the TV and lay on the couch. Surfing religiously through all of the stations available from the cable station, the remote control ceased at the soccer game between the United States and Brazil. Shortly after placing the remote on the coffee table, I fell sound asleep.

A thunderous rapping on the front door awoke me, and assuming it was Angelo, I jumped up quickly and flew open the door. Two clean-cut young men with dark suits filled the doorway. The gentleman on the left advanced his foot onto the threshold, preventing door closure.

"Are you Ben White?" the unyielding black man inquired with a matter of fact quality.

"Well, yes," I answered, still surprised that it was not Angelo.

"We have a few questions to ask you," the other agent barked.

"Who are you?"

Both men simultaneously retrieved identical looking identification cards with badges from their inside coat pockets.

"We're from the FBI. I'm Agent Barnes and this is Agent Orlando."

"What do you want?"

"We would like to ask you a few questions about what happened at the Sand Dollar Bar last week."

"I don't know what you are talking about," I answered, trying to exhibit a consistent demeanor.

"Can we come in?"

"Well, I guess so, I don't know if I can be of any help."

"Were you at the Sand Dollar Bar last Tuesday evening?"

"I don't remember, I probably was."

"Do you remember sitting next to a woman at the bar?"

"Do you mean the one that cold-cocked William, the cook?" I answered, sensing that they already knew I was there and that there had been a disturbance.

"Yes. Do you know this woman?"

"Hell no!" I answered.

"There were several people in the bar that have reported that you left the bar with her."

"I left the bar after she did," I corrected Agent Barnes.

"Did you see her after you left the bar?"

"No, I went home." This was the first time that I had ever perjured myself in front of law enforcement.

"Have you seen this woman since that night in the bar?" Agent Orlando asked immediately.

"No," this was my second lie. I hoped that my deceit would not come back to haunt me. I also hoped that I would never be subjected to a lie detector, as I would clearly flunk.

"Here is my card. Call me if you see or hear from her again. You can leave me a voice mail message at this number or page me at this number," Agent Barnes explained as he pointed to the business card.

"What did this lady do?"

"We just need to ask her some questions. Routine FBI work," he answered.

As the two agents left, I observed them for a while through the curtain in the door. The agents stood briefly on the lawn, pointed towards the main house, then wandered back in the direction of downtown Beaufort.

Again, my recollections raced to Karen. Surprised that I first lied to Mindy at the Sand Dollar, I followed up with lies to Margaret Smalls at the bookstore and now I had lied to the FBI. These were not small white lies. They were serious untruths. Moreover, in some strange way, I did not feel guilty. Fatigued of the mundane routine I once knew, I welcomed the new unique challenges that presented themselves.

Was it Karen that had changed me? How could it have been? Did I enjoy her company or was I envious of her adventurous lifestyle? Too many questions. We had not even touched.

I grabbed a Heineken from the fridge, my last residual luxury from my working days, and after taking a shower, I yet again trolled the bars downtown.

Five

After Sunday came and went, I resolved that on Monday I would hit the job search boards heavy and start calling back on previous contacts. Scheduling time Monday afternoon, I set aside time to be creative about starting my own business.

The early morning heat became too much for the inefficient air conditioner and sweat dripped down my back as I cooked eggs in the kitchenette. Transforming from quiet to business hustle bustle, the work crowd outside my bungalow returned to work after a South Carolina summer weekend. I remembered my work life with intense pleasure.

Another knock on the door and Karen came to mind again, but she never would knock, just pick the lock, and show up when I would least expect it.

At the door, a gray haired businessman dressed in very posh business casual clothes, heavy gold chain disappearing into a bushy chest, stood impatiently waiting to deliver some information.

"Hey, where's Angelo?" the man commanded in a haughty tone.

"He's not here."

"I thought that he came down this weekend."

"Look, I don't know what to tell you, but he is not here." I was reluctant to supply information about my boss and landlord, learning a little in my years in business.

"My name is William Bradfield. I'm a business associate of Angelo's from New Jersey."

"Ben White," I interrupted his speech and extended my hand.

"Nice to know you Ben. Do you know where Angelo is?"

"I really can't say."

"You can't say because you don't know or you can't say because he told you not to?"

"I really can't say."

"Then I know that you know. Can you get in touch with him?"

"I would rather not."

"Well, let me tell you. I am interested in buying this house here in Beaufort."

"This property?"

"Yes. Tell him that I am ready to make him an offer today. A very lucrative offer," Mr. Bradfield explained confidently.

"I can't guarantee that I will be able to contact him."

"Why don't you give me his number?"

"I won't do that. I will do my best to contact him. Why don't you come back right after lunch? What do you want me to tell him?"

"Tell him he's a sonofabitch and that I was hoping that we could celebrate this sale together. Tell him that I won't go home until we have come to an agreement."

"I'll do my best."

"Thanks Ben. I will see you at 1:00 sharp. I will have a written offer with me. If you need me before that, I'm staying at the Beaufort Inn."

So much for my plans to seriously look for work that day. As I looked for the card that had the Miami phone number on it, it occurred to me that if Angelo sold the house, I would have to look for another place to live.

The telephone rang five times until a young woman with a Cuban accent answered.

"Bennett's Personal Vacations. This is Maria, how can I help you?"

"Hello Maria, my name is Ben White. My boss gave me this number in case I needed to get in contact with him."

"What is his name?" she asked professionally.

"Angelo Columbo."

She paused while she was obviously locating his name in their records. "It might take a few hours. I am assuming that this is an emergency. Mr. Columbo is on vacation and we try not to disturb the precious few days that our clients get for vacation," she announced as if reading off a cue card.

"I've thought about that, and I believe that he would want to be contacted."

"Very well. What number should he return the call to you? Are you sure that you will be at that number for the next few hours? You will not be able to call him back except through this number."

"845-555-2225. I'll stay close to the phone."

"I will get a message to him. I cannot guarantee that he will want to call you back."

"I understand. Thanks for your help."

"Good bye Mr. White."

Quickly logging on to the Internet, I checked my e-mail. Reluctant to stay on the computer very long because of only one phone line, I hurried so I would not miss Angelo's call. Since I had no e-mails, I logged off.

Placing the phone on the coffee table, I lay down on the couch. As I picked up a book that I had not read for months, I tried to start reading at the bookmarker, but needed to reread the previous chapter to get into it. As I reached my old starting point, I fell asleep.

The ringing phone woke me. I sat up quickly and looked at my watch. It was 10:30am.

"Hello."

"Is this you Ben?"

"Yes sir," I recognized Angelo's voice.

"Actually, I knew that it must be you because you were the only one that has my number. What's up? Everything all right there?"

"Yes sir. It is. I had a visit from a Mr. William Bradfield."

"No shit? I guess he was serious about coming down. Sometimes you just don't know if it's just bullshit," Angelo spoke in words and a casualness that I had never heard from him previously.

"Yes. He said that he would like to buy your house in Beaufort."

"No shit?"

"He said that he would be back at my place at 1:00pm with a very lucrative offer."

"Wow. That's great news, Ben."

"Should I fax this offer to you sir?"

Surprisingly, Angelo responded immediately, almost as if he expected the offer and had already worked out a plan, "no."

"No?"

"No, I want you to bring it to me. I am having a lot of fun here and I do not want to leave. Are you busy for the next couple of days?"

"Well, I guess not," I answered, trying to think of reasons not to go, "I . . . my passport has expired."

"What makes you think you need a passport?"

"Aren't you in Venezuela?" I asked, forgetting how I had acquired this information.

"I never said that I would be in Venezuela. How did you know?"

"I guess that I snooped a little bit on the Internet using the phone number you gave me."

"Then you know where I am and what I am doing."

"I believe so sir."

"Do you have your original birth certificate?"

"Yes."

"That's all you need. I'll call my secretary in New York and have her book a flight this afternoon. Felicia will call you with the itinerary as soon as she books it. You can pick up the tickets at the Savannah airport. Pack for a couple days. And don't forget to bring the offer."

"All right, I'm not doing anything else productive. I might as well."

"Good man, Ben. You are going to have a great time. I'll have someone pick you up at the airport in Caracas. Oh, tell Bill that I'll call him as soon as I read the offer."

"Thank you sir."

After hanging up the phone, I retrieved the suitcase from the bedroom closet and thought about whom I should advise on my trip to Venezuela. However, after a second thought, no one would care if I was leaving the country for a couple days, except of course Angelo Columbo. Packing a few pair of shorts, some Dockers and some short sleeve collared shirts; I acknowledged how proficient I was at packing.

At 12:00 noon the phone rang again. It was Angelo's secretary. She provided the itinerary that had me leaving Savannah at 3:30 that afternoon and arriving in Caracas at 11:30pm. Hoping Mr. Bradfield was prompt for his 1:00 pm appointment, I detested the drive to the airport in Savannah with limited time available. At precisely 1: 00pm, I witnessed Mr. Bradfield out the kitchen window, strolling across the yard and down the sidewalk to the servant quarters that I might soon have to leave.

"Did you contact him?" he asked.

"Yes sir."

"Are you going to fax this to him?"

"No, he wants me to bring it to him. Mr. Columbo said that he would call you as soon as he reads the offer. Do you have a number where he can contact you?" Angelo had not asked for this, but I thought that it was pertinent.

"When will he get this offer?"

"Tonight. Late. Tomorrow morning at the latest."

"All right. Don't lose it, Ben White."

"I won't sir."

Although I normally left the computer turned on all of the time, I decided to shut it down for the three days I was to be away. I also disconnected the phone line, turned off the lights, and turned up the thermostat. Halfway out to the pickup truck, I remembered that I had left the manila envelope with the offer on the coffee table.

The long-term parking lot at Savannah Airport was half-empty and I located a spot very close to the terminal building. With a short line at the Delta ticket counter, I was ticketed and at the gate within minutes. Since Mr. Columbo was wealthy, I had expectations of first class, but settled for the coach seat his secretary booked.

It was not easy to get from Beaufort, South Carolina to Caracas, Venezuela. After flying to Miami, I connected through San Juan, and finally on to Caracas. My fellow passengers became more Spanish speaking on each consecutive flight. Concerned about the connections after I arrived in Caracas, I visualized some miscommunication based on the language barrier, but in the end, trusted that Angelo would take care of all details.

A Spanish speaking voice on the intercom woke me as the DC-10 descended toward the Simon Bolivar International Airport. Millions of lights lit up the sky as the city of Caracas welcomed me on a lucid night. It reminded me of the late Friday night flight across Lake Michigan into Chicago.

English and Spanish signs crowded the airport terminal ceiling directing the arriving international passengers to immigration and customs.

"What is purpose your visit to Venezuela?" the uniformed officer barked across the immigration counter.

"Business," I answered, hoping that it would also be a bit of pleasure.

"Where will you be staying, Mr. White?"

"I am not sure. I am meeting someone here at the airport. I'll find out my accommodations from them."

"Very well. Welcome to Venezuela," he said without smiling. "Next."

Folding tables with open suitcases cluttered the customs area. I claimed my dirty black suitcase in Baggage Claim and the Customs Officer waived me though without inspection. Perhaps he did not want to get his hands dirty, I thought.

Just outside the customs area, passengers greeted family and friends while I frantically searched for someone with a sign. Moving through the crowd a young well-dressed Latino held a Bennett's Vacations white board with "Ben White" illegibly written on it.

"I'm Ben White."

"Good evening, Mr. White."

"I am Paulo. I am to drive you to the hotel. I will take this bag. How was your flight?" Paulo asked with perfect diction.

"Okay. Thanks." I allowed him to carry the suitcase.

The silver Peugeot whisked us away through the narrow streets of Caracas towards the beaches to the North. At 12:45am, we pulled into the reception area of a Sheraton resort hotel in La Guaira. Paulo popped the trunk and carried my suitcase up to the check-in counter. He spoke with the well-tailored hotel representative in local Spanish, I signed a card and I was off with a bellman to my room.

"I will pick you up here in the lobby at 9:00am. I will escort you to the island where Mr. Columbo is, per his instructions. Feel free to order breakfast from room service. Mr. Columbo will take care of all of your expenses. You will be returning to the hotel tomorrow evening, so leave your personal items in the room." Paulo instructed as he shook my hand and we parted company.

Gaudy exorbitantly pricey drapes and bedspreads distinguished the dark cherry brown wood of the chiffonnier and king size headboard. The full moon reflected off a calm ocean as the 10th story view made its way out to the Caribbean. Lights on the horizon led me to believe that an island situated a few miles off shore might be the island where Angelo was staying.

After unpacking, I showered, dressed, and then rode the elevator up to the bar on the roof of the hotel. Brilliant neon lights lit the dance floor where several couples danced to an upbeat ten-year-old rock song. A scattering of men hovering over Latino women occupied more than half of the tables. It was 1:30am.

A very lavish mahogany bar finished the room on the left. I selected one of the three open stools between two couples.

"What'll you have?" a very engaging bartender placed a napkin between her and me.

"What do you recommend?"

"What do you like?"

"I like drinks with rum. Surprise me," I answered wanting a change from my normal Heineken.

"Somehow I don't think that anything would surprise you," she played back laughing.

"You're wrong, I'm just a rookie."

Sasha brought back a red colored drink with fruit anchored at the rim, "should I start a tab?"

"Sure."

The groping dancer's reflections in the mirror during a slow song made me think about vacations that Kathy and I had taken during the beginning of our marriage. We spent a week every spring at some island in the Caribbean. For an instant, I felt more alone half way across the world than I did at home for the entire last year.

The man to the right of me was obviously trying to pick up the woman who sat next to him. Black dress pants with a black sweater shirt accentuated his well-oiled jet-black hair. He worked very hard convincing the classy lady that he was important. I did my best to listen in. Maybe I could learn something, I thought.

"So, what do you do for a living, Warren?" she asked him after sipping a clear drink on the rocks.

"I work for the government."

"Which one?" she asked, making jest of his answers.

"United States Government," he answered and they both laughed.

"That's not too specific. Is it a secret? Are you the President?" Her quick wit reminded me of Karen.

"Actually, I am a Deputy Director in the Office of Special Programs from the Health Resources and Services Administration of the Department of Health and Human Services," he answered, too proud to recognize her ridicule.

"That's more specific. Just what do you direct, deputy?" she smiled and I tried not to laugh aloud.

"Well, basically . ."

I hated people who started a sentence with "basically". This overused word made a person sound so stupid they could not understand anything that was not "basic". I did not know this guy and already I did not like him.

"Basically, I oversee a newly created program that was assigned by the National Organ Transplant Act. I worked on a congressional committee that wrote the act. Then I was hired to administer the department."

"You appear to be awfully young to have that much responsibility," she observed.

"Well, I don't know, I have BBA and a Masters in Public Administration. I developed this national database to store the names of those individuals who are in need of organs for transplant. You see, there have historically been problems with quickly matching donor to recipient. My system is available to donating organizations and prioritizes recipients ranging in condition from non-urgent to urgent."

A few words in his sermon struck a familiar chord. Where had I heard something about organ transplants? Then it hit me. It was the newspaper article about Jonathon Stone; the conversation I had with Angelo. I turned my head to better hear the conversation, although our modern day Don Juan was sufficiently loud.

"Sounds important to me. How did you ever get that job?"

"It probably didn't hurt that my father was the Senator from Florida," Warren explained.

"Your father is Clark Smithson?" the businesswoman looked for a resemblance in his face.

"Yes."

"Well, it is a mighty small world," she admitted.

I removed a bar napkin from the stack and retrieved the pen near the cash register. "Clark Smithson, Warren Smithson," I wrote on the napkin and stuffed into my pocket. Just more fodder, I thought, for my Internet search craving.

"Do you know him?" Warren Smithson asked.

"Let's just say that we know each other. Look, Warren, it is time I called it a night," she abruptly modified the pace of the conversation.

"But, the night is still young."

"And it seems to be getting younger. Thanks for the drink and chat."

"But, wait a minute. . ."

"Sorry Junior, gotta go," she left before he could argue further.

Warren Smithson stared as his most recent victim left the bar, then scoped out the rest of the room in search of other prey. I shook my head in disbelief. This must be how they do it today. Must be nice, I thought, to have the money to jet down to Caracas, Venezuela and cruise for chicks. Hell, I had a Masters Degree, why didn't I have the money to do the same thing. The answer was simple; I did not have a job. I came back to my senses and then felt worse. I signed for my drink and went back down to my room.

six

The wake up call from the hotel front desk performed per plan at 7:00am. Strolling to the window wall filled with a view of the Caribbean, I glanced down to see a few gray haired people chased by the waves as they strolled the beach beneath me.

After ordering a large breakfast from room service, I showered, dressed with swim trunks under my Dockers and waited for the delivery. After devouring breakfast, I retrieved the manila envelope from the dresser and rode the elevator to the lobby. Paulo was waiting there for me.

"Did you sleep well?"

"Yes, very well. Thanks," I answered as professionally as he asked.

"We will be driving down the beach for a few miles and then we will catch a boat to the island."

"How far is the island?" I asked, trying to get an idea of what was in store for me.

"Just a few miles from the mainland. It just takes a few minutes, and is the only way to get to the island," Paulo explained.

The silver Peugeot sped to a small dirt driveway leading to a weathered dock with a small open fiberglass boat tied to it. Straight out from shore, a small island with palms lining the powdery beach approached quickly. Small indigenous huts nestled down beneath the palms with sand extending to their front doors. Wide double hammocks hung from the supports of the porches on each hut.

We tied up to a small dock and I followed Paulo to a larger shelter with pool situated amongst a scattering of palms. Gray haired men surrounded the pool on deck chairs in small private coves fashioned from the tropical landscape. Young attractive Latino women lay out next to each of the men, all of them topless, some wearing no bathing suit at all. A few unattached young women playfully splashed each other in the pool.

Half way around the pool, I spotted Angelo, wearing flowered green trunks and reflective sunglasses. Next to Angelo, a fit young girl, not more than 19 years old, lay face down on the lounge.

"Ben. Come on over and sit down."

"Good morning Sir. Interesting place," I acknowledged, stealing a quick look at the topless girl lying next to him.

"The best that money can buy."

"I can see that."

"Ben, this is Suzy. She doesn't speak a word of English, but we seem to get along just fine."

Extending my hand to hers, she accepted it into her own and then rubbed the top of my hand with her thumb. It got my attention.

"Well, what do you have for me?" Angelo asked.

"This is the offer sir."

"Let me see this," Angelo took the sealed envelope, opened it, and started to skim the ten pages of contract language.

"This is not bad. I am going to need to crunch some numbers for a couple hours. Did Mr. Bradfield leave a number that I could reach him?

"Yes sir," I searched my wallet for the card that Angelo had given me on which I had written the phone number for Mr. Bradfield.

"Here sir."

"Did you bring a suit with you?" Angelo asked.

"I'm wearing it."

"Good. These young girls in the pool are unattached and with a little coaxing, you might convince one of them to escort you to my hut. I have left a hundred dollar bill on the dresser, which should be plenty."

"Thanks a lot. Which hut?"

"Number 3, down that way."

Walking quickly to an empty lounge chair, I stripped down to my trunks and slipped into the water. The girls welcomed the companionship as they quickly surrounded and stroked my arms and legs, almost as if rehearsed. Glancing back at Angelo, I witnessed him retreating to the resort office. He smiled on his way and gave me a thumbs up.

None of the girls spoke English and I did not know Spanish, but we mutually understood the physical language of pleasure. We caressed in the water for a few minutes, and then Natalie, Jasmine and I departed the pool for the privacy of Angelo's hut.

Bamboo walls, palm fronds, and wooden floors adorned the inside of the cabana. Mosquito netting gathered above the bed and spread out over the sides. Already topless, the young girls peeled off the bottoms to their suits and crawled under the netting onto the king size bed.

What a fantasy for me after many months of frequenting singles bars hoping beyond hope for a relationship, any relationship. How could I have ever earned this kind of opportunity to be lying on a bed on an island off the Venezuela coast with two young beautiful Latino girls? Was it fate? Others have said that it was being at the right place at the right time, but sometimes I wondered.

Jasmine, maybe a year older than Natalie, could not have been more that twenty years old. Shoulder length black hair framed a dark soft perfect complexion. A well-tanned body with slight tan lines defining a minimal bikini bottom augmented a very young toned frame. Medium sized firm breasts accompanying a small waist and a cute white smile would have triggered a heart attack for any of the men back at the Sand Dollar Bar.

Natalie seemed slightly more spiritual, seldom smiled, but her eyes captivated me. She also carried shoulder length jet-black hair with a much slender figure. Completely void of any fat, Natalie had muscle definition in biceps, legs and tummy.

For the remainder of my life, I fondly remembered the hour spent with Jasmine and Natalie. Completely exhausted, the three of us lie on the bed with the ceiling fan blowing full strength. Suzy walked into the hut, uttered some words in Spanish to the girls and exited to the bathroom for a shower.

Stepping out of the shower into the bedroom without concern for her privacy, Suzy toweled herself off in front of the three of us. What a morning it had been for me.

"Angelo!" Suzy said pointing toward the pool area.

Assuming she brought a message for me from Mr. Columbo at the pool, I resolved that my fantasy had come to conclusion. Rolling to my right, I kissed Jasmine fully on the lips. To my left, I forced my leg between Natalie's and kissed her on the cheek. She wrapped her arms around my neck and pulled me close.

While dressing slowly, I intently watched the three girls as long as I could, imprinting the scene in my brain, where I hopefully could replay it at will. Finding the hundred-dollar bill on the dresser, I held it up so that Natalie and Jasmine could see it.

"Thank you very much," I said slowly, hoping that they understood.

"Mochas Gracious," they said in unison with smiles.

"Bye."

Strolling exhausted through the palms along the path towards the pool, I imagined how great the life for those who could afford happiness. Angelo, now sitting at a table on the porch of the resort office with fans turning slowly above him, gestured for my attention.

"Ben. Come on over and sit down."

"Thanks."

"Have a good time?"

"Yes sir. Thank you very much for the opportunity."

"My pleasure. Thanks for coming down. I have already called William and we have come to an agreement. I need you to take this document back tomorrow. Your flight leaves tomorrow at 6:00pm. At least you will have this afternoon and all of tomorrow to enjoy Venezuela."

"So, you're selling?" I asked.

"He made me an offer that I couldn't refuse, as they say."

"Does that mean that I will be looking for a place to live?"

"Probably. He said something about a niece or nephew attending University of South Carolina and they would stay in the servant's quarters. In any case, you probably have two months to find another place to live."

"Well, that's too bad. I kind of like your lifestyle."

"I work hard at it. Here is the signed purchase agreement. William Bradfield's phone number is inside. Call him when you get back to Beaufort. Paulo is waiting for you down at the boat. Thanks again Ben."

"Thank you sir."

Before stepping onto the boat, I glanced back one last time toward the pool and saw Angelo with arm around Suzy. To say that I was jealous would significantly understate my feelings at that moment. On the ride back to the mainland, I decided to get serious about making money and someday return to Venezuela and this island. I only hoped that I would not be too old to enjoy it.

I spent the entire afternoon soaking up the near equator sun on the beach in front of the hotel. The English speaking women wore full bathing suits while Spanish, French, and Dutch speaking women felt comfortable topless. In any case, the scenery was very acceptable to me. I remained all day, applying generous amounts of sun block, afraid if I left, I would miss something.

Room service brought lobster with a baked potato and a local vegetable. The fiery orange sunset spectacle from my hotel room complemented the pure delight of dining perfection. What a day it had been!

What a life it could be too, if I only had money. Lack of money had always been an issue with me, however some income was significantly better than no income. Angelo was not that smart. How hard could it be? The key is a good idea, I thought. Unfortunately, I still did not have one.

In the quiet of the hotel room, I lay on the bed and starred at the ceiling. I had not thought about God for at least the last year. I used to pray but lost interest in the previous few years. Since nothing else was working, I decided to give it another try.

God, I know that I do not deserve any favors. I know that I am not the ideal person. I have never struggled this much looking for direction. Can you please give me some kind of sign? Something. Anything.

At 10:30 pm, bored with my unsuccessful thoughts for a new career, I rode the elevator again to the roof to check out any female prospects in the bar, hoping to continue my stretch of good fortune.

Soft music from the jukebox played and only two older couples sat quietly near the dance floor. Two men sat together on the far side of the bar drinking martinis while a middle-aged man occupied the side of the bar toward the entrance. I selected the stool two away from the single man.

"Hi," I nodded to the man dressed in Dockers and a sport shirt.

"How ya doin'?"

"You speak English?" I asked.

"Yep, I'm from Texas."

"Oh yea, where abouts?"

"Dallas," the man answered.

"What do you do?" I asked, knowing that this was the normal first question when you meet someone, almost as if work was everything in your life.

"Actually, I'm a headhunter."

"Really?" I asked.

"Really."

"Work for a big firm?"

"Well, I own the business," he answered, not at all boasting.

"No kidding, good for you."

"How about you?" he forced himself to return the conversation volley after a few quiet moments.

"Unfortunately, I have been out of work for the last seven months."

"Any prospects?" he asked.

"Few and far between. A few interviews, but no offers."

"Where are you looking?"

"The Southeast mostly," I answered.

"Some say that the job market is down right now," he offered to make me feel better.

"What do you say?"

"I haven't had any problems placing clients."

"Do you think it is my age?" I asked.

"How old are you?"

"Forty eight."

"No, that shouldn't be a big contributor. You've got another good 15 years of service."

"That's the way I feel," I admitted to him but thought differently.

"You know, I was probably just like you. I had twenty years of service in HR with a medium-sized company and then was laid off when a larger corporation bought out the company. I was off from work for six months, when I decided to take the bull by the horns. I knew a lot of people in the industry, and I knew a lot of people that were out of work just like myself."

"So what did you do?" I showed significantly more interest in his latest rhetoric.

"I decided to start my own business as a headhunter. I called on some of the customers of my old company, some of the larger suppliers, and then I called on my previous company. Slowly but surely, I started to place some of my friends with these other corporations, and the money started coming in.

"Before too long, I couldn't handle all of the company clients and prospective candidates, so I hired some help. I also advertised on the Internet and my volume increased tenfold. I now have offices in ten major cities in the South employing a hundred and fifty agents. All because I decided to take a chance. With an initial investment of $1000 for incorporation, I worked out of my house for the first year."

"Wow, what a success story," I said.

"It has been a lot of work, but nothing like what others said it would be. I work as much or as little as I want."

"So I take it that this is vacation."

"Well yes, but I'll write it off of course. Because we talked about work. Thanks."

"My pleasure."

Sensing he was not going to help me find a job, I decided to call it a night. "By the way, Ben White," I said and extended my hand for a handshake as I stood to leave.

"Tom Williams."

"Nice chatting with you," I added politely.

"Yea, good luck."

"Thanks."

Retrieving a white napkin from the bar, I left the bar, and while waiting for the elevator, jotted down "Tom Williams – Dallas – Headhunter".

Still beating myself up over my recent inability to make money, I needed the boost from the conversation with Tom Williams. As I rode the elevator down to my floor, I developed a plan in my head to search the Internet for recruiters in South Carolina as soon as I got back home. I would find out if the area was saturated, interview with a few recruiters, and determine the feasibility of starting a business.

When I reached the hotel room, I took the hotel stationary from the desk drawer and started writing notes.

1) Check Internet for Headhunters in SC and in Southeast

2) Call headhunter and find out information about the business

3) Search Internet for small business incorporation

4) Search Internet for free web page listing

After reaching into my pocket for the folded napkins, I added to the list:

5) Warren Smithson - National Organ Transplant Act

6) Clark Smithson – Senator

7) Tom Williams – Dallas – Headhunter

seven

At the Savannah Airport at about 11:30pm, a large group of family and friends waited in the gate area for others from my flight. I excused myself, passing by the people hugging and kissing in the aisle near the check-in desk. Young women greeted husbands away on business trips and grandmas and grandpas hugged their grandchildren. There was no one there for me.

Light traffic from Highway 95 kept me alert as I turned onto Highway 278 towards Hilton Head and Beaufort. Reflecting on the unforgettable experiences I had the opportunity to share over the last few days, I was deeply impressed by what money could buy.

#

The hard drive on my computer whirred while energized for the first time in three days. The anticipation of e-mail was overwhelming. The sight of one particular e-mail from Karen excited me.

Ben,

It was good to hear from you. Things not going as well as expected for me. I may be swinging back through your area. If I do, you may see me.

Friends,

Karen

Strange as it might have seemed, I again felt a renewed sense of anticipation in my life. I sensed that I knew Karen like no one else knew her. She had shared with me things that I was convinced no one else knew about. I decided to write a note back.

Karen,

Sorry to hear that your not doing well. You know that you are always welcome at my place. I just returned from Venezuela. It is a long story that I can tell you about when you visit.

Please Come,

Ben

Unpacking my suitcase for the first time in over a year again reminded me of my working days. I dismissed any negative thought quickly with my renewed attitude towards creating a new job.   Setting the alarm for 6:30am, I retired to the bedroom for some well-earned sleep.

The next day, I awoke with a heightened enthusiasm. As promised, I telephoned Mr. Bradfield, and met him for breakfast at Louie's Restaurant on Bay Street. Paying for breakfast, he also tipped me $50.00 for all my trouble. Too bad I did not have the fifty back on the island, it certainly would have been better spent there than in Beaufort.

Stopping at the Beaufort Public Library, I initiated my research on the job placement industry. Several recruiters were listed in Hilton Head, Savannah, and Charleston, but none in Beaufort, South Carolina. That discovery was encouraging.

When I reached the servants' quarters where I was soon to be evicted, I started down the list of items on the list I previously drafted in Venezuela. Jotting down telephone numbers of some of the recruiters in Savannah and Hilton Head, I followed up with a few quick telephone calls to answer preliminary questions that I had about the profession.

Searching for recruiters in Dallas, I identified "Professional Recruiters, Inc.", listing Tom Williams as the owner and principal agent.

Typing the name Clark Smithson in my browser, I read articles about a successful political career and untarnished voting record. Though finding a few articles on scandalous behavior with some women from his re-election committee, nothing prevented him from re-election for five straight terms. I turned my exploration to his son.

Entering in the name Warren Smithson into the browser, six links returned to the screen. I followed the first link for the Department of Health and Human Services. According to the home page, "the Department of Health and Human Services is the government's principal agency for protecting the health of all Americans and providing essential human services, especially for those who are least able to help themselves".

I then clicked on the link to the Health Resources and Services Administration. This agency, the (HRSA) "directs national health programs that improves the Nation's health by assuring equitable access to comprehensive, quality health care for all". I still was not deep enough into the agency's web site.

I followed the link to the Office of Special Programs. According to the words on the home page of this organization, this agency "was created in 1997 to provide leadership to three divisions", which among these was the Division of Transplantation. The Division of Transplantation also had its web site, more flashy and professional looking than the preceding ones, most likely due to the young age of Director Warren Smithson.

Near the top of this web page, a large image of Director Smithson seated on a walnut desk in front of a wall of bookshelves, dominated the page, similar to the fashion which he overshadowed the bar in Venezuela. The black hair slicked back and well-tanned face conjured up characteristics of a shady executive. The paragraph below the picture described the responsibilities of the Division of Transplantation, which included: "Federal oversight of the Organ Procurement and Transplantation Network, the Scientific Registry of Transplant Recipients, and the National Marrow Donor Program Contacts."

The button labeled "Organ Recipient List" was one of the many buttons listed along the left side of the screen. Curious if I could find Jonathon Stone's name on this list, I quickly clicked on this button.

A password window popped up in the middle of the screen requesting login and password. I minimized the window and saved the web address as a favorite on my computer so that I could come back to this screen after hacking the login and password. Once I closed the window to the Internet, I loaded the EasyHack program.

The whirring from the hard drive on my computer continued for 10 to 15 minutes attempting to find a login and password for the Division of Transplantation site. When the screen finally came back to me, there was a note across the screen that read "Unable to find a suitable Login ID and Password".

I must have stumped it. Now what do I do? Karen had not covered this scenario. I could go back in and try the simple combinations, but thought that the EasyHack program would be able to pick up those combinations. Once connected again with the Internet, I started my research on the incorporation of my small business.

Finally finding an attorney that specialized in incorporating small businesses, I sent an e-mail describing my intentions. After finding a web site that walked the user through the creation of a business plan, I started to write my new business plan including sections for marketing, competition, capital requirements, cash flow, and facilities. I was pleased with my progress working towards a definite goal again.

Over the next few days, visiting the limited Beaufort Library, I searched the Internet, and contacted a recruiter in Savannah inconspicuously seeking information about his business. Completely consumed with the task at hand, I stopped thinking about Karen as much.

One afternoon while sitting at the computer, I noticed movement in the corner of the window by the couch. Slipping into the bedroom, I peeked through the slit between the closed blinds and the window casing toward the side yard where the movement originated. Stretching to the bottom corner of the window on tiptoes balanced on a concrete block was a red haired woman dressed in black jeans and a black tee shirt. As she glanced back towards the bedroom window, I recognized her. It was Karen.

I sneaked through the living room to the front door and escaped down the steps and around the house. "You're busted!" I barked out almost out of breath.

Karen turned, the block tipped and she grabbed a frond of the Palmetto palm as she fell backward. "I knew you were there," she lied confidently.

"You know, you could just knock on the door."

"I wasn't sure that you were alone."

"I'm always alone. FBI still chasing you?" I asked.

Karen put her index finger in front of her lips, "can we go inside?"

"I like your hair. Something new?"

"Got to keep them guessing," she said.

"You want a beer?" I asked once we got inside.

"Sure. So what's this about Venezuela?"

We sat together, Karen on the couch and I in the side chair, while I recounted the story of Angelo, Mr. Bradfield, and Bennett's Personal Vacations. Excluding the elements about Jasmine and Natalie, I included some sensual details about Suzy, sufficient to let Karen know I was interested in such things. I described the encounter with Warren Smithson and Tom Williams, the recruiter from Dallas. Then I explained my plans regarding a recruiting business. "I'm assuming that you're still running," I tried to realign the conversation towards her dilemma.

"I'll always be running."

"So, what are you going to do about work? About making money?"

"Good question," she answered.

"What are you good at?"

"You really don't want to know." I recognized the same look that I received in the Sand Dollar bar as Karen stood over the unconscious body of William the cook.

"Look, Karen. I am a 48-year-old man who worked very hard for the same company for 25 years. That compassionate company fired me seven months ago. I have divorced. My children do not talk to me anymore. No one will hire me. I am a loser. The only thing that I have in my life right now is a part time relationship with a woman who beats the crap out of men over twice her size and can't tell me anything about her past. I need your companionship right now. Moreover, I think that you need me. Why can't you trust me?" I hoped that my honesty would provide my best chance with her.

"I'm sorry Ben. I have been trained not to trust anyone. I have been extremely independent for the last 15 years because of my profession, and I am not sure that I can change that. I have created my life just the way it is and I do not want to answer to anyone. The only thing . . . "

"The only thing is what?"

"I'm not sure that I can easily change what I do or how I feel."

"Why do you feel that you have to?" I asked.

"Because there is not a great demand for my work."

"Look, why don't you stop dancing around and tell me your big secret. It can't be that bad and if you feel uncertain after you tell me, then kill me," I offered in jest.

Karen pulled her feet onto the couch crossing her legs beneath her and leaned forward towards me, my question obviously weighing heavy on her mind.

"You have to realize Ben that I have never told anyone about myself. I don't have any friends. Both my parents have passed away not knowing what their daughter did for half of her life. And now that I have lost my job, I no longer have a life. But, I'm going to trust you Ben. You may very well wish, some day, that I had never told you and that you never met me."

"Let me have it. I can take it," I encouraged her.

I did not know exactly why I did encourage her. Was I really interested in her life's story? Did I actually want to be sensitive to her needs? On the other hand, did I just want to get Karen in bed with me and do or say whatever it took to make that happen?

"You'd better get us another beer," that perfect smile returned to her face with perhaps a little uncertainty in her voice as she started her story.

"I graduated very high in my class in high school. I was a good student. It was easy for me. I knew in my junior year that I would not be attending college because my parents did not have much money.

"Since my father was a chief petty officer in the Navy during World War II, it seemed like I was destined to join the Navy and go to school on the GI Bill after the service. I enlisted the week after graduation.

"I was a tomboy growing up mostly because there were no other girls in my neighborhood. In order not to get pushed around, I played hard with the boys and after a while, they learned to respect me. I think that I have always been plain, maybe a little more intriguing when men feared me.

"I did well during boot camp and took leadership positions when offered. When I met with the training officer to decide what I was going to do in the Navy, I told her that I wanted to do something different from the normal recruits. I found out about the NECEP program, which allowed me to attend 4 years of college while being in the Navy. After college, I owed the Navy six years of active duty, but as a Naval Officer. I accepted the opportunity and attended college at Washington & Lee University.

"I majored in political science with a minor in law enforcement. It was my goal to get out of the Navy and get a job as a FBI agent. My first assignment as a Naval Officer was for the Naval Criminal Investigation Service – Special Programs working with foreign counterintelligence. The Washington Navy Yard was my duty station.

"I worked for a married captain who had a crush on me and wanted me out of his command before he got in trouble with his wife. A group within the Executive Branch was creating a force for special assignments. Even Congress was not aware of our existence. At first, the architects of this new group had not considered women to be effective, but when my commanding officer made a midnight recommendation, I was approached."

I sat up straight and listened intently to each word as it slid out of Karen's delicate lips. I started to get aroused, partially from the once in a lifetime story she told and partially because she was strikingly beautiful and was trusting in me.

"They did not tell us much about the group at first, only that we would be receiving a lot of training, especially in psychology, chemistry, computer science, and self-defense. We never knew the real names of our trainers or leaders. Although the Seal program did not allow women, I had the opportunity to go through the same Seal training with the rest of my group.

"They explained our mission only after two years of grueling meticulous training. I can't tell you what a hard time I had in dealing with a mission to eliminate American citizens."

"What do you mean eliminate?" I finally broke her speech, anticipating that I was close to hearing her secret. My heart raced as my questions turned the pages of her story.

"I mean killing, wiping out, medically taking their life without any trace of foul play."

"What was the name of this group?"

"It really didn't have a name, but the limited number of people who knew of us called it the Death Lab," Karen answered. "It all made sense that day. Their final instructions to us were that we would be contacted with targets, and it was our job to investigate each target, find out where they lived, what their habits were, and how they could be killed without raising suspicion. We were never privy to why they were targets but we understood that they must have pissed someone off pretty bad.

"At the end of our instructions, they explained if caught, the Government would deny any association with the individuals of the group or the mission. You know, a lot like the television show Mission Impossible."

I nodded.

"Although I did not care for our mission, I had to look tough in front of the other members of the group. The only thing that the leaders ask is that we identify a city as a home base. Since I had visited Charleston in the past and it was not in my parent's hometown, I picked it. They handed me an envelope with $20,000 as we left the meeting room, and then instructed me to buy a car, get an apartment, and get settled. Information and additional money came with each new assignment.

"Being conservative, I bought a used car, and rented a small apartment in an inconspicuous neighborhood in the historic section of Charleston. I bought some books to catch up on reading and did a lot of walking.

"After a couple of weeks, as I was wandering down by the Battery watching the sailboats in the harbor, a man quietly came up behind me."

"Don't turn around," he commanded.

"I didn't argue. He placed an 8 X 10 envelope under my arm and quickly walked away. I continued to stare out across the water for a few minutes until I was sure that my contact was out of sight. I walked home with a tight grip on the envelope and a definite fear of what might be inside.

"When I reached my apartment, I closed the shades and double locked the door before opening the envelope. In the envelope was a black and white photograph of a man in his forties, dressed in a suit looking as if he just stepped out of his Manhattan office building. The name written below the picture was Kevin Johnson. The address written below the name was 1200 Michigan Avenue Apt 15B, Chicago, Illinois. There was also an envelope labeled expenses with $10,000 cash inside."

"Jesus Karen, so what did you do?" I asked chasing the lump in my throat down into my stomach with a slug of beer.

"Well, I took a train to Chicago, got a hotel room down in the Loop and started to gather information. On a Monday morning, I stationed myself outside his apartment building and waited for him to leave for work. At 7:00am, I identified my initial target, and a strange empty feeling covered me. I was very nervous and extremely paranoid. I followed him to work staying far behind him to avoid any suspicion. I knew that if I lost him, I could just pick it up again the next day. I was cautious.

"As it turned out, Mr. Johnson was an attorney. He was a bachelor that dated many girls, frequented the same upscale bar, and visited a classy strip joint every Friday evening. His routine was very predictable. I watched him as he picked up women at the bar and escorted them back to his apartment. After a few hours, the girls left his apartment alone, and the doorman secured taxis for them.

"I broke into his apartment one day while he was away and found a file on medical bills. According to one of the office visit receipts; Mr. Johnson suffered from a heart condition passed down by his father. Angina Pectoris is a heart condition where the heart muscle does not get enough blood. It normally occurs during strenuous activity but sometimes can be caused at rest. Mr. Johnson's diagnosis of coronary artery spasm could happen at any time."

I wondered how much training could give someone that depth of knowledge, and then for the purpose of taking lives, not saving them.

Karen continued, "I broke into his apartment for a second time and replaced his nitroglycerin tablets with a placebo that looked and tasted exactly like the nitro, ensuring that he not have any residual drug in his system. On his normal night to visit the bar, I was there and sat at the bar very near where he normally sat. When he came in, he sat next to me, bought me a drink, and within an hour we were headed back to his apartment.

"I made sure that the doorman did not get a look at my face as we walked through the door and entered the elevator on the way up to his fifteenth floor apartment. We had a few drinks in his apartment and I could tell that he was expecting sex. I was able to slip a vial of chemical, heavily induced with caffeine and other blood pressure elevating drugs into his drink. I stripped down to bra and panties while Mr. Johnson lay naked spread eagle on the bed."

I moved forward in the chair spellbound by Karen's tale, trying to cover up the degree that her story and her body turned me on. As she sat there on the couch, I was able to visualize through her clothes and see the stark white bra and panties she wore that day.

"I reached into my purse," Karen said, "and retrieved some soft restraints that I attached to the far corners of the bed. Physical restraints caused marked excitement in Mr. Johnson. I straddled his body moaning and groaning pulling at the cups of my bra and watching his response. His heart rate and respirations increased, his face turned red and he began to sweat. He forcefully pulled at the restraints and pleaded for release. I rolled his socks into a ball and forced them into his mouth.

"The pain lasted for about thirty minutes and must have been unbearable. Five minutes after his heart stopped beating; I got dressed, cleaned any fingerprints from the scene, and removed the restraints. I returned the nitroglycerin tablets to the bottle and tipped the bottle over on the nightstand to make it look like he was in distress. I placed the receiver of the phone in his hand, left the apartment, and exited out the back door to an alley.

"I monitored the newspaper for the next few days and on the third day after Kevin Johnson passed away, there was an article and an obituary. The article explained that Mr. Johnson died at home of an apparent heart attack brought on by an existing heart condition. I returned by train to Charleston."

"So how did that make you feel?" I didn't know how to respond to Karen. Of course, I was shocked that I was sitting in the same room with a murderer; albeit, a petite foxy looking murderer who chronicled her story with very little emotion.

"Pretty shitty actually. Nevertheless, it got easier after that. I learned how to channel the emotion out of my thoughts and kept focused on the logic and mechanics necessary to be successful. And being successful meant not getting caught."

"So, how many people have you a . . e . liminated?"

"Sixty three."

"Sixty three! Jesus Karen! Anybody that I would know?"

"Let me think. Oh yea. In the mid-seventies, there was a serial killer that picked up, raped, and then strangled girls on their eighteenth birthday. All of the girls were picked up less than one mile from I-10 from Jacksonville, Florida to New Orleans, Louisiana."

"Didn't they call him the 18/10 Killer?" I asked.

"That's the one."

"So, what happened?"

"One of the girls that was abducted, raped, and strangled was the daughter of a United States Representative from the State of Florida. This representative happened to have a close friend who ran the Justice Management Division in the Department of Justice. The Assistant Attorney General knew something about the Death Lab and subsequently, I got the assignment.

"I secretly acquired a copy of all of the local police and FBI records without the knowledge of either of the two agencies. The serial killer abducted, raped, and killed yet another girl during the three months I worked alone gathering information.

"Following an instinct regarding the I-10 sales route of a popular beer and wine distributor, I was able to identify a single male employee who fit the profile of a serial murderer, who also had the opportunity to commit each of the murders. Witnessing this salesman's behavior for a few days, convinced me that Clarence Todd was not only the serial killer, but was planning his next victim.

"Linda Davis, beginning her freshman year at Florida State University in Tallahassee, worked evenings at a breakfast chain restaurant on Monroe Street less than a block off I-10. The salesman/serial killer stopped at the restaurant one evening and as I watched through the restaurant window, witnessed him in many conversations with Ms. Davis in the hour while he was there.

"After finding out the identity of the waitress/FSU student, I also checked out her birthday. Linda Davis would turn eighteen years old on the Friday following the initial confrontation with Mr. Todd. I also found out that although she had asked for the night off, she was scheduled to work that evening, but only until 9:00pm.

"I arrived in the restaurant parking lot at 8:30pm and shifted parking spots as they became available until I had appropriate views of the restaurant door and Linda's powder blue 1965 Corvair. At about 8:55pm, Clarence Todd maneuvered the company van next to the Corvair parked in the back corner of the parking lot."

"God, Karen. Weren't you scared?" My mouth dropped open in disbelief. Although I was overwhelmed by the private memoirs of Karen, the adventure began to sound intriguing to me.

"There was no time for that. Stay in control," Karen continued. "Linda Davis opened the restaurant door waving to the other waitresses as she departed. Once she got back to her car, the van door flew open and Clarence jumped out, wrapping one arm around her and the other over her mouth. The van shook for a minute and then backed out of the parking spot heading for the exit.

"I followed the van out of the parking lot, onto I-10, and then as soon as we were a few miles away from Tallahassee, off onto an exit and then down a small dirt road. I proceeded with my lights off until the van came to a stop out of sight from any house or side street.

"I removed the inside lights fuse from the fuse box and left the car door open as I wound my way on foot, through the underbrush to where I could see and hear the van. The van again began to shake and the sounds of Linda struggling and screaming through the tape placed over her mouth were obvious. Maneuvering in front of the van, peering through the windshield, I was able to witness Clarence Todd straddling Ms. Davis' restrained body, ripping her waitress' uniform from her.

"Squatting in front of the van, I reached down, picked up a sizable rock, and hurled it behind the vehicle. Surprised that Clarence Todd heard the thud over the muffled cries from Linda

Davis, the side door of the van opened slowly and Clarence stepped out. With 38-caliber pistol in hand, he stared first in the direction where the noise had come from.

"The first bullet from my silenced 45 struck him in the back about an inch under his shoulder blade. The force of the bullet dropped Mr. Todd to his knees and then face down on the gravel. The pistol fell out of his hand several feet from his stock-still body. With my foot, I rolled his body over onto his back, aimed the 45 at his head, and while he was gasping for his last few breaths, placed another bullet midway between his eyes. Surprisingly, there was not much blood at the entry point."

I took a deep breath. The way she told the story was so vivid, I felt as if I were an accomplice. "What happened to the girl?" I asked, trying to keep the story alive.

"I left her there. I could not take the chance of her identifying me. I stopped at a pay phone not more than a mile from the scene and gave the local police the information about Linda's whereabouts. I called the FBI informant line and explained the situation with Clarence Todd, so as not implicate me in any way."

"So you must have felt better about that job than the first one you told me about."

"You bet I did. But I seldom know why the victim is selected. This one just happened to be a high profile case."

"Sixty three of these stories?" I reaffirmed, amazed at what she had shared with me.

"Would have been sixty four, but the target decided to fight off the chemical or I didn't receive the advertised strength of the reagents. In either case, I failed, and I didn't cover my tracks well enough."

"So now we are both looking for work." I complained, happy to change the subject for a few minutes.

eight

Much to my disappointment, we both drank too much beer to enjoy a romantic night in bed together. Karen crashed fully clothed on the couch while I made it to my bed. Waking the following morning to the sound of pans clanking and the smell of bacon, my head ached as I groaned and scoured the bathroom for aspirin.

"I'm hurtin' for certain," I complained, stumbling to the chair in the living room, steadying my head from vertical movement.

"I'm not feeling to good myself. Breakfast always helps. Come and sit at the table. Have some coffee." Karen looked as pretty and fit as ever, wearing shorts and a tee shirt, displaying perfectly proportioned legs; not too skinny, but no signs of cellulite at all.

"I'm surprised that you're still here," I countered.

"Why is that?"

"Cause now I know your secret."

"So."

"So, I think that makes you uncomfortable."

"Well, it does. However, right now, I guess that I need someone. And that someone must be you. And, if you double cross me, I'll just kill you," she added jokingly however, chased it with a serious as death look on her face.

"I'll bet you say that to all the guys," shuffling to the table, I forced a smile.

After breakfast, I cleared the dishes and with Karen again in front of the computer, the pangs of the modem soon echoed through the living room.

"Hey, I finally found an Internet site that I couldn't hack," I admitted.

"At least not yet. Right?"

"Yea, right."

"EasyHack can't break them if the Webmaster forces the use of special characters in the password."

"Now you tell me. So I guess Hacking 101 doesn't cover that chapter. So how do you break into those sites?"

"You have to be at least as smart as the Webmaster."

"That leaves me out."

"What's the Internet address?"

I led her to my list of favorites, and told the story about Jonathon Stone, Warren Smithson, and Jennifer Jackson.

"Why are you researching organ donations?" Karen turned to acknowledge my body language as well as my answer.

"Just for fun, I guess."

"I guess that if it were me, I would find a local doctor who accessed the site and somehow find out from him what his ID and password is."

"Sounds like more work than I care to do," I admitted.

A loud knock on the front door completely took both of us by surprise, but immediately shifted Karen into a business mode I had witnessed only once before. My heart started to pound. In that moment, I visualized the dark suits kicking down the door, bullets stinging my flesh.

"Shh!" Karen held her index finger in front of her lips.

"Is there another way out of here?" she whispered into my ear. As Karen's body pressed against mine, it was the closest she had ever been to me. I could smell her perfume and feel the warmth of body.

I put my hand on her back as she leaned in towards me. I didn't want her to move; however I pointed towards the rug by the kitchen table. "This leads down to a tunnel that comes out by the main house. I think the original owner used to sneak through the tunnel and visit one of the slave women," I whispered back.

Moving the rug, I lifted the trap door beneath it. Karen quietly slipped down the four steps. After handing her a flashlight, I softly closed the door, cautiously replacing the rug.

The rapping on the door repeated louder than before.

"Just a minute," I bellowed trying to allow Karen a few more moments to escape. I opened the door to acknowledge Mr. Bradfield dressed in a blue suit. My blood pressure immediately diminished and my face felt cooler.

"Good morning, Ben. I thought that I should let you know that Angelo and I have come to an agreement and we will close on the house in a few weeks. I am sorry, but I have a nephew that will live here in the servant's quarters. Therefore, you'll have to vacate. I am sorry if this inconveniences you. Angelo said that you didn't sign a lease with him."

"That's right. Just give me the final date and I will be out of here."

"How much of this furniture is yours?" Bradfield asked.

"Just the computer."

"Well, you can have what you want of it. I will be buying all new stuff."

"That is very thoughtful," I replied, thinking it was the least he could do for kicking me out. Knowing I would be searching for an unfurnished apartment immediately soured my new business research.

"If you could be out by the end of this month then?" Came his question that didn't sound much like a question. It sounded more like an offer that I couldn't refuse.

We shook hands, I closed the door, and I immediately threw away the rug to open the trap door. Peering down the small staircase under the servant quarters, Karen was gone. As soon as Mr. Bradfield vacated the property, I searched the length of the tunnel and the remainder of the property but Karen had disappeared. I retrieved the flashlight from the rear steps to the main house. I lost Karen again.

#

Walking the seven blocks to the bookstore to purchase the current Beaufort Gazette, the warm Beaufort sun raised some perspiration on my tee shirt. Cars lined Bay Street waiting for the close of the drawbridge spanning the Beaufort River. I crossed Boundary Street in the middle of the block around the waiting cars. As I continued down a side street and then across Waterfront Park, I stopped to sit on one of the swings facing the river.

I opened the single section paper to the classifieds and searched for inexpensive places to move. After circling a few possibilities, I marched off to find out about the living arrangements. Crossing off each opportunity because of excessive cost or inadequate living condition, I convinced myself that more opportunities would exist in the Sunday's paper, so I finished the walk back to the house.

As I passed Dr. Carl Lyons' office on Port Republic Street, I remembered what Karen stated about a doctor's password into the donor database. Dr. Lyons had been our family doctor for the previous fifteen years and he and I golfed together once a month before I lost my job.

The bell on the heavy oak door clanged as I approached the receptionist desk. Dr. Lyons' nurse, Christine, glanced up from a chart that spread out in front of her. Christine accompanied me home from the Sand Dollar a few months earlier. As she glanced up at me, it was obvious that she was surprised to see my face again.

"Ben!"

"Christine!" I answered in the same tone.

"I thought you said you were going to call me." Hadn't I used that line once or twice before?

"I've been busy," I said.

"Find a job yet?"

"No," I answered bowing my head slightly.

"So why are you here?"

"I came to see you. Where is your boss?"

"Where do you think?" she answered.

"Golf Course?"

"Where else?"

"So you here by yourself?"

"Yep. No patients today. Just answering the phone."

"Meet me at the Sand Dollar tonight?" I asked.

"What time?"

"How about seven?"

Christine was late forties, a little overweight, and recently divorced. I had not called her back because I could not take her mouth running 24 hours a day, even during sex. She came along when I really needed a partner and when I was a little drunk. Now I needed something else.

I walked behind the counter and started to massage her shoulders. She quickly relaxed to my touch pushing her shoulders into my hands.

"What is going on here?" she looked up at me.

"Just trying to be friendly."

"Are you sure that's all?"

"I signed up for organ donation today," changing the subject, I began my quest for information that I needed for my latest hobby.

"That's great. The world needs more people like you."

"How does that work exactly?"

"What do you mean?"

"I mean, when I die, how will they know that my organs will be donated?"

"Well, your name goes into a database, and I'm assuming that you have a card that you keep in your wallet. Since there are people out there already waiting for organs, they match up your organs with someone who is at the top of the list."

"How do they know who gets my organs?"

"There is a new Federal program which has all of the names of people needing organs. Carl went to a seminar on it a few months ago."

I knew I was on the right track. "How do doctors get to know the names on that list?" I asked, trying not to be too leading.

"It's on the Internet."

"No kidding. What is the address?" I asked.

"Well, I filed that information in Carl's office last week," Christine unlocked the door to her boss's personal office and returned with a manila folder.

"Right here. www.HRSA.gov."

"Let me write that down," I quickly scanned the official letter with CONFIDENTIAL bolded across the bottom.

The middle of the page listed: "Logon: Carl.Lyons Password: *C*Lyons$$". I memorized the two lines while writing only the web address, though I already discovered the web address at home.

"Thanks," I closed the folder before Christine realized the confidentiality of the information she was providing.

"I'll see you tonight."

As soon as I closed the front door, I wrote the login and password on my hand and hurried to get back to my computer.

A 50-foot moving van parked in front of the main house reminded me of my own eventual eviction. White wicker furniture balanced over the shoulders of dark black laborers filed up the ramp and on to the truck.

After grabbing a beer from the refrigerator, I immediately headed for the computer. Logging on to the Internet, I typed in the address that I had hastily jotted down only minutes before. The address took me right to the Health Resources and Services Administration site that I had previously found using other links. I followed my past paths to the login screen.

I typed in "Carl Lyons" followed by "*C*Lyons$$". A window popped up in the middle of the screen reminding the user of the confidential nature of the information contained on the screen to follow. I clicked on the "I Agree" button, and the computer whizzed off to finally display a list of names, addresses, doctors names, dates, and organs needed. The list was sorted by organ by date by region.

I quickly scanned the list for Jonathon Stone's name. I could not find it, but as I was looking, I noticed a note that read, "This list was updated today." Since Jonathon already had the surgery, I concluded that they removed his name from the list.

I further scanned the list, curious if I would recognize any names. The names at the top of each organ list had been on the list for up to a year. It occurred to me that there were two ways to have your name removed from the list: to finally receive an organ or to die waiting.

Third on the list, waiting for a heart was Christian Flynn. Recognizing his name from some old movies, I searched Internet sites to discover that he was an actor very popular in the 1960s. After several years of success, he faded from stardom. I concluded that his health finally failed him, and sick actors do not get work. I wondered how I would feel if it was I that was waiting on the list.

I glanced at the top two names on the list: Margaret Branch of St. Louis, Missouri, number two on the list and William Lewis of Dallas, Texas, number one on the list. I transcribed the names, rocked back in my chair and stared out the window precisely where I spotted Karen the day before. Where did she go when she left? When would she return?

Pushing on to learn more about Christian Flynn, I switched from site to site looking for address, phone number, newspaper and magazine articles, and information about his family. Mr. Flynn lived in a multi-million dollar home in the desert east of LA. Apparently, he invested the money he made from films and parlayed it into a small fortune. It was unfortunate for him that no money could save his life now. The more that I read, the more I liked him.

The afternoon light faded into darkness without announcement as I continued my investigations. It was fortunate for me that I not only enjoyed the investigative work but also was proficient at it.

Margaret Branch, a retired elementary school teacher, lived in a small home in a suburb of St. Louis. At 86, she no longer drove a car, and divorced caregiver daughter was in poor health. Candidacy for a heart transplant did not seem to fit for an 86 year-old woman, but I guess the government and doctors followed their prescribed standards.

William Lewis held 10 jobs in as many years, working mostly as unskilled labor in or around Dallas. Mr. Lewis had a drug problem and served time in the Texas State prison near Austin. When a valve in his heart started to leak, the Warden finally released him from prison. Heart surgeons did the best they could to repair the valve, but put him on the list for a new heart when it did not repair itself adequately after surgery.

After researching the top two heart transplant candidates, I began to feel sorry for Christian Flynn. He had to wait for three heart donors with the same blood type to die before he could get his new heart. In addition, the two recipients higher on the list were not as worthy as he and certainly not as prominent. Since Christian offered much more to society than the others, shouldn't he have a second chance at life before the others?

Copying all of the information I had gathered into a Word document, I stored it in a folder marked "Organ Recipients".

I glanced at the time in the corner of the computer screen and sighed in disbelief at how quickly the time had passed. It was after eleven o'clock when I realized that I had forgotten about my meeting with Christine at the Sand Dollar Bar from earlier that evening.

After deciding to revisit the list of organ donors that I had found earlier, I monitored the list, discovered when a heart donor dropped off the list and attempted to match it up with a prospective recipient who received the heart.

Since William Lewis lived in Texas, I downloaded just the heart organ donors that lived in Texas into an Excel spreadsheet and labeled the column "Sept 10".

I had 20 days before I had to vacate my home. Each day I monitored the donor site, downloaded the heart organ donors from Texas, and downloaded the list into a new column on my spreadsheet. About every other day, a new name supplemented the list but no names came off. Finally, on September 18 I noticed a name drop off the list.

Renata Newman, a 43 year-old mother of two, lost her life to a brain aneurysm, according to the obituary in the Huntsville, Texas Gazette. The article even confirmed that she donated her heart to a Texas heart recipient. However, the evidence that confirmed the donation was that William Lewis' name came off the Organ Recipient list stored on the Health Resources and Services Administration web site. Excited about my ability to track the entire process, I pushed on for even more information.

Over the next few days, I read as much as I could about organ donation, while alternately pursuing my future in the recruiting business. On September 20, I received an email back from the attorney that specialized in low cost incorporation. He left me a phone number to call and a schedule of when he would be available.

Returning his call the same afternoon, I emailed him a copy of my business plan, and discussed my plans for the business. His quote for services was $950 and his schedule could complete the work in one week. Taking the $950 out of savings, I would only have $225 left, plus the unemployment of $190 a week that was to run out in five more weeks.

Since I had no other prospects for a job, I decided to write the check, and establish Manufacturing Services Recruiting; a South Carolina Corporation, Benjamin E. White –President.

nine

After continued investigation, I concluded that recruiting services saturated the Florida, Georgia and South Carolina areas and manufacturing businesses were now moving away from the Southeast towards the Southwest. I considered a move out West. If Tom Williams could make his recruiting business work in the big state of Texas, there must be room for me.

I spent several hours researching the recruiting business in the larger cities in the Southwest. My findings suggested that Houston Texas would offer the highest probability of success.

Afraid that I would never see Karen again, I left email messages everyday. Explaining my new business ideas, I also admitted how much I missed her. Repeatedly expressing my desires for her advice on moving to Texas, I finally received an email from her on September 29.

Dear Ben,

Sounds like you got a plan. Sorry that I have been inaccessible. I am out of country trying to make some contacts. Let me know where you end up. I will look forward to seeing you again.

Love,

Karen

I read her email again. Did she end the letter with the word love? I wondered if that was her intent or if she treated that word casually. What an odd relationship we had. Perhaps, after I settled somewhere besides South Carolina, Karen would decide to settle down as well.

Borrowing $2,000 from my 401K account, I rented a U-haul trailer to make my trek across America to the land of opportunity in the State of Texas in the city of Houston. After packing the trailer to the ceiling with almost the entire contents of the servant's quarters, I logged off the computer for the final time on September 29, knowing that I would not log on again until settled in Houston. Placing the computer on the Nissan's passenger side floor, I wrapped the monitor in a towel and placed it on the seat next to me.

The Sand Dollar, packed with regulars I had spent a lifetime with, called me for one last night out. Overhearing a group at the table behind me complaining about their jobs forced me to cut the evening short. After hugging the bartender, Mindy, I walked into the kitchen to shake William's hand.

Waterfront Park, packed wall-to-wall that evening with the rowdy party crowd from Beaufort County, celebrated the annual Shrimp Festival. Smoke from several barbecue troughs billowed up through the Spanish moss dangling from the many live oaks in the park. The smells of the grilled marinated shrimp and chicken hung over the park filtering out towards Bay Street luring the many curious tourists. The Shrimp Festival and the Water Festival were very big summer and fall events in Beaufort drawing large crowds and providing many memories.

Living in Beaufort for the majority of my life, I was acquainted with many of the people at the festival and had the opportunity to stop and visit with several of them. Coming out of one of the port-a-potties, I recognized Christine chatting with two other women waiting in the beer line. She had not spotted me yet, so I shielded myself from her until I was safely out of the park and on my way back home.

Thinking again about Karen, I knew that I had to close that chapter and move on. It also concerned me that I had not considered my ex-wife in the same thought. Why was it so easy to push that part of my life deep into the background?

Back in my house by 9:00pm, with all of my life now packed in a five foot by eight-foot trailer and a small pickup truck, I decided to get my trip underway. Easing the trailer out onto the street, I headed west down the often-photographed Bay Street. Driving through the few downtown blocks, I would miss the patches of sea grass in the marsh at high tide and the funky smell during low tide. At 10:00pm, I reached the South Carolina/Georgia border and by midnight crossed over the Florida State line.

Following Interstate 10 through the Florida panhandle, reminded me of Karen's story about the 18/10 serial killer. I finally stopped at a cheap hotel at 4:00am. Setting the alarm for 8:00am, although exhausted from the packing & driving, I found it difficult to sleep in a strange place. After sleeping off and on, I finally got up, showered at 7:00am and checked out of the hotel.

Fog hung on the interstate with a light mist slapping on the windshield with every passing 18-wheeler. Slowing for several accidents, I pulled off the road to stop when the rain pelted the windshield and visibility was impossible. I made horrible time, averaging only 40 miles per hour. Finally, I spotted the sign announcing the Alabama State line, and at 2:00pm stopped for gas and food.

Devouring a hamburger and fries in order to return to the road, I set a goal to be in New Orleans before dark. Just past Mobile the rain started to let up and the clouds dissipated. Relaxation returned, my grip on the steering wheel loosened, and I enjoyed the countryside while trying to anticipate my moves once I hit Houston.

After exiting Interstate 10 at Orleans Street in the greatest party city in the US, I checked in to a small run down hotel a few blocks from the interstate. I disconnected the trailer from the pickup after backing into a parking spot in front of the hotel room. After a quick shower, I marched past the rundown storefronts to the French Quarter, turning when I arrived at Bourbon Street.

Laughter and music spilled out of the clubs and onto the famous Mardi Gras street, littered with plastic glasses and wine bottles. Tourists and locals stumbled in and out of doorways and out onto the street, blocked off at night for pedestrian traffic only. Selecting a walk up outdoor bar, I ordered a rum punch. Noise levels on the street were intense as most of the visitors carried plastic glasses filled with alcoholic drinks of many colors. Two girls across the street shouted to men up on a second story porch. The blond handed her drink to the other girl and then pulled up her blouse exposing her suntanned breasts. We are not in Beaufort anymore, I thought.

Wandering past the vendors selling palm reading and tarot card readings, I declined, reluctant to know exactly what my future held in store for me. I continued down the street with a strange new sense of adventure.

I settled into a restaurant that had an empty chair at the bar. Noise levels in the bar were deafening as the other guests screamed in order to overcome the clamor of several jazz bands from adjacent bars. No singles frequented this bar, just couples and groups of people, mostly young ones. After finishing the rum punch, I ordered another. New Orleans was by far the rowdiest party town that I had ever seen.

A black man dressed only in a thong danced on top of a bar in one of the corner bars. The crowd of men standing shoulder to shoulder clapped to the dancer's gyrating body movements taunting the mostly gay audience.

The crowds in the street swelled as I left the restaurant to check out the other bars and entertainment. The absence of light in the topless bar took me several minutes to readjust. Finally, I made my way down toward the stage, sitting in one of the empty chairs. To my surprise, there were a number of men who had brought their wives and girlfriends into the club with them.

Feeding each of the dancers a dollar, I watched about ten young women strip to a g-string while dancing and tempting the crowd. None of the girls were very attractive but a few had decent bodies. After two more rum punches, I abandoned the club and continued down Bourbon Street. It was hard for me to believe that the crowd in the street had grown in size again. Difficult to navigate the overflowing assembly while balancing a drink, I paused in alleyway where the smell of vomit in the nighttime heat became overwhelming.

Finding another of the straight bars, I entered and sat at a stool next to a woman cab driver. She clocked out at 10:00pm and was trying to get as drunk as the rest of the crowd. After buying her a drink, we encompassed the range of conversation from religion to politics and back again. We had absolutely nothing in common and without doubt traveled in different circles. I could not help thinking about Karen and the last time that we were together.

Saturated with alcohol, weary of the woman's rhetoric, disgusted with my choice of company, I left the bar. Recognizing as I stood that I probably was too smashed to locate my hotel, I inconspicuously stumbled back into the bar's disgusting rest room and splashed handfuls of cold water on my face. Planning to sleep in until noon the following day, the 5:00am hour was not all that upsetting to me.

As I meandered farther away from Bourbon Street, the noise and light diminished swiftly. Cutting across through an alley to arrive where assumedly my hotel was located, challenged my concern for security. Light from both ends of the alley was not sufficient to light the center and at the halfway point, I became worried about my decision. Hearing suspicious noises behind me, I saw nothing but shadows when I turned. Carefully advancing down the alley, I realized that the noises were coming from in front of me.

When I stopped, the noises stopped. When I started to walk again, the noises continued. As I cautiously moved closer to the end of the alley, I recognized the shadow of a man sitting against a building. As I quietly turned to walk back the other way, the man spoke to me. I turned back to look but could not see his face.

"You need to follow what you are good at," the words came out with a quiet, educated confidence.

As I prepared to run, the voice came back, "wait."

I decided to answer, "I'm just going back to my hotel. Sorry I bothered you."

"Oh, you didn't bother me. I've been waiting for you," he advised, not sounding at all inebriated.

"This is too weird for me. I'm out of here," I turned again to walk away.

"You are out of work, aren't you?"

My intense curiosity coupled with my alcohol-induced courage made me turn again. When I had decided to make New Orleans a stop on my cross-country trip, I was surprised to read about the voodoo, black magic, and fortune-telling that was prevalent there. Incomprehensible though, is why a fortune-teller would be selling his services in an alley at 5:00 in the morning.

"What do you want?" I asked.

"I can only tell you that you should pursue what you are good at. And your hotel is this way," the figure's hand came into the light pointing towards the brightness at the end of the alley.

Apparently, that was all that was on his mind. I shook my head in disbelief and walked on the other side of the alley, trying to catch a final glimpse of this figure as I passed by. As I moved farther away, I picked up my pace and when I reached the source of the light, I recognized the street and saw my hotel immediately.

Setting the alarm for 10:30am, I did not remember anything else until I finally attempted a sitting position on the side of the bed at about 11:00am. Suffering the worst hangover for a long time, I struggled to the shower and received low-pressured lukewarm water at best. As I finally brushed my teeth, my tongue, and the roof of my mouth, I began feeling slightly better.

Once I checked out of the hotel, I visited a nearby breakfast restaurant, and fed my empty stomach. After hooking up my Nissan up to the trailer, I headed west again toward Texas. Contemplating my experience in New Orleans, I vaguely remembered my early morning hike back to the hotel. Far exceeding my normal limit of alcohol, I could not distinguish what was real and what I imagined.

Finally reaching the Texas line at 4:00pm, I was surprised at the number of trees and green grass. With expectations of vast desert plains with tumbleweed and cowboys, I saw none. Expecting oil wells and fields of cattle, I saw strip malls and major highways. This definitely presented a different impression of Texas.

After an hour of heavy traffic, I crossed the I-610 loop into downtown Houston. I checked into a small motel on Lockwood Street, blocks away from the 60 story buildings in the heart of Houston. Purchasing a Houston Chronicle from a nearby street vendor, I opened it up to the classifieds and then to the unfurnished apartment listings. After buying a street map for the downtown area, I spread it out next to the newspaper across the bed.

Circling several possibilities for the next day's apartment hunting, I walked two blocks to a local bar & restaurant where the motel manager suggested. I limited my dinner to three beers and the check came to twelve dollars. Walking back to the truck and trailer in the motel parking lot, I glanced over at the computer in the passenger seat of the Nissan. I could not wait until I had it plugged back in to the Internet. Although I had closed the book on Karen, I still wanted to check for any e-mails from her.

At twenty-five dollars per night, I knew I could not remain in the motel more than two nights. Yellow residue from years of smoking guests stained the once white walls of the old and neglected motel room. As I lay on the bed, staring at the ceiling, I remembered the nights at the four star hotels when traveling for the company. Two hundred dollar dinners with customers, and now I could not afford twenty-five a night for a motel room.

Placing my alarm clock on the nightstand, I set it for 7:00am. Sleep came easy after a long and traumatic day of unsettled beginnings. I wished for better times.

After waking with an incredibly clear head and a strange enthusiasm, I showered and dressed in my best business casual. I started down my list of circled apartments going from the least expensive to the highest that I could afford. After finding the address or name on the first two apartment homes, I drove by without stopping. My situation forced me to be desperate, but I still had limits. Amazed at the Hispanic influence in downtown Houston, I was also shocked at the many other races walking around town and working in the shops. Houston was different from Beaufort in many ways.

Stopping at the third apartment, I located and then entered the apartment office. An Asian woman probably in her mid-fifties greeted me and seemed surprised when I told her I was looking for an apartment.

"You no look like man who live here," she admitted in her best English.

"Well, I'm new in Houston, and I need an affordable place to stay until I get my business started."

"We have one bedroom open now and two bedroom in two weeks."

"I would be interested in seeing the one bedroom."

Trash overflowed the dumpster in the parking lot that ran between the two apartment buildings. We passed a parking lot filled with cars, surprising me for that time of morning.

"Why are so many cars still here?" I asked.

"Many people work night shift. Sleep during day."

I was a little worried as the available one-bedroom apartment was a first floor apartment in an area of Houston that was prone to flooding. The apartment door, rotted at the bottom, also had a latch that barely kept it shut. Jiggling the key in the lock, she twisted the handle to the left then to the right and the door opened. Must be a combination lock, I thought.

Tan painted walls masked the smoke stains but retained the smell. The tan carpet, appearing recently cleaned, was at best 15 years old. The air conditioning unit situated beneath the window in the living room clanked and shuddered, but cool air began to filter out the vents and the fan on high pushed it out at my face.

Water stains decorated the outside wall of the bedroom from an old roof leak. The toilet in the bathroom flushed and the shower spit out water. I did not wait for hot water, not wanting to push my luck.

"How much?" I asked.

"Three hundred a month. First and last month and two hundred deposit," she answered as if she had been through that many times before.

"I can give you two of the three, but not both," I replied.

"It policy to get first and last month, two hundred deposit," she said firmly.

"Well, I guess I will look elsewhere."

"Wait!" she added as I turned for the door.

"You like apartment?"

"Yea, I could stay here."

"Okay, I waive deposit. When you want move in?"

"How about today?"

"Let's go office, sign lease."

"Great."

Back at the motel by 10:30am, I checked out and again hooked up the U-Haul trailer. Fortunately, a vacant parking spot in front of my apartment was available when I returned. I backed the trailer into the parking spot and disconnected the Nissan. The thermometer moved through the eighty degrees mark going to a high of eighty-five by midday.

Three hours of soaking sweat and the trailer was finally empty. Leaving the boxes packed, I turned the air conditioning up to the maximum, locked the door behind me and headed for a U-Haul agent that I had passed earlier in the day. After picking up hamburgers from a nearby McDonald's, I decided to eat back at the apartment.

The parking spot in front of the apartment now filled, I parked on the end of the building away from the other spots. The apartment was cooler, but not cool enough. I opened the blinds and allowed the Texas sunlight to pour into the living room. After I had the computer hooked up, I walked back down to the office and called the phone company.

Employing a different approach with the female phone company representative, I was sweet, sympathetic, and appreciative. In return, the woman moved up the hookup of my phone for the next day. Her first position was 10 days, so I reveled in my ability to persuade her to pull in the date.

They transferred the electric service the first day I moved in. I decided to hold off on subscribing to cable until I started to bring some money in. Utilizing a small antenna, I hoped I would not be watching much TV anyway.

"Where is nearest grocery store?" I turned toward the rental manager who was still amazed at my immediacy.

"Two miles north. Same street," she pointed in the general direction.

"Thanks. I'm sure that I will see you later," I felt her stare as I left the office.

I passed by the food store that she referred only because the building looked thirty years old and there were only a few cars in the lot. Instead, I took the luxury of a ride around town. I got on I-610 that looped around the downtown area of Houston and rode the circle, noting the stores and other landmarks as I went.

Stopping at a small strip mall with a Kroger store, I bought a week's worth of groceries. I also purchased the cleaning supplies necessary to make sure that the apartment was clean. On the way out of the store, I picked up some of the help wanted advertisements, locally known as the green sheet, as well as the latest home sales and rental properties.

By 6:00pm, I was laying on my couch with the radio thumping out an old Fleetwood Mac tune. Pleased with how I had handled the move and made the decisions to get me to that point, I decided to rest. The next day, I would look for a part time job, and start planning for my second career.

ten

Waking unexpectedly at 2:00am to the sound of three gunshots, I rolled out of bed onto the floor, reached for my glasses from the nightstand, and crawled over to the window in the bedroom. Gently pulling the corner of the blinds slightly away from the window, I peered out. The parking lot, so serene at mid-morning when I arrived, now was full of life with people talking in groups of three or five or more.

None of the other residents seem to be alarmed at the gunshots and I noticed them pointing nonchalantly towards the apartment complex to the north. Shortly after that, I saw the blue flicker of a police car light blur by at the street and the sounds of the fading siren follow swiftly behind it. After rechecking the lock on the front door, I returned to bed.

A flicker of sunlight shining through a missing slat in the blinds crossed my eye and I opened my eyes for the second time that morning. Glancing over at the alarm clock, the face was black. Attempts with the light switches proved unsuccessful as the lack of power kept it dark.

"Great!" I spoke aloud with no one to hear my disappointment.

Opening the blinds for light, I turned on the shower and waited. After five minutes of waiting, the water heated to lukewarm, so I stepped in. Lukewarm must have been maximum for that day. I refused to allow this unfortunate beginning to drag down the first day of my new life in Texas.

While pouring a glass of juice, I hoped that the electricity would return before the week's worth of fresh food spoiled in a warm refrigerator. I lifted the phone hoping for a dial tone. There was silence on the other end. I marched down to the apartment office to find out about the electricity.

"It off all round neighborhood," explained the apartment manager sitting quietly in her darkened office.

Sitting in front of the light from my living room window, I perused the help wanted section of the classifieds. I decided against the jobs that I was qualified for but had previously been turned down. Sporting a new corporation, I was bound to succeed at recruiting. Nevertheless, to pay the bills, I needed a part time job.

After making several calls from a phone booth at a strip mall, the most interesting prospect was a position as cashier at a small hardware store. As the owner answered the phone, he asked a few questions about me, and then gave directions to the store. I experienced my first job interview in Texas.

Brown weeds crept through the cracks in what was once a blacktop parking lot in front of Sam's Ace Hardware Store. The faint broken yellow lines guided me into a parking spot next to a 10-year old pickup. Retrieving my interview folder, I marched toward the barred front door. It occurred to me that the impending interview could have been me over 25 years earlier.

Silver-white hair and a close cut beard graced the head of Sam Black as he turned towards the ringing bell that hung from the door.

"Mornin'!" he chimed, waiting for a similar response.

"Good morning. Ben White," I announced as I approached the counter.

A careful stare examined my eyes as if Sam were capable of assessing my character merely by the way I returned his glare. I obliged by seeming confident in myself even though I had certainly been knocked down by several pegs over the recent several months.

"Sam Black, I own this store."

"Yes sir. I am the one who just called you on the phone about the cashier's position."

"Well, Ben. It is not much of a position, it's a job," he acknowledged sarcastically.

"That's what I meant."

"Why in the hell are you here, Ben?"

"I need a job," I admitted and finally allowed my head to bow in humility.

I explained about the 25 years with the same company, the layoff, the separation from my wife and children, and the previous seven months of agony. Sam seemed interested and sympathetic.

"Do you have a resume or work history?"

"Of course, and it cost me nine hundred dollars to have this resume professionally formatted and sent to over 100 executives throughout seven states in the South, so please enjoy it."

"Let's take a look." Sam denoted the sarcasm and pondered over the ten different positions of increasing responsibility and prestige.

"So as Director, how many direct reports did you have?"

"Eight direct reports and forty under them," I answered, pleased to again talk about my past career.

"It says that you got your MBA from Baldridge College, where is that?"

"South Carolina."

"Jesus Ben, what has happened to you? And what is the matter with this country."

I just shrugged my shoulders, as there was nothing gained by listing my dissatisfaction with the corporate world.

"Ever been arrested?" Sam turned to the table behind him and grabbed a form.

"Not yet," I answered smugly.

He laughed, "well Ben, I can tell that it has taken a lot for you to come here and I am not going to turn you away like all of the others have. You are so overqualified for this job; I think you just might enjoy yourself. I hate to ask you to fill out an application, but I need to know address and phone number.

"What I was looking for is someone who will watch the store from about 3:00pm to 7:00 pm. Monday through Friday and help me out some on Saturdays. I currently close the store about 5:30pm and I think I am losing business. I hope that ninety more minutes will be worth more than your wages. I would be willing to start you at eight dollars per hour. That is a far cry from the sixty-five thousand that you previously made, but look around, you know I can't afford any more than that."

"Eight is fine. I feel that I need to be honest with you also. I am trying to start my own business. It will not in any way affect my work here, but you need to know that I am probably not a long-term employee. Since the last seven months has drained the severance that I received, I need to put bread on the table. I hope that you will be able to trust me and I will give you one hundred percent while I am here."

"I appreciate that Ben. When can you start?"

"How about now?"

"All right. I'll start showing you where the product is and by the end of this week you can probably work on your own."

I locked my paperwork back in the pickup and returned for my on the job training. At 5:30pm with no customers in sight, Sam closed and double locked the front door.

"When do you want me here tomorrow?"

"Why don't you show up about 10:00am."

Driving back to the apartment, I felt good about my early successes in Houston. The light in the bedroom was on and the air conditioner hummed as I entered my new digs. Checking the refrigerator, it was cold. I hoped that the week's worth of groceries were still edible. Upon lifting the receiver of the phone, a dial tone resonated in my ear. Maybe my luck was changing.

Opening my interview folder, I removed the compact disk that I received earlier that day from a local Internet company. Upon placing the disk in the CD tray, I booted the computer for the first time in Texas. Per the store instructions, I input the phone number and the modem whirred and clanged until a logon screen appeared. I entered the password that I had setup in the Internet provider's store.

Loading the address for my e-mail account, I found five new e-mails. One was from Angelo who apologized for the eviction, thanked me again for my work on the sale of his house in Beaufort, and explained that upon receipt of my new address, he was returning my last month's rent of one hundred dollars.

The second e-mail was from my attorney explaining he would mail the corporation documents for me to sign as soon as I would e-mail my new address. I received two e-mail rejection notices from earlier job interviews, one from the interview at Carolina

Manufacturing Technologies in Charlotte, North Carolina. I deleted both of them quickly.

The last e-mail was from Karen. I fanaticized about what it would say before I actually opened it.

Dear Ben,

I guess that you have moved and are somewhat settled by now. Unbelievably, I have already found your new address. You are on several published lists as a new apartment renter in the Houston area. I am not far from you now and I have a few things that I want to talk to you about. You may have stumbled on to some moneymaking opportunities.

I hope to see you soon.

Love,

Karen

There was the love thing again. Unable to imagine what moneymaking opportunities she was referring to, I let my thoughts drift on to other things. I typed in the address for the Organ Transplant Recipient list to see how it had changed in the few days it took me to relocate.

Margaret Branch was still the number one name on the list of subjects needing a new heart. The actor, Christian Flynn, was still number two and now third was a retired senator from Idaho. James Bradford had been on the list for nine months after resigning as United States Senator from Idaho.

Senator Bradford was two months shy of completing his third term but during his campaign for re-election, received a diagnosis of Rheumatic Endocarditis. His heart specialist ordered minimal strenuous activity and added his name to the organ recipient list for a new heart. At 52, the Senator had an excellent chance for many more years with someone else's heart.

Of course, I could not leave this information alone, and looked up Rheumatic Endocarditis on the Internet and found a wealth of information. This disease was most likely caused by a previous streptococcus infection, probably early in the Senator's life. Tiny vegetations grow around the valves of the heart and thicken them, forcing the valves not to close perfectly around the orifice. In the Senator's case, it was the Mitral Valve; the valve that allowed blood to flow from the left atrium to the left ventricle.

The more information I found, the more I wanted. Wondering if the Senator had any idea that someone was researching all of his personal history, I decided to close the book on his story.

Finding the list of heart donors from Missouri, I copied and saved it in my donor folder. After creating a spreadsheet with heart donors on one-side and heart recipients on the other, I drew an arrow from Renata Newman from Huntsville, Texas to William Lewis from Dallas, Texas. Noting the date of death from my previous Internet investigations, I copied and filed it in the donor folder.

While Karen's e-mail was fresh in my mind, I decided to reply before I made myself something to eat.

Karen,

It was great to hear from you again. I got a part time job today in a hardware store and will be starting my new business as manufacturing recruiter very shortly. I do miss you and cannot wait to tell you all of the things that have happened to me since I have seen you last.

Obviously, the computer is up and running and I have food and beer in the refrigerator.

Hope to see you soon.

Ben

The alarm woke me in the morning and I tried to shower before any of my apartment building neighbors had a chance to use up the hot water. The strategy was successful. I booted the computer and looked for an e-mail from Karen, but found none.

As a courtesy, I arrived for work clean-shaven with my best business casual twenty minutes before Sam wanted me there. Being early was a habit of mine that I found impossible to break.

"I'm restocking shelves. Come on back and take over for a while. I need to place a few orders," Sam said, trying to quickly establish that he was in charge.

After arranging the shelves with the new stock, I walked the store noting locations of product and straightened shelves as I went. Noticing a few dust balls in the corners, I found a broom in the back room and swept the shop from front to back. From time to time Sam would look up from the phone and smile, knowing that he was getting a lot for his money.

Taking notes on the short stock, I reviewed the list with Sam between phone calls. He explained his method of re-ordering and I listened intently and consequently learned his method. This was not to admit that I thought his method was right; there was plenty of time to assess the situation and make recommendations later. This was only my second day.

After a quick lesson on the cash register, I was on my own checking out the few customers that had wandered in. I checked on a few items with missing prices and Sam knew them by heart. He took the time to show me how to find a price in the computer if it was not marked on the product. I picked this up quickly.

"Why don't you use the computer to flag you when you need to re-order?" I asked.

Sam appeared threatened as he glanced from his supplier statements, "because I don't."

"I understand," knowing that I had crossed the line; I knew not to bring it up again.

We walked out at about 5:45pm that evening, but opened back up when a car came into the parking lot. It was fortunate that we did because we sold five gallons of paint at $18 per gallon. Based on Sam's excitement, I concluded that paint prices contained a high markup.

As I dodged the potholes in the apartment parking lot, I noticed a cable company's truck parked directly in front of my apartment. The technician dressed in a khaki uniform and a ball cap worked on the cable box outside my front door.

"Are you hooking up my cable?" I inserted my key in the door knowing that I had not yet ordered cable.

"You look like you might need the services of a cable guy," the technician barked in a false voice.

As the technician turned around and removed the hat, her blond hair fell out and identified the owner. It was Karen.

"Oh my gosh, what are you doing?" I asked as a wave of happiness enveloped me.

"I'm hooking up cable for you," she smiled with confidence.

"Are you serious?"

"Absolutely!"

"For free?"

"Isn't that the best way? Can we go inside?" Karen asked.

Once inside, I extended my arms for a hug and she hugged back, still a little tentative.

"So, how have you been?" she pushed me back slightly to start a conversation.

"I'm okay. I am working now, at least part time. In about a week I will be working afternoon & evenings. That will give me a chance during the day to start learning the recruiting business and develop some clients."

"Sounds promising. You had dinner yet?" Karen asked.

"No, I have some food here though."

"No, I think we need to celebrate your new job. Let's go out. My treat," Karen smiled.

"Sure, let's go."

"I know this Italian restaurant in the Hyatt a few blocks from here."

"Am I dressed okay?" I asked, always cautious about the proper protocol.

"Sure, am I?"

Driving us through the maze of 50 story buildings to the Hyatt, I parked on the street around the corner from the main entrance.

"So what is with this cable thing? When did you get this job?"

"Oh, I'm not working for a cable company. It's a cover I've been working on."

"Well, you sure fooled me," I said.

"What is going on with the organ donation project that you were researching?"

We ordered and received drinks and the meal while I rambled through a long explanation. I explained about Christine at Dr. Lyon's office and how willing she was to help me. Surprisingly, Karen seemed fascinated.

Describing the individuals who were on the organ recipient list waiting for organs, I further explained how I had researched the information on them. When she heard the tale about Christian Flynn and his life without a new heart, Karen hung on my every word. I was confused and a little suspicious why she was so interested.

We left the restaurant and drove the fifteen blocks back to the apartment. I was a little unsure about what would happen next and Karen sensed this.

"Look Ben, I really like you. However, I am different. I think that our government made me different. I don't know if I can have a normal relationship. I have lived by myself and with myself for many many years now. I have worked for an employer for a long time and I will never get any awards, in fact, if I do not keep in the shadows, I myself might be eliminated.

"Now, I know that you have not asked, but I can see that you just have one bed. I will stay with you tonight, but I will not sleep with you. I have some things I want to talk to you about tomorrow night, and I don't want to confuse you with any emotional ties."

"Fine. Please let me take the couch and you can have the bed. Here is a second key, please feel free to come and go as you wish." I was just happy to share her company if that was all she was willing to give.

"Thanks, but I already made myself a key. I have a key-making machine in the cable service van. And the couch is fine for me, but thanks for the offer."

We both laughed at that and got ready for bed in a dim bedroom. Turning on the small TV on the dresser, I surfed the 50 different channels that now came in crystal clear. "Great perks you get when you share your apartment with the cable guy," I bragged. I quickly surfed through the movie channels passing over the barroom scene from the movie Starwars.

"Turn it back," Karen said abruptly.

"To what?"

"Back one. Right there. This is a classic."

"Starwars? Starwars is a classic?"

"You bet it is. My favorite movie. I love this movie. Can we watch a little of it?"

"Sure. So who are you in this movie, Princess Leah?" I asked, propping the pillow up against the headboard to the bed.

"More like Darth Vader, I think." She took the empty side of the bed, sitting not laying.

eleven

My eyes opened the next morning and I immediately remembered that I had spent a sober night with Karen. I noticed a blurred flickering light from the living room and concluded that Karen was already up and on the computer. I glanced at the alarm clock on the nightstand. It was 5:15am.

"I didn't wake you, did I?" Karen asked as I shuffled into the living room behind her.

"No, I'd be getting up in a few minutes anyhow."

"You want me to make some breakfast?"

"No, I'll just have some juice."

After another cold shower and some small talk with Karen, I headed for door and then to work.

"You going to be here when I get back?"

"You never know, but I hope so. We need to talk," Karen turned away from the computer looking as fresh, young, and alive as ever.

As I puttered around the hardware store, Sam's eyes followed me. I sensed that he noticed a difference in my attitude. Waiting on most of the customers, I helped them all find what they wanted, and was successful in selling them additional products. I felt Sam's eyes on me throughout most of the day, sensing an increased confidence in me.

Sam left during lunch to run an errand across town. He left his cell phone number and encouraged me to call him if I was stuck. When he returned I bragged to him about how well I had done without him. Working alone from 5:00pm to 7:00pm that evening, I closed the store precisely as Sam had instructed.

The delightful aroma of broiled steak filtered through the apartment when I opened the front door. Potatoes sizzled in the frying pan in front of my newest diversion. As previously recognized by my new employer, I was acting differently. Maybe I was beginning to feel happiness again.

Karen and I enjoyed a delightful dinner sharing small talk about the hardware store and my opinions of Sam Black.

"So, have either of you caught on to the fact that he is black and you are white?"

"What do you mean?"

"Sam Black and Ben White." she answered

"Ha ha ha."

"I thought it was pretty clever," Karen finished putting the dinner dishes into the lime stained dishwasher.

We sat facing each other in the living room. Karen was uneasy about something as if the situation may offer a defining moment in our relationship.

"Let's talk," she leaned forward in her chair.

"About what?"

"I want you to keep an open mind about something."

"Sure," I said, thinking she wanted to talk about our relationship.

"I am interested in your research on the organ donor program."

"You are?" I answered somewhat surprised by the topic.

"Based on what you have said, I think that you probably know more about this program from both sides of the fence. You know how to gain access on organ donors as well as organ recipients. You know where to find information about the donor lists and now you know how to find out about individual's personal lives. That is a lot of power to have."

"I guess that I really hadn't thought about it."

"Let's go to the computer and look again at the latest Donor Recipient list."

"Sure," I agreed, as I had not seen the list for a couple days and I wanted to impress her with my new skills.

When the list popped up, I looked at the top of the list and was surprised to see that Christian Flynn was now number one on the list of heart recipients. Since I was curious, I searched the St. Louis paper for Margaret Branch, expecting an article on her heart transplantation. Instead, her name popped up in the obituaries with a sentence explaining her cause of death and her surviving daughter.

"Wow, I guess she didn't live long enough for her new heart," I concluded.

Karen stared into my eyes in an unusual way, "I guess not."

"I knew that there were two ways to get off of this list and I guess that Margaret took the second."

"Christian Flynn lives in LA, doesn't he?" Karen led me with her pointed questions.

"Yea."

"Why don't you look up the donor list in California and find a couple of donors that have the same blood type as Mr. Flynn."

After an hour of searching the donor list and expanding the personal information on potential candidates, we identified a 45-year-old man in Bakersfield and a 49-year-old woman in LA.

Juan Alvarez was a single man working as a landscape laborer for the city of Bakersfield. Renting an apartment in the slum area of the city, he had no record of any medical visits to any of the hospitals within Bakersfield. The Mayor of Bakersfield was strongly in favor of the organ donor program and in January of the previous year signed up over two hundred city employees to register their offer of organ donation.

Debbie Shultz was a Viet Nam veteran's widow who never remarried. She lived by herself in a mobile home drawing a survivor's pension from the government as she had for the previous 35 years. Debbie visited her daughter once per month at a mental hospital close to San Bernadino. She was a member of the Baptist church that was a few blocks from her mobile home but had not attended for several years.

"I'm shocked at the information we can find on these people with just a little ingenuity," I admitted.

"Why don't you give Mr. Flynn a phone call tomorrow and see what he knows about his position on the recipient list?"

"Why?"

"Don't you think that the people on the Organ Recipient list would like to know where they are on the list?" Karen drilled me.

"Probably," I answered after some thought.

"That's what I am thinking. Maybe it would be worth some money for Mr. Flynn to know where he is at on the list."

"You think it would?" I asked, somewhat concerned with where Karen was going with this line of questions.

"Only one way to find out. Make sure that when you call, you call from a phone booth, preferably away from the apartment or the hardware store. Try not to stay on the phone long. Do not identify yourself. Control the conversation. Let him know that you'll call him back. Ask him what that information might be worth to him. Do not even suggest that you'll tell him how you have come across this information. Be his friend."

"I don't know. I'm trying to look at this from their perspective and I don't think I would pay any money," I admitted.

"That's just it," Karen interrupted. "You can't put yourself in their position because you are still healthy. Your mind hasn't been programmed by months of despair."

"I still don't think that it's right," I repeated.

"If he has been waiting over a year for a heart and if he loves life, he will want to know how much longer he has to wait. You will be doing him a favor. You've got good news to tell him."

"All right," I said. "Tomorrow is Saturday and I work in the morning, so I'll call him on my way home from work." I don't know why I finally agreed to the phone call unless I was trying so hard to please Karen.

"Give it your best salesmanship. You were in Sales for 3 years, close the deal."

Searching back through our conversations, I could not remember ever telling Karen about the 3 years in Sales. "You staying here tonight?" I hoped her answer was yes.

"Sure, but I'm leaving first thing tomorrow morning. I might be back late Sunday. By the way, I will be in California. If Mr. Flynn is interested in the information that you have, I can go to him on Saturday night, pick up the money, and give him the good news. I will call you early evening to find out what he says."

Karen fell asleep on the couch early while I pecked away at the computer, picking up e-mail and trying to find out more about

Christian Flynn. I printed out the list of films that he had made and the co-stars and leading ladies that he worked with.

Adjusting the blanket that outlined the curves of a perfect feminine form, I turned as I left the living room and silently blew a kiss in Karen's direction. Lying awake, I wondered if I would ever be able to be intimate with her. Maybe I needed to tell her exactly how I felt about her and take my lumps if she did not feel the same.

Just as on the previous morning, Karen awoke before I and busily pecked away at the keyboard. As I wandered past her to the kitchen, I noticed an official-looking government document displayed on the screen and the name Debbie Shultz listed in bold letters across the top. I was still not fully awake and could not remember where I had seen the name before. She quickly switched to another screen and we again exchanged small talk about sleep and mattresses and bed companions.

Gathering my papers on Christian Flynn, I stuffed them in a folder and headed for the door. "Have a good flight!" I yelled to Karen.

"May the force be with you, Luke!" she answered and we both laughed.

The few hours at the hardware store went quickly and Sam Black provided less and less coaching each day. I must have been learning at a much faster pace than most of his previous help. Leaving the hardware store at 12:30pm, I drove about 2 to 3 miles across town to the Galleria district.

After finding a phone booth away from the busy street, I opened the folder on the shelf provided. I punched in the numbers for the phone card I had purchased a few minutes earlier and dialed the number in California for Christian Flynn.

"Hello?" came an older voice with Spanish accent.

"Could I please speak to Christian Flynn?" I spoke the words slowly.

"Who eez calling?

"William Reed. I was in a film with Mr. Flynn many years ago," I was perfecting my ability to lie using the information I had found the previous night.

"I will see if he can talk to you."

There was the clanking sound of the phone hitting the table and then the faint sounds of Christian's domestic help announcing my call.

"Bill, how are you? It's been a few years," Christian acknowledged.

"Mr. Flynn. I'm sure that you can tell, this is not William Reed, he is in fact deceased now."

"Who is this?"

"Please don't hang up, Mr. Flynn. My name is Pete Rogers and I am in possession of some information that may be of interest to you."

"What kind of information?"

"Well, Mr. Flynn, I am wondering if you would at all like to know where your name is on the list for receiving a new heart?"

There was a pause for a few seconds. "You can't know that, it is a closely guarded secret. My doctor doesn't even know, I have asked him and asked him," Christian exclaimed with conviction.

"Well, Mr. Flynn, suppose that I can convince you that I do know that information and I would be willing to share that information with you. What do you think that it would be worth for you to have that knowledge?"

"I think that this is preposterous and I can't believe that you would prey on a dying man and take advantage of his declining health."

His words cut into me like a sharp knife. This had definitely not been my style. My only rationalization was that Mr. Flynn would be better off in the end, knowing where he was on the list. Nevertheless, it still hurt me.

"Mr. Flynn, I want you to think about it and I will give you a call later this afternoon for your answer. Have a nice day."

Amazed at my delivery and my ability to keep a constant tone throughout the conversation, I wondered how well I was able to set the hook.

Driving home to an empty apartment, I decided to gather my laundry and head for the apartment laundry facilities. When I finally found the small room near the office where three washing machines and two dryers lined the walls, I discovered that only one machine actually worked and that there were two residents in front of me waiting.

Opting for the Laundromat that I passed on the way to work each day, I was considerably more successful. After my laundry finished, I returned to the apartment and waited for 5:00pm to call Mr. Flynn again. I anticipated the call, wondering what Christian would say, and how powerful information was when you had it and others wanted it. Most of my work life it had been the other way around.

Driving to another phone booth a little closer to my side of Houston, I dialed the numbers and a different person answered the phone this time. She seemed much older and significantly more polished in her diction.

"Could I speak with Mr. Flynn? You may tell him that it is Pete Rogers."

"A Mr. Pete Rogers, for you?" she announced.

"Thank you dear," a muffled voice said as Christian picked up the phone on the table next to him.

"Yes?"

"Mr. Flynn. Good evening. I wonder if you have had a chance to think about the conversation that we had earlier today?"

"Well, Mr. Rogers. Although I really think it stinks what you are doing, I would like to know the information that you have." With the receiver pulled away from his mouth, he whispered, "could you get me some coffee, Dear?" He, no doubt, was trying to disguise from his wife of thirty years, exactly what the conversation was about. After a short pause, he said into the phone, "how can I be assured that the information that you claim to possess is factual?"

"Mr. Flynn, you can't for sure. However, I will tell you where you are on the list, how long you have been on the list, and how long you have been at the position where you are."

"I am assuming that this is not totally legal and above board."

"You could assume that."

"Well, to cut to the chase, I would be willing to spend about $1000 for that information."

"The going rate for this information is $3,000," I repeated cautiously.

"In that case, I will give you $2,000."

"Deal," I snapped back.

"All right, what is it that you know?"

"I have an assistant that will call on you later this evening. After you pay the money, she will give you the information. If the adequacy and correctness of the information is not satisfactory to you, she will return the money to you while she is there." The added guarantee that I presented made me feel a little better about taking his money. "Good evening, Mr. Flynn."

Like a child going home with a 100% on a test, I could not wait to share my success with Karen. Driving home though, I wondered whether this plan would actually work out. I played solitaire on the computer and waited for the phone to ring. Karen finally called at 6:00pm and got right to the point, "did you talk to Mr. Flynn?

"Yes."

"Well, what did he say?"

"He said yes," I answered, allowing myself to smile.

"How much?"

"Two thousand."

"Two thousand?"

"You think that's enough?" I asked.

"I think that's a great start. Did you tell him that I am coming over?"

"Sure did. You are on. Don't screw it up," I laughed.

"I'll see you tomorrow night. Good job, Ben!"

Pleased that Karen and I were getting along, maybe this little partnership would bring us closer and get her to trust me.

I immediately accessed the computer and started to research further down the list of recipients, looking for someone who had the money to pay me for the information that I was retrieving easier each day. Focusing on Senator James Bradford, I determined that his family controlled a significant amount of money. Maybe he had the power to find this information out himself and I should bypass him. I still pressed on for information and decided to talk about it with Karen when she returned.

Sunday allowed more work on the computer, mixing research on my recruiting business with more research on potential organ recipients. The sound of the front door opening awoke me from an afternoon nap on the couch.

"You going to sleep all day?" Karen strode in with uplifting energy.

She had a white envelope in her hand, walked over to the couch, and handed it to me. I opened the envelope and counted $1,400 in $100 bills.

"I thought that he was going to pay two grand."

"He did. Fourteen hundred dollars is your split. I already have mine."

"Well, I'm no mathematician, but two thousand divided by two used to be one thousand."

"My cut is only 30%," she said.

"Why is that, you did all of the work."

"No Ben, you did the research. After all, this whole thing was your idea."

"It was?"

"That's the way I see it," Karen answered.

"How did he take the news?"

"He was very grateful. Very happy. Until I told him that the previous holder of the number one spot waited for three months as number one and finally died waiting."

"Why in the hell did you tell him that?"

"Just in case we could get some more money from him."

"How is that?"

"Well you know, if we could make arrangements for a heart to be available."

"I don't understand."

"Well, just start looking for another client, maybe from the kidney or lung recipient lists," she answered, quickly changing the subject.

twelve

Karen showered and dressed quickly the next morning saying only that she had some business out of town. She instructed me to get a commercial bank account under the name of Manufacturing Services Recruiting and to deposit the $1,400 in it.

After running a few errands in the morning, I drove to the hardware store. Work at the store was easy for me and I enjoyed the relationship that I had developed with Sam, believing that he took pleasure in my company as well. I buried myself in my efforts at the hardware store and my research on the Internet. Things were finally looking up for a change.

On Tuesday morning, visiting the main office of the Lonestar Bank and Trust on McKinney Street, I had taken the corporation papers that the attorney had drawn up and completed commercial checking account applications for about an hour. My initial deposit of $1,400 was exactly the instructions that Karen had given me. Returning to the apartment, I created a checking account register on the PC and labeled it Manufacturing Services Recruiting, and logged my first deposit.

Investigating deeper down the organ recipient list, I documented personal information about each potential recipient and assessed his or her ability and probability of paying for our information. On Tuesday night after closing the hardware store, I logged on to the Internet and again accessed the organ recipient list.

On this evening, I was very surprised to discover that Christian Flynn was no longer number one on the list. Using the Internet, I checked the Los Angeles Tribune web site and read a two-column article summarizing the career of Christian Flynn and describing a successful heart transplant operation.

There was reference to a 58-year-old donor from San Bernadino who passed away from respiratory arrest. The article further explained that an unknown person transported this woman to Los Angeles General Hospital. Although the death was not suspicious, the Los Angeles Police Department asked for information about the person who brought her in. The Tribune neglected to list the heart donor's name.

Again, since Christian Flynn was once a celebrity, the Tribune took the opportunity to educate the public about the ever-growing need of organ donation and the ease at which a person could register their wishes to donate some or all of their organs or tissues.

Revisiting the organ donor list, I concluded that the heart donor from San Bernadino must have been a Debbie Shultz. There was nothing listed in the Tuesday's paper from San Bernadino but obituaries sometimes didn't make the papers for a few days.

Updating my spreadsheet by drawing a line from Debbie Shultz to Christian Flynn, I filed the spreadsheet in my research folder.

Senator Bradford, now number one on the recipient list and based on my research, seemed like the perfect candidate for our information sales. Of course, I would wait for Karen to return, but I had all of the information summarized for my visit with her.

Karen strolled in the door at about 9:30 that night. I advised her about the bank and described the article about Christian Flynn.

"You act like you already know this," I commented.

"I . . I saw it on a news program today," Karen answered cautiously.

"I watched the news tonight at the hardware store, and I don't remember any story about it. I'm sure that I would have remembered it."

"I saw it on a local station," she tried to recover.

"From LA?"

"Yes"

"So you were in LA?"

"Da, I guess so," she answered and walked to the refrigerator to grab a beer. "You want one?"

"Sure. Hey, I got some information that I need to share with you."

"Let's do it," she said.

"I have done some more research on the heart recipient list. The number one candidate is an ex-Senator from Idaho. His father started his own company, grew it to 100 million dollars, and sold it five years ago. James Bradford's father funded his campaign for the last election. The family has money."

"What, you want to do this again?" Karen asked, knowing the answer.

"Like you said, I think that there is money to be made."

"How long has he been on the list?"

"Almost a year. He has been back in the hospital three times in the last month. I think that he is more than ready."

"Don't you think that since he has been a Senator, he won't bite on a proposition like ours?" she asked.

"I think he might. He was investigated during his first term for accepting large donations from a defense contractor in Idaho while he was on the Defense Appropriations Committee."

"You're getting good at this!" Karen put her arm around me and pulled me close to her side, "it might work. Why don't you give him a call tomorrow?"

"I'll give it a try," I told her.

"Why don't you look up some possible donors from Idaho that have a blood type match. How long will that take?"

"Do I need to do that tonight?" The sense of urgency puzzled me.

"Don't you try to match donor and recipient on your spreadsheet?" Karen asked.

"Yea, but not till after the transplant operation."

"You work on that, and I will go out and get us some pizza. Be back in about 45 minutes."

Although tired, I labored quickly to identify potential donors, so I could present something to Karen when she returned. Identifying three potential donors from a list of 250, I searched my favorite address and phone finder, copied the information to a Word document, and printed it. The printer ejected the paper just as

Karen returned with pizza in hand. She traded the pizza for the piece of paper.

"I'll call you tomorrow about noon and see how you did with your phone call to the good Senator," Karen suggested as we finished the last piece of pizza.

Knowing better than to ask Karen her travel plans for the next day, we repeated our routine of preparing for bed in different places. Karen still insisted on taking the couch in spite of continual pleas from me to take the bed with or without me in it. Just like other mornings, Karen was gone by the time I woke from sleep. Just once I would like to wake up, roll over to find her next to me, and then make love until it was time for me to go to work. Maybe someday.

"This is Dr. Andrews calling for James Bradford," I falsely announced to the woman from Idaho Falls.

"Well, Dr. Andrews, he's back in the hospital. I thought that you might know that."

"Is this Mrs. Bradford?"

"Yes."

"Mrs. Bradford, I was called by Mr. Bradford's heart doctor for a consultation."

"I have not heard about you, Dr. Andrews. Where are you from?"

"I am currently practicing at the Mayo Clinic." She was making it difficult and I had to think fast to keep up with my improvisation.

"How is your husband doing?"

"Not very well . . . Doctor . . . Andrews. I think that he is losing the battle. He has waited so long for this transplant. I hope that he can hold on long enough."

"Has you heart doctor told you how long he may have to wait?"

"No! The doctor said that he not only does not know but it is impossible for him to find out. I thought that you would already know that," the Senator's wife proved to be much smarter than I planned.

I had a choice to make. Should I end this call and try to contact the senator at the hospital or should I try to deal with his wife. Mrs. Bradford was certainly engaged with her husband's care and had a determined interest in his future. My silence made her impatient.

"Doctor?"

"Mrs. Bradford. As you have probably have figured out by know I am not a doctor."

"Who is this?" she asked in a stern voice.

"Please don't hang up ma'am. I have some information that I believe you might be interested in."

"There is no information that I would want from a fraud."

"Don't sell me short. You know the information that the doctor told you was impossible to get?"

"Yes."

"I have that information. I can tell you the position that your husband holds on that donor recipient list. With that information, you can reassure your husband about how much longer he will have to 'hold on'."

"How much?"

"Well Mrs. Bradford, I know that this information might be just the thing to save his life. I think that this information should be worth $5,000."

"That's absurd. I am not going to pay you that much. Do you think I'm stupid?"

"No Mrs. Bradford, I think you are very practical. How much is your husband's future worth to you?"

"Look, I have about $2,500 that James doesn't know about. However, I will need to see you. I'm not just going to hand over $2,500."

"I think that is the right thing to do Mrs. Bradford. My associate will contact you at your home sometime this evening. She will give you the information and will only take your money if you are satisfied."

"What makes you think that I won't call the police on you?"

"Because I think that you are tired of waiting on the list. Because you love your husband and you want your life back. Because it isn't fair to you."

"I won't be home from the hospital until after seven," she said.

"I'll make sure my associate waits until then."

I left the phone booth and drove back to the apartment to wait for Karen's call.

"Well, how did my best salesman do?" Karen asked without even a hello.

"A little twist this time."

"How's that?"

"It seems that the good senator is back in the hospital."

"So you didn't talk to him?" Karen asked.

"No. But I talked to his wife."

"And?

"And, she is going to pay us $2,500."

"When?"

"After 7:00pm tonight. Can you get there by then?" I asked.

"Yea, probably."

"I'm counting on you. I had to work hard for this one."

After lunch, I drove to the hardware store. Sam had had a good day and was in a pleasant mood. On his way out the door, he handed me a check.

"What's this?" I asked.

"You weren't going to do this all for fun, were you?"

"No sir. Thank you."

"You're welcome. You are doing a good job. Don't disappoint me."

"You can count on me."

Back on the computer after arriving at the apartment that evening, I again inspected the list. It was obvious that Senator Bradford would still be at the top of the list because I had just talked to his wife. I collected data until 8:00pm and then got off the computer in case Karen called.

Karen called at about 10:00 o'clock to make her progress report. "That wasn't hard at all," Karen admitted.

"A walk in the park?"

"You could say that."

"You were right Ben, I think they are oozing money."

"Maybe I didn't ask for enough."

"You did fine. You know it is extremely pretty country here, near the mountains and all. I think that I am going to stay here for a couple days."

"Great, I'll just stay here and work," I answered sarcastically.

"See you in a couple of days. Another good job, Ben."

"Thanks. Good night. Hurry back."

After breakfast the next morning, I went to the Lonestar Bank to deposit my paycheck from the hardware store and withdraw some cash. Very different from the paycheck I had deposited a few days earlier, I folded the deposit slip in my pocket and then stopped at the grocery store on my way back to the apartment.

Loading the check register program on the computer, I entered $150 as a deposit. As I was just about to store the deposit slip in my accordion file, I noticed the balance printed on the bottom of the slip.

Eight thousand five hundred and fifty dollars was the number printed below the word balance. I punched the numbers on my calculator and identified a seven thousand dollar problem on my account. I could not believe that the bank would make a sizable mistake in my favor. Rationalizing that I had only opened the account a few days earlier, I decided to wait until my next deposit to determine if they caught the mistake.

thirteen

Bored with my research on the heart recipient list, I switched over to the list for liver recipients. Number one on this list was Paul Butler, an unemployed disabled Vietnam veteran from Dallas. Checking a few personal items on Mr. Butler, I quickly dismissed him as a candidate for our information business.

Billie Silverstone, second on the list, possessed definite potential. I quickly learned that Billie was the lead singer for Southern Cross, a country band from the 1970s. Although she stopped performing five years earlier, she kept up her consumption of alcohol until she developed Laennec's Portal Cirrhosis, a liver disease that eventually placed her on the liver recipient list.

I further ascertained that prolonged overuse of alcohol destroys liver cells and those cells are replaced by scar tissue. The scar tissue surrounding the portal areas, eventually leads to death of the patient. In spite of a previous liver lobectomy, Billie continued to partake of the liquid toxin several months after the operation. Her last chance at life would be a liver transplant.

Billie's father instilled in her a much-disciplined fiscal responsibility that allowed her to save and invest her many years of success. In short, she had money. My only concern was that she could negotiate better than I could. After I wrote out several possible dialogs for our future conversation, I started a new file folder labeled LIVER DONORS.

Pulling up the donor lists in Dallas and Nashville, I identified a couple of names from each state where the blood type was identical to Mr. Butler and Billie Silverstone. For each, I got address, phone number, some financial information and current job.

The standard issue olive drab shorts and shirt of the United Parcel Service stood in the doorway of my apartment that morning. The letter size package came from a name I had never heard of. Inside the package were round trip airplane tickets to Frankfurt, Germany, reservations for a car and one night hotel stay in Germany, all with my name on them. The date on the reservations was for the upcoming Thursday. I knew that an explanation, probably from Karen, would present itself eventually.

I diligently continued my research after another day of easy work at the hardware store. Hoping to hear from Karen so I could share my latest findings, I logged off the Internet at 9:00pm in case she would call. A few minutes later, she obliged.

"Having a good time up there in the mountains?" I asked.

"It is nice up here, Ben. How are things back in Houston?" I could tell by her tone that she was waiting for a briefing on my research.

"I have started looking at the liver recipient list as well as the heart list."

"And?" Her phone etiquette became more and more businesslike.

"And I think I have a possibility."

Spending the next 30 minutes providing information on both Paul Butler and Billie Silverstone, I included information on the donors as well.

"Where did you say Billie Silverstone lives?"

"Nashville. I doubt if Paul Butler has any money and I don't think he would be a very good target."

"I agree. Let's go after Ms. Silverstone. When can you call her?"

"Tomorrow morning if that fits your schedule. Aren't you coming back here?"

"Not now. I will head for Nashville tomorrow. By the way, did you get the tickets?" she asked.

"Oh, so you are the one who sent the tickets. What makes you think that I wanted to go to Europe?"

"I wasn't really thinking about whether you wanted to go there. You need to go there," she said.

"And why is that?"

"You need to open up a bank account there."

"I already have the commercial bank account that you asked me to get last week," I said.

"You really need to get an account in Switzerland."

"Why?"

"So that your clients can wire you money. The banks in Switzerland will ensure that your name is never given out if there is ever an investigation."

"An investigation?" my heart rate went up immediately.

"Don't worry Ben, it will never happen."

"How do you know?" I asked.

"Because we are very cautious."

"Can't I just get this account over the phone?" I pleaded.

"No, they will only issue a new account if you are there in person."

"Are you going too?"

"No, you'll do fine. I have e-mailed you the name of the bank, the name of the bank manager, and the directions from Frankfurt. Will you have problems getting off from work?"

"No, I'll talk to Sam. So far, I have done everything he has asked and then some."

"I'll call about noon again," Karen said.

"Maybe we can spend some time together after this assignment."

"We'll see. There is still a lot of work to do. You want to make some more money don't you."

"Of course," I admitted.

"Not again." The computer monitor went black and the room darkened quickly.

"What's wrong?"

"Oh, we lost power again. It happens about every other day here."

"Maybe its time you moved out of that apartment. With the money you'll be making, you can afford better. And get two phone lines so you don't tie up the phone line while you are on the computer."

"All right, I'll look around when I get back from Switzerland."

"I'll talk to you tomorrow. Do a good job, sounds like this one won't want to part with her money."

With money now in the bank and no electricity for the computer, I got in my Nissan and headed across town where I had located a strip bar a few days earlier. The lot was almost full with the finest machines ever made. BMW, Jaguar, Mercedes, Cadillac, and Lexus. Parking the Nissan there was an embarrassment.

Inside, the club was as obscure as my apartment, but the pounding beat, the rising smoke, and the extraordinarily beautiful women reminded me of exactly where I was. Sitting at an empty table near the center stage, the other stages eventually came into focus. Two of the three stages had dancers, both down to their G-strings. Once I consumed my first Heineken, I began to feel at ease.

Rachael approached me and asked if I wanted some company. With D-size breasts protruding from the mini bikini top and shoulder length blond hair, it was difficult to carry on an intelligent conversation. She sat close to me and nuzzled in towards my neck. She slid her hand down between my legs.

"Oh! How about a table dance?"

"What is the going rate for table dances?"

"Twenty plus tip of course," she displayed a forced smile.

"All right then. How about the next song?"

"Okay Baby."

I enjoyed Rachael for four more dances, paid her a hundred, and ordered another beer. The ten o'clock crowd arrived and the tables filled with anticipating executives. The twenties were dropping fast and the girls were working hard. It was fun to watch the other men out of their element and the girls into theirs.

Carefully maneuvering the streets of downtown Houston, I watched out for Houston's finest all along the way. When I reached the apartment, the sign on the street was dark, even though there were lights across the street and one block away. Lighting a candle, I got ready for bed.

The next day, I drove to yet another phone booth and repeated the phone sales process that I was beginning to perfect. Since most of these people within the public eye are skeptical of solicitors, I needed to assume a believable character. "Good morning, this is Carl Hudson from Nashville Today. Could I speak with Billie Silverstone please?"

"I'm afraid that she is not available," came a young man's voice from the other end.

"Could you tell me when she might be able to talk to me?"

"What is your business, Mr. Hudson?"

"Well, like I said before, I'm from Nashville Today, a new radio program from 98 WSIX. We are doing a segment on Tammy Wynette and those that knew her best."

"Tammy Wynette?"

"Yes sir. Are you Billie's agent or manager?" I asked.

"No, not exactly."

"Look, could you ask Billie if she would like to say a few kind words about Ms. Wynette?"

"Hold on . . . she said that she would be with you in a minute. Please only five minutes. She is not feeling well."

"Thanks a lot for your help."

"Mr. Hudson?" a weak but upbeat Billie Silverstone answered.

"Thanks for taking the call Billie."

"You're welcome. How can I help you?"

"I am not Carl Hudson. I do not work for any radio station. I have some information about your position on the liver recipient list. I know that you have not announced your latest condition to the general public. I am not going to lie to you; I am willing to sell you this information for five thousand dollars. I am not trying to hurt you but help you. I have been laid off of work for eight months and I am just trying to make a living."

"That is the strangest telemarketing call I have ever had. I will tell you Mr. Hudson, or whatever your name is, I am dying, but I enjoy a good joke when I hear one."

"I appreciate your enjoyment, but I can assure you that what I say is the truth," I said.

"I am relatively young, too young to die. I made my share of mistakes but I have been one of the fortunate ones. I have lived the good life."

"Just hang up, Billie," came a muffled command from her male companion.

"And you should live a lot longer. Don't you want to sing again?" I asked, trying to pour on the drama.

"Sing? What in the hell do you know about me?" she asked.

"Actually I know quite a bit about you. I have amassed three pages of your early life, your family, and your first marriage. I know about your addictions, your previous surgeries, a very detailed medical history, and I know that you are very provident with your spending."

"Mr. X, I can tell you have done your homework. I do not agree with your choice of occupation, and what I would really like instead of your information is a normal size pinkish red liver that has not been pickled by the likes of someone like me. Can you sell me one of those for five thousand dollars?"

"Sorry, I'm only in the information business," I answered.

"So you are. So you are. What do you want from me?"
"To be exact, I want your money. My associate will come by your house tonight at 7:00pm. She will give you the information and if you are not satisfied, don't pay her."

"You know, I have some pretty tight security here."

"I have confidence that my associate would be able to get to your door, but if you are willing, you could open the front gate for her."

"I'll think about it. Nevertheless, it was interesting to talk to you. Perhaps if things do work out for me we could talk again."

"I would like that, but it would be better if you forgot about me."

Billie gently placed the phone back on the hook and I reveled at the uniqueness of the people I had crossed paths with in my most recent life. I rushed back to the apartment for my phone call with Karen.

"Where we at?" Karen's conversation was turning our relationship into that of business associates.

"Strange conversation. She was not mad at me but mad at herself. I'm not sure if she is going to pay."

"So how did you leave it?"

"I told her that you were going to show up at her front gate at 7:00pm tonight. I ask her if she would open the gate for you."

"That really wasn't necessary. The stone fence surrounding her house and grounds is only six feet, no barb wire and only two surveillance cameras."

"You've been there?" I was again amazed at how proficient and careful Karen was.

"You know that I have to check these things out before they know I'm coming," Karen said.

"I don't know. I don't think that she is ready to die. I think that she might pay the money."

"Let's hope so."

"I don't know how happy she will be to find out that she is number two on the list," I sympathized.

"Number one actually," Karen corrected me. "Paul Butler passed away yesterday. I took the cable repair van to his house in Dallas last night to do some more in depth research, but his live in girlfriend said he had passed away earlier that day. He'll probably come off of the official list tomorrow."

"Whoa, that is too freaky," I said.

"So, have we got time to do one more before your trip to Switzerland?"

"No, let's take a break."

"All right, but you have got to keep me busy," Karen insisted and hung up the phone.

Where had I gone wrong with this relationship? While I wanted to get closer, she was keeping me at arm's length. While I wanted nothing more than to see her, she always found reasons to be away. I did not really mind the idea of making money, and although it was not altogether honest, I didn't believe that I was hurting anyone. Most of the time, we provided information making the clients happy. Maybe our information provided our customers the strength to continue waiting.

Feeling significant guilt, I asked Sam for a day or two off work and lied about why I needed it. Closing the hardware store an hour later than normal to compensate for my personal time off, I brought in five more customers during the hour. I bought a paper from one of the street vendors on my way back to the apartment.

Perusing the classifieds, looking for a more expensive apartment in a better neighborhood, I was attracted to the high-rise apartments in the Galleria area of Houston. Still downtown with all of the action, the apartments had strict security provisions that, after my experience with the slum apartment, became more attractive to me. Maybe I could turn the second bedroom into an office and buy some nice computer furniture which was previously unaffordable.

My first trip to Europe came up quickly and I found myself a little excited about the trip. After drawing five hundred dollars in cash from the Lonestar Bank for expenses and two thousand to start my new account, I studied the withdrawal slip that the teller handed me. Expecting to see a correction in the balance reducing it by seven thousand, the balance showed seven thousand higher and read fifteen thousand eight hundred dollars.

I did not understand. Turning to go back and ask the teller, the person behind me in line was already at the window. Well, I just will not spend it and when they catch the error, I will be okay, I thought.

Back at the apartment, I logged onto the Internet and turned on the TV for the first time in two days. Switching the TV to CNN, I glanced at it as I quickly checked my e-mails. Once I logged onto the organ recipient site, the corner of my eye caught a picture of the ex-senator James Bradford filling the TV screen.

"Senator Bradford was flown by helicopter to Boise Idaho where he received the gift of a new heart today. His doctor's are claiming that the senator is doing very well and is not rejecting his new heart. The donor was a twenty-seven-year-old nurse from Idaho Falls that suffered from acute asthma. She went into respiratory failure and passed away on her way to the hospital. By request, her family has withheld her name.

"Her family, satisfying the wishes of their daughter, immediately advised the emergency room doctor of her donor status. Within an hour of death, they rushed her to surgery, where they removed her heart and prepared it for a trip to the Boise Medical Center. Senator

Bradford arrived at the Medical Center about one hour before the heart arrived.

"The shortage of acceptable donors has remained the same in the past several years while the list of patients waiting for organs has risen by over 25%."

How timely was our pitch for information. One day after we advised the senator's wife of his position on the list, he gets a new heart. In the months previous, I had not experienced such a speedy fulfillment of new organs. Pleased with the outcome for the Senator and his wife, I rationalized the acceptability of my information sales.

Retrieving the folder for heart recipients, I placed James Bradford in the recipient column. Loading the Word file that listed the personal information for the three potential donors that I had previously handed to Karen, I reviewed the information.

Kristin Johnston was from Sugar City, Idaho and was 59 years old, so she was out. Mitchell Sluman was a man, so he was out. Barbara Billings was 27 years old, just changed addresses to Idaho Falls, where her parents lived. She recently hired on at a doctor's office in Idaho Falls after finishing nursing school in Boise.

Barbara Billings had to be the donor, but I still could not be sure. Inspecting the web site for the hospital in Idaho Falls, I finally matched Barbara's name on the emergency room admittance list. I jotted her name down on the donor side of the sheet and drew a line between her name and that of Senator Bradford.

Removing the airplane tickets from the plain manila envelope, I reviewed the simple itinerary. Searching on the Internet for Flughafen Frankfurt, I located the customs area and the rental car counter. Karen secured reservations from Europcar, located within Terminal One on the ground level.

Next, I pulled up a map program on the computer that determined the route from Frankfurt to Zurich. Two hundred forty four miles in an estimated 3 hours and 45 minutes. The car ride would take me through Darmstadt, Karlsrue, Baden-Baden, Offenburg, Freiburg, and Basel. Never traveling in Europe before, I was excited yet apprehensive. I searched for the Banque Privat web site and printed information about the company, its security policies, and the map to the office in Zurich.

Removing the old clothes stored within my suitcase that I had used on many previous business trips, I began packing for my flight to Germany.

fourteen

B right colors and neon lights accentuated the new airport terminal building as I stepped onto German soil for the first time in my life. Hundreds of young accomplished tourists jetting off to cities in Europe and America crowded the modern airport. Newness, cleanliness, and orderliness were obvious but unexpected.

Traveling with a lone medium size bag, I cleared customs with little trouble. "Business" – "Switzerland" – "Three Days," I answered the Immigration Guard as he rhythmically repeated his rehearsed dialogue. Highway A5 stretched out wide in front of me after completing a quick rental car transaction. The green-blue clock display read 7:00 pm.

My itinerary specified a night's stay at an Inn at Freiburg. Breathtaking scenery met me around each curve and over each hill like flipping through the pages of a German landscape calendar. All of my presumptions of Europe countryside were accurate. Evening sunlight cooperated with my ignorance of the area and allowed discovery of the Inn before the sun completely disappeared behind the mountains to the west.

The plump middle-aged innkeeper called to her equally plump 18-year-old daughter in order to communicate sufficient English to complete the check-in. The Inn staff and guests were extremely helpful and after navigating the hallways to my room, I showered in the shared bathroom. Returning to the lobby, the staff pointed me in the direction of the Freiburg Biergarten.

Verbose German-speaking locals challenged my ability to block out the unfamiliar conversations. I pointed to the Sauerbraten on the menu and beer seemed to be a universal language.

The single tap and lack of glass-doored refrigerator indicated there would be no choice of beer. Well, bier is the same as beer, I thought. I was wrong. Before the warm mug reached my mouth, the pleasing aroma teased my senses as never before. The warmth lingered in my mouth while the taste sensors attempted to identify the unique tastes. I guess that bier is not beer.

An older gray-haired man who recognized my distress with the language shuffled over and sat next to me.

"First time in Germany?" the executive-looking mid-west customer asked, as noted from his accent, or lack of one.

"Yes actually. Very nice to hear something I understand."

"It takes a little while but you will get use to it. John Palmer from Indianapolis," he reached across the bar and offered his hand.

"Ben White," I answered happily.

"You here on business?"

"Yea, kind of."

"Vacation?" he asked.

"Some. How about you?"

"Well, I have taken a couple months off, but I'm looking for new customers in Europe."

"What business are you in?"

"I sell information," Mr. Palmer stated.

"What kind of information?" I asked quickly, then, realizing we were in a similar business, I wanted to know more.

"Whatever someone will buy. I started out selling lists from the State of Indiana Department of Motor Vehicles," Mr. Palmer confessed with a bold confidence.

"Is that pretty lucrative?"

"Very. I didn't know how much until one day I received my bank statement and my savings were over a million dollars."

"So, who do you sell to?"

"Whoever will buy. I am not too particular. I used to be but if I don't sell it, someone else will."

"Companies or individuals?" I asked.

"I beg your pardon?"

"Do you sell your information to companies or individuals?"

"Both, though sometimes I am not aware whether it is a company or an individual. A while ago, I dealt with an individual and supplied some information on a celebrity. The following day I read about it in one of the supermarket tabloids. I concluded that my contact either worked for the tabloid or sold information to the tabloid. The information was quite damaging to this particular celebrity, but I got my money, and I continue to work for that contact."

"You don't have problems living with yourself?"

"No. Working for myself, I can take off a few months and get back to the grind when I feel like it. Life is short."

"It sure sounds inviting."

"You didn't tell me what line you are in," he said.

Honesty for me became an infrequent trait and since Mr. Palmer's pursuits paralleled my own, and the fact that Karen's instructions about trust were foremost in my mind, I decided to keep my latest vocation to myself. "Actually, I'm starting a business as a job recruiter."

"No kidding. How are you doing with it?" obvious by the look in his eye, I had not achieved his economic level.

"I've just started."

"Well, good luck to you Ben White. I have to get back to my room to make some phone calls."

"Nice chatting with you."

After that fastidious snub and swift retreat of my American friend, I considered the strangeness of our meeting and the sameness of our method of making money. It just seemed so contrived. Mastering the art of name recall was difficult for me. Once introduced, I seemed to erase from memory the name of every new acquaintance I met. Yet, this businessman remembered my name as if he already knew me.

My way of life had certainly changed paths in the previous year. There I was, in Freiburg, Germany, traveling to Switzerland to open a bank account where individuals could wire money in return for information that I had illegally extracted from the Internet. Who would have guessed that this was what was in store for me?

Instead of being apprehensive, I congratulated myself for the success that I had made in the previous few months. Well not completely by myself. Karen had helped. She actually had done more than that. She was a big part of the program. Should she be getting only thirty percent of the take? I would talk to her about our arrangement when I got back to Houston.

Early the next morning, powerful smells from a bakery and pastry shop a few doors down from the Inn lured me inside. Strong black coffee and rich pastries afforded significant energy to face another day of uncertainty. I steered the rental car back onto the A5 road to Basel and then into Switzerland. I reached Zurich by 10:00am and when I entered the Banque Privat, the Account Manager was expecting me.

He explained the privacy policy that the bank employed and assured me that they had hundreds of clients very demanding about their anonymity. I deposited the thousand American dollars into my new account and placed the account number and password in my wallet. The instruction from the bank manager was to memorize the two numbers and dispose of any physical evidence.

As a separate precaution, which Karen was not aware of, I decided to open a second account, which seemed like the right thing to do at the time. I deposited the other thousand dollars in the second account.

While returning to the car, I passed several quaint outdoor cafes and was drawn to the laid back atmosphere that Europe offered. People watching became rich with many opportunities, so I attempted, at least through lunch, to become one of the subjects. After feeling that I overstayed my welcome in the café, I decided to tour some sites in Zurich before heading back for Frankfurt. When I strolled past the library, I took a chance and entered. As long as I did not speak, people accepted me as one of their own. As anticipated, the language barrier prevented me from reading or searching for information.

I spotted a table with a bank of computer terminals so I wandered over and sat in front of one. Although the menu items were in German, through trial and error and my high school German classes, I managed to open up my favorite search engine and retrieve my e-mails. There was a message waiting from Karen.

Ben,

Hope you are having a good time in Europe and that things went well at the bank. Hurry back and we can make some more money.

Love,

Karen

Well, that was that. Short and sweet. The love thing at the end of the message obviously did not mean a thing. Karen probably signed all of her letters that way. I am sure it meant nothing to her.

Quaint shops and upscale boutiques in historic buildings along the main streets in Zurich closed one after another on that Friday afternoon, as the only life anywhere to be seen seemed to be tourists, acting like the Europeans. Rather than stay in Zurich to witness such drama, I decided to return the rental car and take the train to Amsterdam.

Before the trip to Europe, I spent several hours on the Internet researching the hot spots in each country. The overwhelming hot spot that appealed to my current lack of female companionship was that of Amsterdam. The apparent activity in the "Red Light District", completely legal and thriving, was a necessary visit for me. Since I could not imagine when I would be back in Europe and did not have to be back to Frankfurt until Sunday noon, I decided to go and enjoy myself.

Central Station Amsterdam bustled with locals and tourists traveling all over Europe. Three blocks over from the train station, over one of the main canals, the hotel The Globe was situated among other hotels and restaurants. Sections of Amsterdam were very quaint, clean and quite safe, although most of the action occurred in the other sections of the city. The amenities of that medium priced hotel located several blocks from the "Red Light District" were satisfactory to me, so I registered, dropped my things off in the room, showered, and returned to the streets by 9:00 pm. The City was alive with young adults, hanging out in the parks and outside the bars.

Upon hearing English spoken in a group of young men, I opted for some information on the nightlife. The young men, who were considerably stoned on the marijuana they openly passed around, identified two or three establishments in which I might be interested. None of the teenagers had been inside because they could not yet afford the entertainment. They advised me on the "taxi scam", where the taxi drivers would solicit a fifty dollar referral fee from each client whether they delivered them to the club or not.

Bright blue and red neon lights accentuated the front of the most promising club as I followed the exact directions from the Americans. Taxis lined the street in front where the drivers stood outside their vehicles, cigarettes dangling from their mouths, ready to pounce on unsuspecting foreign businessmen. A very properly attired doorman stood outside the door to the club tactfully soliciting potential guests inside for the prescribed entertainment. His welcome first came in Dutch, then German, then English and finally French.

I nodded to the doorman when he reached the English translation and he opened the door.

"Enjoy your evening sir," his delivery was very proper with perfect diction.

Immediately on my tail was one of the taxi drivers that had been standing out in the street, "sir, you must pay referral fee to me," the middle-aged driver acknowledged.

"I've been here before. You did not refer this place to me. You didn't drive me here either. So, move on," I gave a hand gesture indicating that he should leave. He mumbled something that I did not understand but walked back out the door.

Immediately inside the dimly lit barroom, furnished with several couches, small tables, and a mahogany bar that extended almost across the room, one of the employees met me. A young blond, not more than nineteen or twenty years old, wrapped her arm around mine and went through a similar language routine as the doorman. I stopped her as her rehearsed monologue reached English, "would you like some company this evening?" the scantily dressed girl asked in broken English.

My eyes were still adjusting to the darkness, but I could see well enough to recognize that this girl possessed model class. Her hips pushed against mine as she steered me over to an empty couch in the dim corner of the room.

"Drink?" she asked as she gestured to the lurid waitress standing across the room at the bar.

"Heineken," I answered, acknowledging the connection to the country of origin.

"Would you like to buy me a drink?"

"Sure. What would you like?" I asked, not prepared for her response.

"We can only drink champagne, the house rules."

"Fine."

"And you have to buy the bottle," she blushed.

I did not want to appear like a cheapskate but wanted to make sure that the club would not take advantage of my obviously foreign appearance.

"How much are we talking about?"

"The good stuff is fifty dollars."

"I'm not drinking it, so what is the alternative?"

"You can get a small bottle for twenty five," she admitted.

"Let's do that."

"What's your name?" the model asked as she relaxed into my lap pressing her face into my shoulder.

"Ben. Yours?"

"Angela," the name floated from her mouth on a whisper exclusively for my immediate pleasure.

Angela and I spent the next fifteen minutes exploring each other, talking about Amsterdam, and finishing our drinks. When the need to change our location became obvious, Angela finally asked the standard question, "Would you like to go upstairs?"

"Very much," I could not get the words out fast enough.

The stairs along one wall of the bar led up to an ornately carpeted hallway with about six doors on each side. The hallway was surprisingly quiet as most of the doors were closed. The third door on the right was open, so we entered.

The small room crowded with full size bed, small dresser, and nightstand offered a view from the window of an alley and the back of another building. The sheer curtains prevented anyone from clearly seeing what went on inside the room.

"What do you like?" Angela asked as we sat together on the bed.

"I like it all," I answered hoping that she would understand what that meant, without having to spell it out explicitly.

"Did you have a amount in mind?" she asked, not preventing me from offering more than she was asking.

"I was thinking three hundred."

"Dollars or Guilders?"

"Dollars, of course."

"That would be fine."

I placed the three bills neatly on the dresser hoping that was the correct protocol. Other than a few simple requests, that was the last of the conversation except for significant moaning and groaning for the next hour and a half.

During the multiple acts of pleasure, I could not help but imagine what the same would be like with Karen. Although I received the negative vibes previously from her, I accepted it as a challenge to continue the pursuit.

Early the next morning, I returned to the Central Station Amsterdam, caught the 7:00am train to Frankfurt then grabbed a taxi to the airport. My entry back to the United States was uneventful and I reluctantly returned to my slum apartment by noon on Monday. Since I slept on the plane back from Europe, I just showered and went in to work at the hardware store.

Talking a mile a minute, Sam demonstrated his pleasure in seeing me again. Instead of taking advantage of my relief, he remained until we closed the store at 7:00pm. He offered to take me to dinner, so I obliged. The subject of my past entered our conversation and Sam began to understand the disdain that I had about the system that positioned me in an unrecoverable spiral of diminishing opportunities.

Once home again, the hard drive on my computer whirred as I searched for my next potential client. Beginning my search for the evening, I stumbled on an idea that would not release itself until I acted upon it. My favorite search engine advertised a survey, which, after completed by the user, would provide a customized report on how the user stacked up against others that also took the survey. I pressed on to find out more.

I reached for my legal pad and began scribing ideas for my own survey. It occurred to me that this would be an excellent opportunity to gather information on my clients without them knowing why I wanted it. The difficulty arose about how I could distribute this survey while remaining completely anonymous. I searched down the heart donor lists from Texas, Oklahoma, Nevada, and California until I identified five from each state. This scheme also required my survey participants to have valid e-mail addresses, which even in the new century still was an issue for some people.

The survey questions quickly flowed off my pen. Age, physical health, physical activity, religion, ethnicity, marital status, work status, profession, time as a donor, and annual salary became the information I would request. Name, address, and next of kin already existed on the donor sites, and the other information was easily obtainable.

I created another fictitious e-mail address from another search engine. I wrote a very convincing lead in paragraph with the survey to follow and I included the name Dr. Carl Adams at the bottom. The e-mail address of Doctor_Adams@FreeMail.com listed a phony address and equally incorrect phone number. Nothing to tie the account back to me. Karen would have been proud.

After I e-mailed the survey questions in html format to the twenty perspective donors, I started to formulate a contrived report that I would send to all the survey responders. In return for the submittal of the survey, I promised to send them a customized report ranking them with the others that completed the same survey and a copy of an article about past famous organ donors and their stories.

With the donor e-mail sent, I knew that I needed to be more careful in surveying the organ recipients because they were aware of the confidential nature of the list. I decided to wait for responses on my first survey.

Glancing at my watch, I was surprised to find that it was three am. I jotted a "To-Do" list for the next day.

1) Check E-mails
2) Research new organ recipient client
3) Sign lease on new apartment
4) Purchase cell phone
5) Sign up for pre-paid mobile phone service

As my eyes closed, I hoped that it would be my last night of faulty electricity, gunshots, and all night parties outside my door. My thoughts toggled between the recruiting business, my organ donor scam, and of course Karen. After 15 minutes of tossing and turning, I decided to get out of bed and pack my clothes in anticipation of a move to the other side of the tracks.

While neatly folding the few long sleeve shirts that I brought with me from South Carolina, I heard a noise in the living room that startled me. As I slowly moved towards the noise, I discovered that the hard drive on my computer whirred as it did when data was stored or retrieved. Moving closer to the computer, I watched the screen change from the screen saver to the modem access screen. I studied the screen as a phone number appeared in the dial-up box and the dial button selected. The modem whirred just like it always had when I logged into the Internet.

The screens changed quickly and stopped on a window where all of my files were being scanned. Files that I had worked on in the previous two days were selected and placed in a window at the bottom of the screen. I still had not touched the computer. Not knowing what was happening and expecting the worst, I did what any respectable user would do in the same situation. I hit the power switch. The screen went black. The hard drive and fan fell silent.

I would check the PC the following morning to see if any damage was done and tried to remember to describe this circumstance to Karen the next time I talked to her.

As my body finally gave way to sleep, I allowed myself to again dream of the better life. The life that I worked so hard for; long hours, going to school, kissing the asses of the many overeducated, under achievers that I was forced to work for and with. In my previous life, I perfected the corporate skill of retaining the company-man attitude while incompetent nonsensical executives made one poor decision after the next and then became promoted.

Maybe the good life was not gone forever. Maybe I would get a second chance. My dream jetted me off to Vegas where I was betting one hundred dollars a hand at Blackjack and winning.

fifteen

Sitting across an ornate mahogany desk from an alluring twenty something apartment saleswoman, I remembered the older Asian woman from my first Houston apartment. The contrast of female forms was just as striking as the change that my life had taken in the previous month. The thirty-five-story apartment building offered a six-month lease, which I accepted and subsequently supplied the manager with the first three months rent in cash.

"When would you like to move in?" Angela Brooks, the stunning apartment manager asked. Ms. Brooks appeared and conversed very professionally, however I believed that she was always looking to her best interests first.

"Thursday, but could I have some new furniture delivered before then?"

"No problem. Just have the store contact me and I will see that they get into the apartment," she explained as if receiving that request many times before.

On the trip back across the traffic-overloaded city to my slum apartment, I visited a wireless store and purchased a cell phone with prepaid time. When prompted by the teenage-looking clerk, I presented a fictitious name, address, and phone number.

The sound of a ringing phone hurried me through the door and into my apartment.

"Hello."

"Ben?"

"Karen. Where have you been?"

"Working and how are you?"

"I'm fine. Coming to see me?" I asked.

"Actually I am in Dallas. Give me an update on the list," Karen answered abruptly, once the small talk was complete.

"I need to get back to it," I admitted.

"When should I call you back?" her response reminded me of some aggressive managers in my previous business life.

"I was hoping that you might stop by. There are some things I wanted to talk to you about."

"What kind of things?"

"I'll wait until we see each other," I answered duplicating her withholding of information.

"Maybe. In the mean time you'd better get busy and get me some work."

"I should have something by early afternoon," I hoped this answer would appease her.

"Great. Maybe we will get a chance to meet next week. There is something else that I need to talk to you about."

"Really?" the notion of changes in our relationship intrigued me.

"See you later."

"I hope so."

The screen saver disappeared as I checked my e-mails and clicked and double clicked to my then favorite sites to view the recipient and donor lists. I jotted down the top three patients awaiting a kidney from the latest kidney recipient list on the scratch pad adjacent to the computer in order starting with number 1 on the list.

Samuel Johnson, a 35-year old ex-marine, checked in and out of the veteran's hospital in Dallas for the previous several months. After his involvement in the Desert Storm war in Iraq, Sargent Johnson's kidneys gradually stopped functioning. For five years, dialysis became a burdensome routine culminating nine months earlier in the addition of his name to the list for a kidney transplant.

Unmarried Samuel Johnson previously lost his parents from cancer. After checking his bank balance, it was obvious that he lived from one disability check to the next. He was not a good candidate for my information sales.

Jackie Armstrong was married, mother of twin 12-year old boys. She, her husband and the two boys resided in an older neighborhood in Omaha, Nebraska not more than a mile from where her parents lived and where she grew up. Jackie attended the Methodist Church at the end of her street, sang in the choir, and married her high-school sweetheart. A car accident eight months earlier left her with internal injuries including damaged kidneys. She had been on the list for new kidneys for a little over eight months. As a stay-home mom, she was also a poor candidate for our program.

Mike Ellerton was the #1 disk jockey in Tulsa, Oklahoma for 25 years. The son of First Bank Chairman of the Board James Ellerton and attorney Marie Ellerton, Mike contracted a disease while vacationing in Boca Chica that irreversibly damaged his kidneys. The most eligible bachelor in Tulsa, Mike dated the majority of the 18 to 35 year-old Tulsa women until he became too sick to work or play. His bachelor pad, within the very high-rent district in Tulsa was on the market for $1.2 million. This family had money.

Per Karen's instructions, I visited at least five donors each from Oklahoma and Texas with matching blood types as those of Mike Ellerton. I jotted down names, addresses, ages, and employers. I created a new list and entered Kidney Recipients at the top of the screen.

I reviewed the survey response e-mails from the Dr. Adams e-mail address. There were eight. Eight out of twenty on the first day surpassed my expectations. I spot-checked some of the information and all the respondents had answered honestly with the information that I previously requested. I organized the data, worked on my survey for the organ recipients, and waited for Karen's call.

My plans for the day included my commute to the hardware store at 3:00 PM that afternoon but Karen's phone call delayed that departure. Pleased with the completeness of my research, Karen agreed that the DJ, Mike Ellerton, would be our next target.

"Why don't you give Mr. Ellerton a call mid-morning and I will call you back about 1:00 PM tomorrow," Karen directed.

"No problem."

"See if you can get a little more information on number one and two, you know, family, past health problems, like that."

"Why? I thought we were targeting number three?"

"We are. I just want to make sure that we haven't missed something."

"I'll do my best."

"Good luck. I hope you are as convincing as you've been previously."

"Yea, me too."

Sam departed the store a few minutes after I arrived and the time by myself allowed me to reflect on some of the things that Karen mentioned on the phone. What could she possibly want to talk to me about? She knew that I wanted to know more about her past, but would she share any more of that information? I finalized a "To Do" list for the following day.

When I returned to the apartment, I searched for more information on number one and number two from the kidney list as instructed earlier by Karen. Again, I came up with a blank on Samuel Johnson; no extended family, poor credit history.

Jackie Armstrong; maiden name Carter, grandparents deceased, two older brothers and one younger sister. Brother number one worked at a gas station in Omaha while the other was a street cop. Her unmarried younger sister worked in an office. For the information that I was in the position to supply, it was obvious that the family would not be prepared to compensate me adequately.

Preparation for the next day's phone call with Mike Ellerton consumed most of the late night hours. I revisited the recipient list specifically for potential heart transplants. I searched down the list of recipients and recognized that there were few changes since I visited the list a week earlier.

The feeling of perspiration dripping down my sides woke me at 7:00 AM to discover that the air conditioning was again not functioning. After a quick cool shower, I drove to a breakfast restaurant with air conditioning and then visited an upscale furniture store to furnish the new apartment.

Back at the old apartment by 10:00 AM, I dialed the number for Mike Ellerton on my newly charged cell phone. The stifling temperature produced sweat on my chest, blotted by the dark colored polo shirt. Dependent on who answered the phone, I rehearsed several distinctive responses.

"Hello," came the reaction in an aggravated tenor.

"Could I speak with Mike Ellerton?"

"This is Mike. Who is this?"

"Mr. Ellerton, my name is Frank James," a fresh name came to my mind to use with the new client.

"Mr. James, I am really not interested in what you are selling," he replied quickly.

"I believe that you might be, Mr. Ellerton, as soon as you . . .," the phone went dead.

Although somewhat prepared for this occurrence, the disappointment of not keeping him on the line weighed heavily on my mind. After a few minutes, I rang the number again.

I spoke faster, "Mr. Ellerton, this is Frank James again. Please do not hang up. I have some information for you. I know that you are dying and I know that you are waiting for a kidney."

"Who is this?"

"I told you Mr. Ellerton. My name is Frank James and I know about your disease and how long that you have been waiting for a new kidney."

"What do you want from me?"

"Actually Mike, I have some information for you about where you are on the kidney recipient list."

"So."

"So, you've been waiting for eight months and I'm betting that you would like to know how much longer that you will have to wait."

"So, tell me then."

"Not quite so fast Mr. Ellerton. I have done a lot of work finding out this information and my time is not cheap."

"You mean that you want to sell me this information?"

"As a matter of fact, yes."

"How much?" Mike asked after a few long seconds of contemplation.

"Five thousand."

"Five thousand! You must think I'm an idiot."

"No Mr. Ellerton, I think that you are a very smart DJ that wants to fix some of your past mistakes and get back into the limelight. I think that you are a man that has some money and you have parents that are wealthy and together, you would be happy to put this disease behind you."

"So how is me paying you five grand going to get me healthy?"

"I'm sorry, you'll just have to pay the money to find out. Look, my associate will be at your front door this evening at 7:00 PM. If you want the information, pay her and she will give you the information. If you don't, I hope that you live long enough to get your kidney, whenever that is," I waited a few seconds, pondering my choice of words and then hung up the phone. I re-questioned my abilities to persuade.

The Asian apartment manager sat behind the counter in the office similar to our first meeting. Her face hardly changed expression as I relayed my plans to move out. Returning to the apartment, I finished packing, then arranged for a junk man to pick up the furniture that I no longer needed.

At 11:00 AM, the cell phone rang and Karen was on the other end, "how'd you do?"

"I'm not too optimistic about this one."

"Why not?"

"I'm not sure that he sees the advantage of knowing where he is on the list."

"So where do we stand?"

"I told him you would be coming by tonight, you would collect the money, and supply the information."

"So what's the problem?"

"I don't know if he will pay the money."

"Of course he will. Relax. You did a good job. Leave it up to me now."

"Don't you want to know how much?" I asked.

"I'm sure you were going to tell me."

"Five grand."

"Five thousand. Good job. Did you get a chance to look again at number one and number two on the recipient list?"

"Yea, I looked, but nothing special. Normal paycheck-to-paycheck families. No need to pursue any further in my estimation."

"OK. Why don't you give me the account number for your Swiss account?" Karen added in the same breath.

"Why do you want that?"

"I will get this payment wired there and then in the future you could direct our clients to the account in your phone call."

"Oh. I hadn't thought of that yet," I opened the accordion file that had that piece of information in it.

"Will you call me back later tonight and tell me how this one goes?" I pleaded.

"Sure. Now give me the names and addresses of the kidney donors from Oklahoma."

I fumbled through the yet unfiled papers on this round of client sales and read off the names and addresses.

"Well, wish me luck. I have to get to Oklahoma," she had already hung up the phone before I could answer.

After stuffing everything in the boxes that I had acquired from the hardware store, I departed to my Houston bank. Upon meeting with one of the managers, I explained my desire to wire all but five thousand dollars into my account in Switzerland. I experienced no problem. Additionally, I withdrew three thousand in cash to purchase a laptop computer. I envied the businessmen traveling on company business busily typing letters into their laptops while at airports or in airplanes.

After about fifteen minutes, the bank manager returned, confirming the successful transfer of eight thousand more than I believed was currently in my account. If these mistakes were the bank's fault, maybe it was a good thing that I was pulling the money out, before they could find the mistake.

On my way back to the apartment, I stopped at one of the chain electronics stores and purchased their best laptop with extra memory and the fastest modem. While I was there, the salesperson sold me a piece of software that would automate my Internet searches and help track people who were e-mailing me.

Back at the apartment, I allowed just enough time to shower and prepare for my few hours at the hardware store. My work at the store was starting to get in the way of my other exploits, but I had made a commitment to Sam and it meant a lot to me to keep my commitment.

After closing the store, I drove back to the dilapidated apartment complex for my final night's sleep there. I discarded most of the perishable food into the already overflowing dumpster and packed the remaining dry goods.

With the phone line plugged in to the new laptop, I began to configure it to my liking. After about an hour, I had transferred all of my files from the desktop computer, including the EastHack software that Karen had provided, and was back reading my e-mails. I had more responses back from my survey and quickly replied with the attachment that I had previously prepared.

While stripping off the files that I wanted to transfer to the laptop, I found a folder labeled "CC", with many executable files that I did not recognize. Clicking on several of the files, I was unable to access any of them. The most common error message was "user does not have sufficient access to view these files". Since I had been the only person accessing this computer with the exception of Karen, I could only assume that this was something that she put on the computer when she was with me in Beaufort.

It was 11:00PM when Karen finally called back on the cell phone.

"A piece of cake," came a confident tone.

"He wasn't hesitant?"

"Well, maybe a little at first, but after we chatted for awhile, he came around."

"Did he have the cash?"

"Sure did. You should see it in your account tomorrow. Oh, by the way, give me your new address. I will be busy tomorrow, but maybe I'll stop in the next day."

"Seriously?"

"Maybe. Anyhow, get working on our next client. By the way, you might want to give your notice at the hardware store. I think that you won't have time for that anymore."

"I'll let him know tomorrow."

I turned off the laptop for the night and tried to sleep. As I lay awake for several hours contemplating my new life and my new business partner, I reflected on the ethics of my new line of work. I remembered the conversation that I had with the businessman in Germany about business ethics and faintly remembered the advice administered by a man in the shadows in a New Orleans' alley. I dismissed my reservations and drifted off to sleep.

The next day, I focused on my move into a new apartment. Although still in disrepair, the old apartment was cleaner as I left it than when I moved in. I retrieved the Asian lady from the office, toured her through the apartment and made her sign a sheet of paper indicating that the apartment was left clean and all intact.

Parked on the street in front of the new high-rise apartment building, I entered the front door into the lobby.

"Good morning Mr. White. Moving in today?" the silver-haired uniformed guard surprised me with his information.

"Um – Yes."

"I am Charles and you will see me here Monday though Friday until 6:00 PM. If you need anything, or if you are expecting any guests during that time, please let me know. The apartment office is on the third floor. It is nice to have you here, Mr. White," he pushed the up button on the elevator and then pushed the button for the third floor after I had entered then he stepped back out.

My apartment and mailbox keys and parking access card awaited me in the office, as well as the assignment of third floor parking spot. I rode the elevator to the fifteenth floor, unlocked the door, and toured my new home. The posh new furniture I purchased a few days earlier decorated the rooms and centered on the dining room table was a large basket of fruit, wine, and cheese, compliments of the management.

A large sliding glass door led to a small balcony overlooking the street. I stepped out to admire the view of my new upscale community with the soaring buildings of downtown Houston in the background. My fear of heights returned abruptly as I peered over the railing. The people below walking to and from business meetings and power lunches revealed the stark contrast from my previous neighborhood.

Punching the polished brass lobby button, I rode the elevator down to the ground level and strolled through the lobby to the street.

"Everything all right, Mr. White?"

"Just fine, Charles."

"If there is anything I can do, just let me know."

The Nissan turned into the apartment building entrance, as I slid the parking access card into the slot opening the gate. The ramp twisted around passing BMWs, Mercedes, Volvos, and Cadillacs until I reached my parking spot on the third floor. A white sign in a black frame identified BEN WHITE in black block letters on the wall in front of me.

The apartment management left a cart for me to use going from the truck to the elevator and from the elevator to my apartment. I moved all of my possessions in two trips up the elevator and into my apartment. I opened the bottle of wine and poured it into one of the plastic glasses also included in the basket, grabbed an apple and stood out on the balcony.

After beads of sweat forced me to wipe my forehead, I retreated to the quiet, cool environment inside and made a list for the supermarket. Riding the elevator back down to the lobby, I asked Charles the location of the nearest grocery stores, and rode back up to the third floor to retrieve the pickup truck.

The grocery store that Charles suggested was only a few blocks away. The store was unlike any I've ever seen before. It was best described as a whole foods market where there is a café ambiance. A bakery, meat market, pizza oven, salad bar, and sandwich line circled the outside walls. You could eat there or take the prepared meals home with you. The clientele was upscale, well dressed, and attractive. I loved my new neighborhood.

Using the same cart that I used to move my household items, I loaded and unloaded groceries in the apartment and then replaced the cart where I had originally found it. I left thirty minutes early for work trying to judge the added mileage. Sam was in a bad mood from earlier phone calls with his suppliers. I questioned whether I should talk to him that day about my resignation, or what ever you call it for my type of position. I had promised Karen that I would, so I waited until all of the customers were out of the store and then sprang it on him.

"I'm afraid I have some bad news," my upper lip quivered a bit when I was nervous.

Sam looked up at me from his reports lying on the counter. I knew that he was aware of what was coming but he did not make it easy. "Now what? It isn't bad enough that my suppliers cheat me and can't deliver when they are supposed to."

"I'm giving my notice."

"Notice. What the hell does that mean?" Sam barked.

"I'm giving my two week notice."

"What the hell for?"

"I've got another job."

"Doing what?" Sam continued his harsh tone.

"You remember that I told you I was starting my own business. Well, it is demanding more of my time now."

Sam wore a mean unforgiving face. "Why don't you just leave then?"

"You don't want me to stay for the two weeks?"

"What would be the purpose? I handled things just fine before you got here. I suspect it won't be any different now."

"I will leave now if you want me to."

"Great."

"Look Sam, I have enjoyed working for you. You will owe me for about 12 hours, but why don't we consider that the last check I received was my final one."

I extended my hand for him to shake but he ignored me.

"Your choice," I acknowledged and walked out the front door.

When I got back to the Nissan, I looked back through the bars on the door and witnessed papers flying across the aisles and settling to the floor. I never looked back again.

sixteen

M y muscles strained as I inched the bulky cherry desk in
front of the window in the bedroom I used as a den. The
three-story mall, Highway 610, and in the distance downtown
Houston were framed by the window centered above the desk. The
lights from the business district high-rises toggled on and off from
my window view. With the laptop in front of me, I connected the
phone line and started to work.

Using the new software purchased from the computer store,
the Health & Human Services Organ Recipient web site popped
up immediately. I directed my search for people needing lung
transplants. After identifying the top three people on the list, I
again began to gather information on them. It was an eerie feeling,
penetrating into people's personal lives. Perhaps the newness made
it so addicting to me. Once the information was loaded into a
database, I called it quits for the evening.

Before logging off, and because I was curious about the
operation of the web site, I retrieved the list on kidney recipients
that I had reviewed a few days earlier in order to develop Mike
Ellerton, the disc jockey from Tulsa. The kidney list was up-to-date
as of that day based on the note on the home page. I was shocked at
what I saw.

Mike Ellerton was now #1 on the list and Samuel Johnson, the
Marine Corp veteran and Jackie Armstrong were no longer on the
list. Surely, this occurrence would raise a flag for the Health &

Human Services Department. Confused and curious about the coincidence, I decided to push on in my research.

I searched the Internet for Samuel Johnson's name and found nothing on the Samuel Johnson from Dallas. Searching the Dallas newspaper, I came up blank as well. Several, if not all, of the hospitals in the Dallas area had web sites however, in spite of my attempts to hack into their patient database, I was unsuccessful. At 1:00 AM, I considered stopping for the evening, but instead called the hospital that was closest to Mr. Johnson's home address.

"Yes, my name is Harold Johnson and I am trying to find out the condition of my brother Samuel Johnson," I explained, hoping that my long shot would pay off.

"I will switch you to the On-Call information desk."

"Patient Information," another voice answered.

I repeated the same request to this new volunteer.

"Let me check. Can you hold one minute?" I heard the tapping of keys on a keyboard. "I'm sorry, but I do not have anyone admitted here by that name."

"Could you check to see if he was there but released?" I asked.

"Let me see . . . I . . . what did you say your name was?"

"Harold Johnson."

"Well, Harold, Samuel was here today, but our records show that he did not have any brothers or sisters."

"What do you mean did not have? Is he all right?" I stuttered a bit to let her know that I was concerned, putting her on the defensive.

"Mr. Johnson, we are instructed to give out information only to family members and I do not have record of Samuel Johnson having a brother."

"We haven't spoken in 5 years, I don't blame him for not acknowledging me as his brother. Look, I need to know whether on not to get on a plane to Dallas. Please tell me he is all right."

"Well, I suppose that it would be all right. My records show that Samuel Johnson passed away this morning at 11:32 AM."

"Oh my God. How? I mean why?"

"Cause of death was kidney failure. I am so sorry Mr. Johnson. I will let the hospital administration know that you called and will instruct them on funeral arrangements."

"Yes, please do," I hung up before she could ask more questions.

I glanced over at the sheet of paper where I jotted down number two - Jackie Armstrong - Omaha, NE. It was much easier to find out what had happened to Jackie, both from direct searches on the Internet and the Omaha World-Herald. *Mother and Two Sons Die in a Fiery Crash* was the column heading on page 2 on the Omaha newspaper site. "Jackie Armstrong and sons Jonathon & James died at 1:25 PM this afternoon when the Ford Bronco that she was driving struck a tree at a high rate of speed at the bottom of the Fletcher Road hill. There were no witnesses to the accident. Unfortunately, the first police officer to respond at the scene was Detective Neil Carter, brother of Mrs. Armstrong and uncle to the two boys. The cause of the accident is still under investigation."

I felt sorry for Jackie's husband who not only had to live with Jackie's past kidney problems with constant hope for a kidney transplant, but now had lost his wife and the two boys as well. The only good fortune that would come out of these timely unfortunate accidents was that Mike Ellerton from Tulsa moved up to the number one spot on the recipient list and would maybe soon receive a kidney.

With the laptop shut down, I fell asleep quickly in the new bed, new apartment and new area of town. At 8:30 am, I reached over to shut off the alarm only to discover that it was not the alarm but my cell phone ringing.

"Hello."

"I'm across the street in the restaurant. Come pick me up in your truck," it was Karen, obviously upset about something.

"What?"

"I didn't know that you had a guard at your building. I can't allow him to see me. Get in your truck and come pick me up. We will drive up to your parking spot and take the elevator to your apartment. Are you awake yet?"

"Just barely. Give me 10 minutes."

With ample amounts of icy water splashed on my face, I dragged a brush hastily through my hair. Once I had donned a pair of shorts and a clean white tee shirt, I darted for the truck. When I reached the ground floor, the gate opened, I turned across traffic and stopped in front of The Gateway Restaurant. Karen's hair was black again and with the sunglasses and shorts, exposing her long slender legs, she still turned me on.

"Sorry I didn't tell you about the guard," I apologized, still intimidated by her terse behavior.

"That's all right, just can't be too careful," she explained.

"Do you just want to go back to the apartment?"

"Yes, that's fine."

After circling the block, I pulled back into the garage, and wound myself clockwise up to the third floor. Karen constantly scanned the surroundings until we parked. We were alone in the parking ramp, the elevator, and the hallway to my apartment.

"Nice place. Business must be good," she said sarcastically.

"Very!"

There was not a corner of the apartment that she did not inspect or a question that she did not ask about the management, staff, neighbors, and neighborhood.

"Good choice. It looks pretty quiet and safe."

"There are a few things that I need to talk to you about," she looked for my attentiveness as we sat on my new couch.

"Shoot."

She commenced to tutor me on how to avoid pursuit, how to recognize when I was being followed, and how to lose the person following me. She went into great detail on the surveillance techniques that the FBI used and a few more that she herself used when tailing someone else. I listened intently.

"Why are you telling me this?" I interrupted her, somewhat fearful of her answer.

"You never know when you might need to give someone the slip. Haven't you ever had the feeling that someone was watching you?"

"Actually, I've never thought that anyone would want to watch me for any reason."

"Well, now you know how to detect it. When you go out in the next few days, practice what I have taught you and satisfy in your own mind that no one is following you."

"Do you think someone is following me?"

"No, why should they?" Karen countered.

"I don't know. I know that the FBI was looking for you and somehow made a connection to me. Maybe they followed me to Houston."

"They didn't."

"How do you know?" I asked.

"Because I have had you followed. There is no one else following you."

"Oh, that's great. Sure glad I don't have anything to hide. This has really been a lot of fun. What else do you have to tell me?" I asked, clearly disgusted with her surprises.

She walked over to my printer, grabbed a blank sheet of paper, and brought it back to the coffee table in front of me. She started to draw a map.

"This is Houston. This is highway 59. This is highway 281 South. When you get to the Mexican border, it turns into a small road with a bridge that crosses the Rio Grande. There is a small immigration station there with just a couple guards. One hundred forty seven miles south of the border is a small town called La Coma. Exactly two point seven miles south of town is a dirt road that snakes east for about a mile up a small mountain. At the end of this dirt road is Rancho Hidalgo. This is my place."

"Mexico? Why are you telling me this?"

"In case anything happens, don't try to contact me. Just meet me at Rancho Hidalgo. It is safe there and no one will bother us."

"What could happen? You are scaring me."

"You never know. What we are doing might not be totally legal and as you have experienced it definitely isn't ethical."

"Well, should I be worried?"

"No! Just keep up the good work and watch your backside like I showed you."

I reached for the paper and started to fold it when Karen grabbed it back from me.

"I don't think so. Take another look at it and memorize the route, the mileage and the name of the city. If they catch you, then they got me. I don't want to make it easy for them."

After I studied the route a while longer, she took the paper to the stove, turned on the fan, lit the paper and laid it in a frying pan. She washed the ashes down the drain. Karen looked around as if she were missing something, "I left my bag in your truck. Could you go get it for me?"

I rode the elevator down to the third floor, grabbed the leather attaché, and was back to the apartment in less than two minutes. I reached for my apartment key, but it was not in my pocket. It was strange that I would have left it somewhere. I knocked on my apartment door, but it was at least a minute before Karen let me in.

"Sorry, I was in the bathroom," she explained, a little out of breath. "Now, what did you want to talk to me about?"

"Number one, I don't think that it is fair that you only get thirty percent of the money."

"What do you think I should get?"

"Well, I don't know. Probably fifty percent."

"But all of this was your idea," she argued.

"Yea, but you're chasing all over the country. You're doing more of the work."

"All right. How about sixty percent for you and forty percent for me?"

"Well, that's better," I said.

"Done."

"Number two, I would like to see more of you. I have gotten to like you and I think you kind of like me," I blurted out after having practiced the delivery of the speech for a couple of weeks.

"Ben, we are partners. Even if I am attracted to you, we need to stay focused on the business so that we do not make a mistake. There may be time for us later."

"Is there a number three?" Karen added, trying to quickly change the subject.

Somewhat rejected, I added, "Yes, number 3. Do you know what happened to two recipients that were number one and number two in front of our latest client, Mike Ellerton?"

"No."

"Samuel Johnson died of kidney failure. Today. Jackie Armstrong died in a car accident. Today. Don't you find that coincidental?"

"I guess so. Didn't Mr. Johnson have kidney problems? Why would it be unusual that his kidneys finally gave out? In addition, people get in car accidents all the time. Coincidental, yes, but I don't think it is unusual. Why are you spending time looking up information on those two? We can't get any money from them. Go get me some more clients," Karen's glare changed to all business as if she was pissed at me for bringing these facts to her attention.

I watched her reaction to my news and she moved through it like a boxer receiving a glancing blow. "Well, I have visited the Lung List and I have a couple potential clients."

Karen studied the listing of pertinent information on the top three candidates that I handed to her. Very seldom had Karen asked for additional information as I had honed my search skills to provide all of the information necessary to get the job done. Waiting for her to memorize the data on the sheet and then burn it on the stove, I was surprised when she folded the paper and put it in her bag.

"Looks like we have some work to do. What do you think about this guy Antonio Simpati from New Jersey? Do you think that he might be connected to any of the families?"

I am sure I had a blank look on my face when she added, "Mafia."

"If he is, you can be sure that he is worth a whole lot more than what it shows in his bank account. You think we can protect ourselves from them? If they get mad, it will be hard to hide from them," I reasoned.

"We can probably use it to our advantage. They will pay whatever it takes to keep their families alive. Just consider the possibilities when addressing them. When can you make your phone call?"

"Anytime actually, I have given notice at the hardware store and I'm all done there."

"Why don't you give this Simpati guy a call this afternoon. I will call you back at around 4:00pm and then you can give me a list of four lung donors from New York or New Jersey. Great job. Let's see how it goes."

"Are you leaving?" I asked.

"I've got a lot to do and it sounds like I have to get back to the east coast."

"You just got here!" I complained.

"We have to make the money when it is available. There will be time to rest later. Don't forget to check your Swiss account and make sure the transfer went okay."

"Don't I have to take you out in the truck to get the gate to open?"

"No, there is a small red button on the wall to the left of the gate if you are on foot. I'll be all right."

Karen was gone again. I ventured out on the balcony to watch her as she crossed the street but never saw her.

As I pulled open the file drawer in the desk and retrieved the folder labeled Account Information, I located the e-mail address for checking my account balance and transactions. When the prompt came up for ID and password, I typed it from memory. The screen came back and asked a question that only I would know the answer and then access was permitted.

There were three transactions: the opening deposit, the transfer of funds from my Houston account, and a new one from the previous day. The latest deposit was for $14,000. My calculations were $5,000 times 70% or $3,500. Something unusual was going on with these deposits and it was not the fault of the bank. I just could not put together the circumstances that would generate that much cash but I was determined to find the underlying cause.

Concentrating on the assimilation of more information on Antonio Simpati from Newark, New Jersey, I forgot about Samuel Johnson and Jackie Armstrong for the time being. Since Karen had suggested a connection to the mob, I checked the newspaper archives for articles but found nothing. I spent the early afternoon reading as much as I could about the families in New Jersey and New York City.

At 3:30 PM, feeling as if I was well rehearsed for the call, I grabbed my cell phone with papers spread in front of me and tentatively dialed the number in Newark.

"Yea," came the terse acknowledgement from a dangerous sounding man, New York accent hanging heavily from a single word.

"I'm looking for Antonio."

"What do you want Tony for?" obviously, the man knew that I was not acquainted with Antonio or I would have called him Tony.

"I have some information for him."

"You can give the information to me."

"Who are you?" hoping my brief daring fronted by the distant phone connection, would gain some acceptance by my forceful delivery.

"I'm his mother. Now what do you want?"

"I know about his problem, his health problem."

"So?"

"So, I know he is waiting for a lung transplant, I know how long he has been waiting on the list, and I know where he is at on the list."

"So?"

"So, wouldn't he like to know this information?"

"Maybe."

"So?" I repeated his one word response hoping for a counter response to break the silence.

"What are we talking about?" he asked.

"Money."

"Not that Tony would be interested, but what kind of money we talking about?"

"Ten grand."

"Go to hell."

"It is not like he doesn't have it," I suggested.

"Well, he has it cause he doesn't waste it on pukes like you."

"Tell him five grand and I'm about ready to hang up." Karen suggested that I might have to talk their language, but it seemed a little foreign to me.

"So hang up."

"Go tell Tony," I demanded.

I heard the phone hit the table and the sound of steps diminishing. Three long minutes elapsed and it occurred to me that I could lose our client. Finally, I heard him shuffle back to the phone.

"God knows why, but Tony wants to waste five grand."

"Great. My associate will be over tonight and after you give her the cash, she will give you the information."

"What does this broad look like so we don't shoot her when she comes to the door."

"Late thirties, great shape, short black hair. Tell Tony thanks."

After I hung up the phone, a sense of pride overcame me and I grabbed a Heineken from the kitchen to celebrate. While finishing my second beer, I searched for the four or five organ donors as Karen had previously and repeatedly requested. I assumed that she somehow used that information when talking to the clients, but I really did not know and never asked.

Karen called promptly at 4:30PM, "how did you do?"

"I think we have a paying customer."

"How much?"

"Well, I was a little greedy and asked for ten thousand."

"And?"

"And he was going to hang up, so I backed off to five thousand."

"And he agreed?"

"Sure did. By the way, I never talked to Mr. Simpati, but another man. A real rough-sounding character. He wanted to know what you looked like so he didn't accidentally shoot you," I laughed but heard silence on the other end. "I told them that you would be there this evening. Are you going to make it?"

"No problem, I am at the Newark airport right now. I will give you a call sometime tomorrow and let you know how it went. Have you got the names and addresses of the donors?"

"Donors?"

"Don't go completely brain dead on me Ben. Donors. The list of donors from New York and New Jersey. Ring a bell?"

"Maybe I need a brain transplant. Here they are," I read the list to Karen trying to understand the circumstances that she could use this information but it continued to escape me.

"Got it. Thanks. Hey, I have been reading a little about bone marrow transplants. Maybe you ought to check into that area," Karen suggested.

"Sounds good. I will. Be careful."

"Always."

seventeen

Thoughts of a burning SUV with Jackie Armstrong and two young boys trapped inside filled my head until I could not leave them alone. Also on my mind was Karen telling me to let it rest. Reviewing the Omaha World-Herald for the following few days, I extracted and read several articles pertaining to the accident, including the obituaries.

Research on Jackie's brother Neil Carter was very interesting. Number two in his class at Omaha Central High School, stayed home to help his family on the farm, served as Military Police in Vietnam. Wounded by shrapnel from a misplaced mine, he returned to Omaha to attend community college. Later, when the bank foreclosed on his parent's farm, he decided to become a cop. Number one in his class at the community college, graduated with honors, selected first in his class by the Omaha Police Department and assigned to the traffic division.

Officer Carter worked his way up through the police department ranks for five years until reaching detective. His relentless investigative skills afforded him the best arrest record in the department. Newspaper stories reported a detective easily more intuitive and logical than all of the other detectives on the force. I guessed that this fact occasionally became a problem for him with the other detectives.

The latest record from the Omaha Police Department's database showed the accident involving Neil's sister still under investigation. The University of Nebraska Medical Center performed an autopsy on the burned corpse but could not accurately come up with a cause of death other than the fire. The police department automotive team went over the scorched remains of the late model Ford Bronco but could not detect a cause of the accident. The crime scene showed no evidence of tire marks on the pavement, just on the curb as the tires hit it at a high rate of speed.

"Something doesn't fit about this accident," read the newspaper article quoting Detective Carter.

"The Bronco had the brakes inspected and reworked three weeks before the accident, and I inspected the job myself," claimed the owner of Spikes Auto Repair where Jackie had always taken her car for work. "I have a complete record of all of the repairs for the last five years," he had claimed to the reporter.

"Other than the problems with her kidneys, she was in excellent health. The kidney problem would not result in a sudden lapse of consciousness," stated Jackie Armstrong's primary physician.

The final quote from the article again came from Carter, "we have not yet ruled out homicide, although we can't conceive of a motive. Everyone liked Jackie. Her volunteer work at church and in the community was exemplary."

Since I worked especially hard gathering information and learning more about the organ donation programs, I decided to venture out for some dinner and entertainment. Remembering what Karen ordered in regards to practicing my surveillance detection skills, I decided to drive out of the apartment and consciously check to see if someone was following me.

With significant traffic on the main roads by the apartment, many of the cars that were driving near me, remained with me for many blocks. After turning right at the next block, I pulled over into a parking spot. Not noticing anything suspicious, I pulled back out on the street and took the next left.

I did notice a white sedan make the corner several car lengths behind me but I did not become suspicious until the sedan followed me into a grocery store parking lot. The suspect car parked two rows from my pickup truck and no one got out of the car. Leaving my pickup and crossing the parking lot towards the store, I constantly watched the white car out of the corner of my eye.

When I returned from the store, the white sedan was parked in a new spot one additional row away but in better view of my Nissan. I pulled out of the parking lot heading back for the apartment and when I reached the first traffic light, I noticed the same white sedan four cars behind me.

Should I try to lose this person like Karen had showed me or should I forget about it and not let him know that I was on to him? I decided to forget about it and drove to the restaurant. When I stepped out of the truck in the restaurant parking lot, I looked around for the white sedan but could not see it. I was not surprised.

Not to appear as if I was looking for someone, when I returned to the Nissan after dinner, I was careful with my actions. After a few drinks at a gentleman's club down the street from my apartment, I returned home with little concern over any followers.

An e-mail from Karen was waiting for me after my evening out.

Ben,

The meeting with Mr. Simpati went well. I wired the money into your Swiss account. I kept 40%. I will be out of touch for a couple of days but please send information on our next client.

Make sure that you provide all of the information on #1, #2, and #3 recipients on the respective lists that you send. In other words, if we select #2 as the client, please send info on #1 and #2. If we select #3, then send info on #1, #2, & #3. You know what I mean.

I will call you in a couple days.

Love,

Karen

Over the next few days, I revisited the heart, kidney, and lung organ recipient lists and researched number one, number two, and number three on each list. Although Antonio Simpati had been on the list for fourteen months and was number two, I was again astounded that his name was no longer on the list.

On another whim, I began to develop a process for researching the status of clients after they had paid us for our information. As I reviewed all of our previous clients, I again was amazed at the fact that all of our clients received their new organs within 48 hours of when we had provided the information to them.

At first, I searched the Newark Star-Ledger for anything on Antonio Simpati. Not finding any match, I switched to Pittsburgh

Tribune-Review where I searched for Brian Flynn, number one on the lung recipient list ahead of Mr. Simpati.

EX-COAL MINER DIES FROM RESPIRATORY FAILURE was the column heading on page four. "Brian Flynn, a 52-year-old ex-coal miner passed away last evening from complications from a long-term lung disease associated with many years work in the coal mines in Pennsylvania. Mr. Flynn had been on disability for 12 months and was on the list waiting for a double lung transplant.

"Brian Flynn served his country as an MP in Viet Nam during the war. His wife Carol and sons Phillip and David survive him. Services will be held . . ."

I began checking the hospitals in Newark for evidence of a lung transplant for Antonio Simpati. Finally, after checking three others, I struck pay dirt at the University Hospital. I managed to hack my way into the surgery schedule from the previous few days and found Antonio's name. I added his name to my list of clients that received a new life and even though I had never actually talked to him and even though he was likely to be involved in criminal activities, I was still glad that he had a second chance. Maybe in some ways, I was receiving my second chance as well.

Returning my focus to the heart recipient list, I initiated my research on the top three candidates. It became routine. Currently number one on the list was a high school teacher from Orlando, Florida. Roger Merrill had been on the heart recipient list for ten months because of a deteriorating heart muscle condition that he inherited from his father. His condition being poor, he had been home for the previous six months, in and out of the hospital many times.

Mr. Merrill's economic status consisted of one hundred fifty dollars in the bank and living on a moderate amount of disability money plus the residual of the five thousand dollars that his chemistry class managed to raise holding a car wash and bake sale. Roger's father had already passed and his mother resided in an adult foster care home. He was an only child. Roger Merrill was not a good candidate for our information conspiracy.

Stephanie Swanson, #2 on the list, possessed serious money. Born into money, she managed to make it multiply. Stephanie's mother, Margaret, who also had family money, developed a line of perfume products that dominated the United States market for 30 years. Stephanie worked in the business until her mother passed away and then inherited what amounted to an estate worth seventy five million.

She lived the millionaire's life with chauffer, yacht, summer home in Martha's Vineyard, and residence on the inter-coastal in Naples, Florida. Stephanie never married, but was still doted over by her father who still ran his own import/export business out of Naples. There was no question that this family had money. The only relevant question was whether they wanted to part with it. I am sure that at fifty-five years old, Stephanie Swanson was anxious to get back to her life.

I quickly gathered data on the number three person on the list, but I knew that Karen would be happy with Stephanie as our next client. I summarized the information on all three candidates and then started my e-mail to Karen. I then remembered the list of five possible Florida donor names and addresses that I knew Karen would ask for. If I could only remember, I would ask Karen about the need for that information the next time we talked. I also made a mental note to ask her about the strange file transfers on my computer when I was back at the slum apartment.

As I assembled all of the information and had the time to reflect on the coincidences of recipient's deaths and our client's subsequent good fortunes, coupled with unexplained amounts of cash in my bank account, I concluded that something was not right. Some things were going on that I did not understand. For my own peace of mind, I needed to find out, and a plan started to develop in my head.

Searching the Internet for more recent newspaper articles on the case of Jackie Armstrong and her brother Neil Carter, I became determined to uncover the truth. Listening to the news portion of the public radio station in Omaha, I picked up bits and pieces of information on the story. Without substantial information from the media, I took my chances at the Omaha Police Department web site. Through significant trial and error effort, I was able to access the police department database.

Stumbling on a folder titled "Open Cases" with a sub-folder named "Possible Homicides" and another sub-folder named

"092500-Armstrong", I became excited with my progress. Inside the folder were about ten text files and ten picture files, mostly of the accident scene. Reading all of the notes that Detective Carter had placed in the file, I waited patiently while the pictures loaded into memory. The pictures were painfully more dramatic than any that might be available in the media. It became difficult viewing the burned remains of Mrs. Armstrong and her two sons. Since this was not the type of information that the public had access to, I felt an overwhelming sense of accomplishment in my quest to get to the truth.

It seemed obvious to me that there was insufficient evidence in the Omaha Police folder that Jackie Armstrong had been murdered. I attempted a anonymous phone call with Detective Carter, hoping to find out if he had more information that was not yet stored in the database file. I thought that I might be able extract some more information from him by convincing him that I had some additional information about the accident.

"Omaha Police Department," answered a female voice.

"Could I speak with Detective Carter?"

"I'm sorry, Detective Carter is not here right now. May I take a message for him?"

"I'd really rather not. I have some information for him about a case that he is investigating. Do you know when he will be back?" I asked.

"He won't be back for several days. He is out of town at a funeral."

"Well, I'll call back next week."

"Great, I'm sure that he will be back from Pittsburgh by then."

Disappointed that he was not in his office, I was nonetheless surprised that the police department would tell me that he was out of town at Pittsburgh for a few days. Believing that this type of information was confidential, I was convinced that had Detective Carter known that his associates identified his whereabouts, he would have strongly disapproved.

On a hunch, I spent the next day seeking out information on the lists of five donors that I had supplied to Karen for each of our clients. The exercise took some time but provided more than enough information to feed my suppositions. In every case, one of the five donors associated with each of our clients was dead. Moreover, not only dead, but dead and donated their organ to our client. I feared that, like the newspaper reporters, I was not just reporting the news but I was creating the news.

Karen answered my e-mail and agreed that Stephanie Swanson would be our next client. I agreed to call Ms. Swanson that afternoon and to wait for another call from Karen to give her the details. Since I had further investigated the historic list of five donors, I did not repeat my concerns with Karen, just supplied the information.

At three o'clock that afternoon from my cell phone, I dialed the number in Naples, Florida. The Cuban housekeeper that answered the phone was not able to supply any information nor was I able to ask for it. Through some more searching, I found the number for the residence in Martha's Vineyard. No answer. After scratching my head for a few minutes, I looked up the number for Richard Swanson at Global Product Services in Naples.

To my surprise, Mr. Swanson answered his own phone.

"Mr. Swanson."

"Yes."

"My name is Carlos Montoya," another fictitious name.

"Really?"

"Yes sir."

"You don't sound Hispanic."

"Mr. Swanson. I would like to talk to you about your daughter."

"You would? Is she all right?"

"Yes, of course. Except, of course, the condition of her heart."

"What do you know about that? Are you a doctor?"

"No. Nevertheless, I do have some information about where Stephanie is on the list to receive a heart. And I'm willing to bet that you and she would like to have that information."

"That information is highly confidential. I have tried to buy that information before. I have even tried to buy my way to the top of the list. It hasn't been easy. How do I know that the information that you have is accurate?"

"Because I can tell you when she was put on the list, how long she has been waiting for a heart, and who the doctor is who put her on the list."

After a few second pause, Mr. Swanson added, "I'm assuming that you want money for this information."

"Yes."

"How much are we talking about?"

"Five thousand," I decided not to go overboard with this client because I had some ulterior motives.

"That's a lot of money just for information."

"Perhaps I should talk with your daughter," I suggested, anticipating his answer.

"No! No. Do not bother her with this. It will just upset her."

"Do you want to think about it?" I sensed his concern that he might never hear from me again.

"No. Wait. You've got a deal."

"Great. My associate will call on you tomorrow evening at your house. She will collect the cash at that time and in return will supply the information to you."

"How do you know where I live?"

"Mr. Swanson, do you think that if I can acquire this highly confidential information about your daughter that I can't find out where her father lives?"

"Good point. What if I'm not satisfied with the information?" The seasoned executive asked in a cool calm controlled voice.

"Ask for your money back."

"You serious?"

"Of course. Money-back guarantee. Look for her about 7:00 PM tomorrow."

Karen contacted me about 4:30 PM and I briefed her on the conversation with Stephanie's father. I purposely set the pickup for the following evening allowing sufficient time for my plan to materialize, however I blamed the timing on Karen's ability to get to Naples. Karen would rather have had the pickup for that evening. It would not be the last time that I disappointed her.

Strolling out onto my balcony, I stared out across the rooftops of the buildings in my neighborhood. On the opposite side of the street facing my building, I spotted a black station wagon with the engine running. This scene looked suspicious to me, remembering my earlier conversation with Karen. In the closet beneath a pile of old beach towels, I found my camera bag. I removed the normal lens and replaced with the telephoto lens and an attachment that doubled the magnification.

Lying on the balcony out of sight from the street, I positioned the lens between the concrete slats and pointed it in the direction of the car I previously identified. The sun, now lower in the sky, provided sufficient light and contrast of the man who was sitting in the driver's seat. Of course, I did not recognize him. I snapped a couple of pictures and then removed the film canister from the camera.

Waiting for another half an hour, I went out to check again. The car and the man were still there. I rode the elevator down to the lobby and Charles was waiting as the door opened.

"Good afternoon Mr. White."

"Charles."

"Is there anything that I can do for you, sir?"

"Yes Charles. Is there another door on this floor other than this front door?"

"Well, yes sir. There is a door down this hallway that you can get out. You just can't come in that way."

"Where does it go?"

"It leads to a small parking lot then an alleyway out to the side street."

"Thank you Charles."

After sneaking out the back door, I quickly tiptoed through the parking lot and down the alley. When I reached the side street, I turned towards the main street and peeked around the corner to see if the man in the station wagon had spotted me. All clear. I continued around the block away from the main street and then down to a camera store a few blocks away. Turning in my film at the store, I asked for one-hour service, and then walked around in my new neighborhood.

After picking up the film, I strolled back to my apartment passing within a few feet of the black station wagon. Exhaust floated out of tailpipe so I knew someone was inside. The tint on the side windows prevented me from seeing inside. As I turned to cross the street to the apartment, I glanced back and caught a closer glimpse of the driver. His head jerked towards me as my presence outside of the apartment surprised him.

"Everything all right?" Charles asked as I entered the front lobby to the apartment building.

"Sure. I had a disability claim a few months back and I believe that the insurance company may have hired a private investigator to spy on me for a while. Not a big deal. Nothing to hide," I tried to camouflage any obvious surveillance that was going on.

"You want me to keep an eye on anyone?"

"No need to bother."

"Oh it's no bother, sir. It would be interesting."

"Well, if you're sure, you could let me know if this black station wagon across the street leaves while you are still here."

Charles peered over my shoulder seeing the car parked on the opposite side of the street without making it obvious to them, "got it. I'll give you a report."

When I got back to the apartment, I was careful not to let the driver of the car see me looking out at him. At seven o'clock, my apartment phone rang for the first time since I had moved in. Since I had not given the number out to anyone, I was somewhat afraid to pick it up.

"Mr. White? This is Charles, down in the lobby."

"Yes Charles," I relaxed again.

"Mr. White, I am going home for the evening, but I just wanted you to know that at 6:45 PM a black Ford drove up behind the station wagon, and a man got out and walked over to talk to the driver of the station wagon. After a few minutes, the station wagon drove away and the black Ford has been there ever since. The man that got out of the Ford is still sitting in the driver's seat with the engine running."

"Thanks a lot, Charles. I thought you told me that you went home at six."

"Well, Mr. White, normally I do, but thought I would stick around a little longer this evening."

"Thanks for your help Charles. Now go home to your family."

"Yes sir. I will keep an eye out tomorrow as well. Have a good evening Mr. White."

Collecting all of the papers that I had printed out on Stephanie Swanson, her father, Roger Merrill, and the 5 prospective donors from Florida, I placed them in the briefcase that had not seen any action for the previous 10 months. I packed my smallest suitcase that I normally took on overnight business trips.

After calling for a cab to meet me at the address around the corner from the apartment building, I was on my way down the elevator when I remembered that my cell phone was on the kitchen table. After retrieving the phone, I slipped through the back door of the apartment building and out onto the street where my cab was waiting.

The cab turned back onto the street in front of the apartment and the black Ford remained across the street with the engine running. The trip to the airport went quick in the light nighttime traffic.

My flight to Tampa was the last of the day and was thirty minutes delayed. Many business travelers, after removing their ties and jackets, collapsed into the seats and closed their eyes after a long business day. The many years of business travel again brought back fond memories of my past.

After landing at Tampa at 11:15 PM and not overly exhausted, I decided to drive as far as I could while the traffic was lightest. Crossing the Sunshine Bridge over Tampa Bay, I spotted the lights from St. Petersburg, where Kathy and I went on a honeymoon, albeit 12 months after our wedding day.

The early years of our marriage were great but as time went on, we started to grow apart. My career had always been number-one in my life and was where I received my identity. I missed many family school functions, all in the name of supporting the company and advancing my career. I turned down offers to work at other firms, assuming my loyalties with the company would eventually pay huge dividends. I only wish I could turn back the clock.

Stopping at Sarasota for the night, I plugged in my laptop, and began finding and printing the maps for all of the addresses that I might have to visit. As soon as the last one cleared the printer, I shut everything down, lay on the bed, and took the time to reflect on my dilemma.

Was someone actually following me? Who were the people in the station wagon and then in the Ford? Had Karen hired someone to watch me? Has someone connected me with Karen and her past? Exactly what did Karen do on her visits with our clients? Many questions came to mind but very few answers. I was determined to find some things out soon.

I slept without dreaming. No one in the world knew where I was.

eighteen

The hotel alarm blared out an upbeat Latin song as I scrambled to find the snooze button. Sitting on the edge of the bed for a few moments, I waited to stand making sure that blood was flowing to my head. I peered out the tenth story window to witness the neighborhood that I missed in the darkness from the night before. Corporate America was back at work.

After I checked out of the hotel, I prudently devoured breakfast in the restaurant, and like the other businessmen and women whom I shared the restaurant, I plotted my day's schedule. I organized the maps and addresses in the order in which I most likely would visit them. My strategy prescribed acquaintance with the surroundings during the day, then re-visiting at night when Karen was to carry out the transaction.

After reaching Naples, I first drove past Global Product Services and acknowledged that the license plate on the Mercedes in the front parking space was in fact the one listed in the Florida Department of Motor Vehicles registered to a Richard Swanson, father of our latest client.

Next, I drove down the peninsula formed by Naples Bay, the Gulf of Mexico, and the inlet to Naples Bay. Fingers of land jut out into the bay separated by fingers of water sufficiently wide and deep enough to handle the power yachts owned by the majority of the homeowners in the neighborhood. Most of the million-dollar homes were equipped with fenced-in yards with power gates across the driveways.

After locating Palmetto Lane, I started to take note of the addresses until I reached 805, the home of Richard Swanson. The one-story sand-colored brick home sprawled out across the acre lot. Fifteen-foot royal palms lined the circle drive and the top of the screened-in back yard was visible above the red-tiled roof. The stern of what looked to be a 50-foot boat bobbed in the slip behind the house.

Stephanie's house was a few doors down from her father's place and was equally as impressive. The overgrown tropical landscaping within the front yard camouflaged a stone and stucco façade. I turned at the next corner and retraced my route first past Stephanie's house and then her father's. Anticipating the actions that seemed probable that evening, I searched out places to park and hide. The large vegetation surrounding these expansive homes made the task significantly easier.

At 6:00 PM, I drove the rental car to a side street that allowed parking on the street. There were already several cars parked there, so my rental was not too obvious. I first walked past Mr. Swanson's house and then doubled back through some hedges and positioned myself in some bushes across the street. A black SUV passed several times slowing when it was in front of me and then returning a few minutes later.

At exactly 7:00PM, the same SUV backed up to the driveway gate and Karen, sporting a new redhead, emerged from the truck and walked to the control box. She was wearing nicely tailored black pants with a short sleeve black sweater. The outfit, coupled with her appealing shape and red-hair really made her hot.

I was too far away to hear the words spoken to the small electronic box but shortly thereafter, the gate started to slowly retract. I knew that if I was to get inside the gate I needed to act quickly. However, instead of walking through the opened gate, Karen re-entered the SUV and backed it in so that the gate could not close. I held back and waited for her to exit the vehicle and walk to the front door. As soon as she moved, I moved.

Concealing myself behind one of the front yard palm tress, I was no more than fifteen feet from where Karen conversed face-to-face with Richard Swanson. Mr. Swanson's facial expression exhibited one of uncertainty and mistrust. After a professional & polite invitation into the house, Karen carefully followed the suggestion.

Sliding in through the plants to the bottom corner of a picture window, I stared face-to-face with a small green lizard. Upon acknowledging my presence in his world, the red pouch below his lower jaw began to swell. I nudged it with my finger, producing an ungrateful hiss. The critter was obviously unaware that I had the power to crush him at any moment, even though my silence was imperative.

I experienced an overwhelming sense of adventure dissimilar to anything I had ever felt previously. The way I had meticulously planned my surveillance and made tactical decisions added to this quest.

Between the chairs, drapes, and lamps, Karen sat, legs crossed, arms swinging in explanation appropriate to a business deal. After a few minutes, noticing a smile creep onto Richard Swanson's face, I felt relieved and rewarded. He jotted a couple things down on a piece of paper and then I saw him hand Karen a white envelope. I assumed that within the envelope was the five thousand that we requested.

With the money exchanged, I prepared myself to move quickly towards the gate, keying my actions to those of Karen. However, Karen remained seated and the talking continued. Mr. Swanson contributed some dialog and the expression on his face shifted several times during those few minutes from misunderstanding, uncertainty, to eventually satisfaction and joy.

Richard Swanson retreated to a room off the front room that, because of the rich wood walls now illuminated with light, appeared to be his office. When he returned a few minutes later, he sat down and peeled off several bills onto the coffee table in front of Karen. Karen collected the bills, stood up, and they shook hands.

The front door opened and I was able to hear the last few words of their conversation before I scurried off towards the gate.

"I will contact you when the job is done," Karen explained as she turned towards the street.

"Great. And after that, I never want to hear from you again," they both laughed, although I sensed the seriousness in his voice.

By the time Karen reached the SUV, I was outside the gate, down the block, and unlocking the door to the rental car. The SUV pulled onto Palmetto Lane and the gate closed immediately behind it. As soon as Mr. Swanson closed the front door and switched off the front porch light, I followed in pursuit of my business partner.

I avoided all of the obvious actions that would allow Karen to recognize that I was following her. Switching lanes when possible, I moved slightly ahead of her and then allowed her to pass. She led me to I-75 North towards Tampa. I cautiously remained back amongst the other traffic speeding up just enough to find the black SUV maintaining the speed limit. Many cars passed us and when we were all alone on the highway, I had to slow down so Karen would not be suspicious.

When we arrived back in Tampa, Karen stopped for gas and a fast food store. It was difficult to remain out of site yet maintain my surveillance. Several times, I thought that I had lost her but each time I managed to locate the SUV and began tailing again.

At about 9:00 PM, the classical music notes of the cell phone buried in my overnight bag interrupted the constant hum of the highway. After four rings, I finally managed to push the talk button.

"Hello."

"Ben. How ya doin'?" Karen said cheerfully.

"All right. What's up?" I tried to control my anxiety.

"I just wanted to let you know that everything went all right with Richard Swanson." With the oncoming traffic lights just right, Karen's silhouette revealed a phone placed to her ear.

"Well, that's great. Where are you?" I purposefully asked to get a sense of her honesty.

"I'm just pulling into the airport in Naples."

"Where you going next?"

"You tell me. Where does our next client live?" she asked.

"I . . . I'm still working on the next client," I struggled with an answer.

"Where are you?" she asked this time.

"I'm at home, the apartment. Why do you ask?" I knew that if she was still having me watched that she would know if I had left the apartment. Moreover, if she could lie, so could I.

"There is a lot of background noise."

"Must be the TV."

"Well, I'll try to call you tomorrow some time, so get me information on the next client."

"I'll get on it. Just want to make sure that we are careful."

As I pushed the button on the cell phone and placed it back into my bag, I watched as Karen pulled the phone away from her ear and then a few seconds later it was back. I waited for my phone to ring again but it had not. Karen must have called or received a call from someone else.

Turning onto I-4 towards Orlando, my suspicions were proving to be true. After the hour and a half ride to Orlando, I tried my best to hide behind cars that traveled the same speed as Karen. As I noticed police cars, I always saw Karen tapping the brakes so as not to be stopped for speeding. She explained many times before that being stopped for speeding would be the most stupid mistake anyone could make.

Karen turned off I-4 onto International Blvd and then snaked back and forth as if she had been in the neighborhood previously. As the traffic subsided, I laid back further, just catching the taillights each time she turned. I recognized Summit Street as the street address for Roger Merrill, number one on the heart recipient list.

Houses on this street were small, most without garages. With several cars parked on the street, disappearing from view became straightforward. The neighborhood was mostly quiet at that time of night. Turning the car around, I backed into a gravel driveway next to a utilities shack on the main road and made my way to Roger Merrill's address hiding behind cars on the way. Karen passed me three times before parking along the street at an empty lot.

I observed her as she got out of the car, grabbed a small black bag from the back seat, and inspected the scene for anyone that might spot her. She slithered behind a hedge and stayed there for several minutes before slipping through the empty lot and the back yards until she reached Mr. Merrill's house.

Karen pried off the screen from a backyard window and lifted herself silently into the house. I adjusted my vantage point to look into the house through another window. The darkness inside prevented me from seeing anything at all. The clanking sound from the window fans drowned out any indication of movement from within.

When I shifted to another window, the noise awoke a dog from the neighbor's back yard. I quickly moved back around to the side of the house and within a few seconds watched Karen lowering herself out the window and carefully replacing the screen. She had been in the house less than ten minutes. She worked as if she had choreographed the movements, anticipating the tools required and the arm motions needed. She was very good.

As she returned through the backyards to the SUV, I cut across the street through another yard and out to the main street not far from where I parked my rental car. As she turned out onto the main road, I again followed in pursuit, far enough behind eluding detection.

When we arrived back at I-4 Karen turned North through downtown. Confused, I turned on a light inside the car and looked at my list of organ donors. Of the five donors that I had selected for Karen, two were from Miami, one from Sarasota, one from Gainesville, and one from Jacksonville. I continued to follow at a distance remaining inconspicuous within the heavy traffic. When we reached I-95, Karen turned towards the North, pointing her in the direction of Jacksonville.

It was 3:30AM when we reached the southern part of Jacksonville. Turning on I-10, Karen stopped at a gas station but did not pull up to a pump. The gas station was void of any other customers at that time of night, but being right off of a major highway, it would not be long before more customers joined her. Karen grabbed a small bag from the SUV, pulled out a bottle, removed the cap, and took a few sips.

After entering the gas station, she wandered about the store for a few minutes sipping from the bottle. After a few minutes, it became obvious that the man at the counter was curious about what she was drinking. Karen approached the counter and appeared to be explaining something about the bottle when she grabbed another bottle from her bag, wiped it with a cloth and handed it to the man. He removed the cap and took several gulps of the liquid inside and nodded in satisfaction.

Karen looked around the store for another minute, then waved to the attendant and left the gas station without buying anything.

I trailed Karen to Jacksonville's airport where she returned the SUV to the rental agency. My supposition was that Karen would visit Harold Nelson at 105 Pembrook Circle apartment #105 and eliminate him just as she had done with all of the other organ donors from previous clients. However, she did not. She went directly to the airport. Well, not directly. She did stop at the gas station. If she did not buy any gas though, what was the purpose of stopping there?

Rather than chase her through the air, which would be much harder to be inconspicuous, I decided to go back to the gas station and see what I could find out. When I arrived inside the gas station, a customer stood impatiently at the counter ready to pay for gas. The attendant sitting behind the counter had his arms folded on the counter and his head lay heavy on his arms. Groggy, the man finally lifted up his head trying to acknowledge the customer, but was too weak to sustain it.

"I don't know what's wrong," he whispered with all his energy.

"Are you all right?" the customer shouted trying to hand him a twenty-dollar bill.

"No. Call an ambulance," the attendant muttered in obvious pain.

The Good Samaritan got behind the counter and lifted the employee under his arms so he could ease him down to the floor. I followed behind the counter and found the phone. The sticker on the phone advertised the number for Harris Ambulance, so I gave them a call.

"Yes, I am a customer at the Shell station on I-10 at exit three and there is an employee here who is unconscious and needs an ambulance."

"Could you please give me your name and the address?" the woman's voice on the other end of the line asked.

"I . . . I am just a customer and I have no idea what the address is. It's the Shell station on the South side of I-10 just a few miles west of downtown," I caught myself just before I compromised my mission.

"Could I have your name?"

Just as the woman on the phone asked for my name a second time, I glanced down at the floor and recognized the name

"HAROLD NELSON" printed on the identification badge pinned above the attendant's shirt pocket. As my mind clouded with a hundred thoughts, I instinctively hung up the phone.

"The ambulance has been called." I said, turned away so that the other customer could not see my face again and hustled towards the door. I don't know what triggered my concern for my fingerprints all over the phone however, I grabbed the shop rag from the counter and quickly wiped the phone clean. With the rag still in my hand, I opened the door and ran to my rental car. Fumbling for my keys for what seemed like two minutes, I sped out of the station, trying to keep my head low in the car. Back on I-95 South, I passed an ambulance moving north at a high rate of speed. Obvious to me at that point that Karen knew Mr. Nelson worked at this station on the graveyard shift, she also would have concluded that this would be her best opportunity to eliminate him. Thinking back at what I saw, the drink that she gave him must have contained a poison. Was she that good? I could only assume that she was and I knew that I did not want to be associated with Harold's death.

I drove back South toward Orlando, not knowing what my next move should be. After arriving in Daytona Beach, I became so exhausted; sleep became my only remedy. Registering at a hotel a few blocks off I-95, I contemplated my immediate future. As suspected, my involvement in this crime was much deeper than I had ever planned. I was not into the killing but I was definitely an unwilling accomplice. Too scared to continue our partnership, I was also afraid of what Karen might do if she knew that I knew. After witnessing her work in person, I knew what she was capable of. I placed the "Do Not Disturb" sign outside the door and tried to go to sleep.

I awoke to a loud rapping on the door.

"Housekeeping!"

"Could you give me some time here? I put the sign outside the door," I barked back acknowledging the inconvenience.

"It's 12:00 noon sir. Checkout time," she said as if rehearsed from many times before.

"I'm so sorry. Give me 15 minutes and I will be out of here." In all my years of traveling for the company, this had never happened.

Quickly showering before the water had reached an acceptable temperature, I washed my hair and body with the shampoo provided and threw yesterday's clothes in my bag.

Walking out of the hotel, paranoid from the previous day's events, I again was careful to notice if anyone was hunting me. After witnessing Karen's actions from the previous day, I expected the police to be waiting in the parking lot to pick me up and haul me away to jail. However, I did not recognize anything suspicious.

The abrupt start to the morning prevented me from taking the time to think through my next move, so I stopped at a local diner for lunch and a few minutes to collect myself. Knowing that I required some research time back at my computer, I decided my next move would be to the airport and then back to the apartment.

I intended on using the two-hour flight to Houston for revising my plan, but the man sitting next to me on the plane wanted to talk. Moreover, he talked for the entire two hours. At first, I was suspicious that he might be a plant by Karen, or whoever was looking for Karen, or God forbid, the police. After the first half hour, I was convinced that he was just lonely and liked to hear himself talk.

#

The taxi dropped me off around the corner from the apartment building then I tiptoed to the corner and peered at where the station wagon and black Ford had been parked. I did spot another car in relatively the same spot with the engine running and passenger in the driver's seat. I walked back behind the apartment building and called Charles on my cell phone.

"Charles? This is Ben White."

"Yes sir. Where are you? I've been calling your apartment."

"I have been out for a while. Do you still see anyone across the street in a parked car?"

"Well, yes Mr. White. That is what I have been calling you about."

"Charles, could I get you to do me a favor?"

"Of course, sir."

"Could you please open the back door for me? I don't want these folks to see me returning to the apartment, because they don't know that I left in the first place."

"Right now sir?

"Right now, Charles."

"Right away, sir."

"Welcome back sir," Charles exclaimed as we both walked down the hall towards the front lobby.

"What was it that you wanted to tell me?"

"Well Mr. White, I watched the cars for the last couple days and always different cars and always switching cars and drivers at approximately 6:00 PM."

"Thanks a lot for your help," I extended my hand to him and turned towards the elevator.

"Just a minute. I'm not finished."

"What's that?"

"Yesterday, the man that was in the car walked over here in the lobby to ask me some questions."

"What did he ask?"

"He wanted to know if you were in the building. He wanted to know if I knew you very well. He wanted to know how often you left the apartment and where you went when you left."

"What did you tell him?"

"I told him that even if I had any information that it is the apartment's policy not to discuss our residents. He tried to give me a hundred dollar bill but I did not take it. He walked out the door in a huff and then went into the restaurant across the street. Five minutes later he came out and sat back in the car."

"Wow, Charles. I guess I owe you."

"No Sir, its my job."

"Well, thanks Charles. I really appreciate your help," I exclaimed as I turned for the elevator.

"Just a minute, I'm still not finished."

"I'm sorry."

"About an hour after the man from the car came in, another two men came in and asked about you."

"You're kidding!"

"No sir, serious. These two men were dressed in dark suits and they quickly flashed badges in front of me. They said that they were FBI agents. They wanted to go up to your apartment, but I told them that they would need a search warrant to get past me. This did not satisfy them, so we called the apartment manager, and the three of them went up to the your apartment.

After about five minutes, the three returned to the lobby, obviously not finding you there. I was given instructions to call them back at the number on this business card when you returned."

"So what are you going to do?" I asked, calm on the outside but churning inside.

"Well sir, because I never saw you come back, I don't have to call them," he handed me the business card.

"I guess I really do owe you Charles. I will not forget the help you've given me. Please don't spend any more of your time watching these guys."

The apartment was quiet and dark and I was glad to be back where I was relatively safe. I popped a frozen entrée into the microwave and started to do some laundry. The thought occurred to me that as good as Karen was at espionage, she might have arranged to bug my apartment with microphones, cameras, and transmitters. I spent the following hour searching, but found nothing.

Logging onto my laptop for the first time in a couple days, I checked my heart recipient list, but nothing had changed. Knowing that Karen would be calling soon and expecting another prospective client and list of donors, I got busy on research. This time I decided to check out the kidney list again.

My mind, occupied by the events of the previous two days, somewhat confirmed what I thought I knew about Karen and her activities. The goal of my previous outing was to observe what Karen was doing on her visits to our clients and perspective donors. All of my assumptions proved to be correct however; I did not really witness her "eliminating" anyone. As I searched for another client, I wondered whether I needed to make another trip.

nineteen

Waking to a rare morning thunderstorm, I checked the street again for the cars that stalked me for the previous few weeks. The exhaust smoke from the black SUV parked a few spaces down from the normal spot swirled upward then quickly dissolved in the rain. Through the slightly tinted windshield, I barely made out the figure seated behind the wheel. How much longer would this continue? Why didn't they just walk in and arrest me? Maybe they wanted to investigate more or maybe they were not law enforcement at all was my second thought.

After checking my e-mails, I immediately clicked my way to the Omaha Police web site to retrieve updated information on my new cyber-friend Detective Carter. Again, accessing the database and folder titled "092500-Armstrong"; two additional files not previously in the file stood out from the rest.

A new text file identified Detective Carter's friend, Brian Flynn, as a 52 year-old Caucasian that passed away under unusual circumstances in Pittsburgh, Pennsylvania. Detective Carter listed his association with Mr. Flynn as a good friend from the Army. The notes go on to describe that although Brian was suffering from lung disorders, doctors did not expect him to die of suffocation. Mr. Flynn's wife explained that Brian had been on the national list to receive two lungs but died before reaching the top of the list.

The other file that I immediately identified came from the Office of Special Programs from the Health Resources and Services Administration of the Department of Health and Human Services web site for Organ Recipients. A picture of the suave boisterous executive, Warren Smithson from the hotel bar in Venezuela, dwarfed the department mission statement below it. Handwritten on the bottom of the sheet, in what assumedly was Carter's handwriting were the previous day's date and the words "phone interview". I found no other notes in the file.

Transferring to the Health and Human Services web site as I had done many times previous, I logged in under 'Dr. Carl Lyon's Password '*C*Lyons$$'. A window popped up on the screen indicating that Login ID or Password was not accepted. Slowing to a computer illiterate pace, I carefully typed in the Login ID and password a second time typing one letter at a time pronouncing each letter aloud. Again, I received the message "Not Accepted". I opened the file drawer and retrieved the piece of paper identifying the web site, Dr. Lyons' name, Login ID, and password. I tried a third time and got the same response.

Taking a break from my logon failures, I logged off my computer, and made lunch. When I returned to my research, I was amazed to find that the login and password that I had been using for the previous several months, which came back denied an hour earlier, now worked fine.

Because I anticipated a call from Karen at any moment, I rushed to capture information on the next client. When Karen had not called by 1:30PM, I pushed back in my new executive office chair, put my feet on the desk and dreamed up another scheme to get rid of my Nissan and replace it with something a little less noticeable and significantly more comfortable.

As with most of my research, I searched the Internet, this time for the address of the downtown BMW dealership. Fortunate for me, the dealership was located only a few miles away and directly across the street from a nice restaurant that I had visited once. For security reasons, I used my cell phone to wire $10,000 from my Swiss account to a downtown bank that I had already setup just for this purpose.

Dressed in a blue pinstriped suit, worn at least once per week in my successful years with the company, I expected a certain level of respect from the BMW salespersons. Searching through the accordion file where I kept important papers, I extracted the title to the Nissan pickup truck.

At 2:00PM and still no call from Karen, I drove the pickup out of the parking garage directly in front of the black SUV. My surveillance vehicle pulled away from the curb and into the lane of traffic three or four cars behind me. After making several turns, I arrived at the bank parking lot and picked an open spot directly in front.

Experiencing no problems at the bank, I again spotted the black SUV parked about a block away with the engine running. The SUV followed in pursuit as I carefully watched in the rearview mirror. Turning into the restaurant parking lot, I parked away from the other cars and close to the busy street.

After retrieving the title to the Nissan from the seat beside me, I placed it in the inside jacket pocket and entered the restaurant. I asked for a table in the back of the restaurant to avoid the window where my stalker could witness my next move. I ordered a large ice tea.

The SUV, parked on the other side of the parking lot, had a clear view of the restaurant front door and could easily see the pickup truck. Placing a five dollar bill on the table, I walked past the restrooms in the rear of the restaurant and out through the kitchen and the back door.

Littered with trash, the alley behind the building reeked from leaky dumpsters and employees on smoke breaks. I continued down one block and then crossed the street back to where the BMW dealership was located.

I was very surprised that a salesman immediately acknowledged my presence in the showroom and asked if he could be of assistance. His BMW name badge identified him as Nelson Jeffries.

"Actually, I am looking to lease a BMW, Mr. Jeffries. I am hopeful that it will be from you because I don't have a lot of time."

"Do you have any idea which model that you would be interested in?" Asked the 40ish executive-looking salesman with hints of gray spattered on the sides of his head.

"Yes, I am interested in the 5 Series, 4 door, 3 Liter 6 cylinder, black in color."

"Coupe or Sedan?"

"Sedan."

"How long of lease are you interested in?"

"Three years."

"Let's sit down and work it out," he acknowledged my time limitation by cutting out the customary salesmanship.

After punching a few numbers into the PC sitting in front of him, he swiveled the flat screen display towards me.

"Looks like that works out to be $650 per month for 36 months with a down payment of $5,000."

"I'm fine with that, except you will have to take the trade in that I drove here today, and I will need to drive out of this dealership with the new car – today."

"Let's see what we can do? What is the car that you will be trading in?"

"It's a 1993 Nissan pickup. Here is the title."

"If I could get the keys from you, I will have our estimator look at it and I can give you a price."

"He'll have to look at it from here. It's parked in the restaurant parking lot across the street. It's the red one," I pointed out the window.

"Doesn't it run?"

"It run's fine. But you will have to make me an offer on it without driving it."

"I'm afraid that I don't understand."

"Look, Mr. Jeffries, it is a 1993 Nissan pickup. It has one hundred forty five thousand miles on it. It is a classic. If you can't handle this situation, I will go to another BMW dealership. I know that you are not the only one in town."

"No, don't go anywhere else. Let me see what we can do from here. This may be a bit unusual, but nothing we haven't handled before."

While the estimator prepared an estimate, I worked with the financial manager in order to qualify for the lease. When it came to the question about the amount of money that I had in the bank, I reached for my cell phone to access my account balance from Switzerland.

After punching in the password, I was again amazed that the balance was significantly more than I expected. I wrote it down on a piece of scrap paper, rotated it towards the finance manager and shoved it towards him.

"I don't believe that we will have a problem here. I'll let Nelson know that you are done in here."

"I have checked and we do have the car in stock that you have described. I'm sure that you would like to drive it before you sign the papers," the salesman stated.

"Why?" I asked.

"Well, most people prefer to drive the car before they buy or lease."

"Why, doesn't it run?"

"Of course it runs," he answered with a polite chuckle.

"No, just wrap it up and dust it off and I'll be on my way. One question, before I leave."

"Yes sir?"

"Are the sales here kept private?"

"Of course sir. Only the Department of Motor Vehicles and the state sales tax folks will have the transactions and they hold that information pretty close to the vest. You would have to be law enforcement or have a court order to obtain the information."

"Thanks, just checking."

Fifteen minutes later and just 30 minutes after I entered the dealership, I was leaving with a fifty thousand dollar car. As I pulled out onto the street, the black SUV remained across the street. When I accelerated, I noticed Mr. Jeffries, running across the street towards the restaurant parking lot. I wish that I could have seen the look on my stalker's face when he witnessed the Nissan driven away by someone else.

I am sure that he would have immediately been on the cell phone to whomever he was working for, explaining that he had potentially lost his subject. Eventually, he would have visited the BMW dealership and interrogated them, because of its close proximity to my disappearance. If he was law enforcement, he could get his information, but if he were one of Karen's employees, he would have to dig for it, just as she taught me to do.

Two blocks away from the apartment my cell phone rang. It was Karen. It seemed extremely coincidental to me that she should be calling within ten minutes of giving my surveillance the slip.

"Ben?"

"Karen. How are you? I was expecting your call."

"Where are you?"

"Actually, I am in a restaurant, waiting to be served," I lied, trying to further determine if Karen ordered the surveillance.

"Near the apartment?"

"A couple of miles."

"Nice restaurant?" she persisted.

"I thought that you called about our next client?"

"I was just making small talk," she answered.

"You don't make small talk, Karen. You always get right to the point. There will be time for play later. Remember?"

"All right Ben, . . . what do you have for me?"

"Can I call you back in a half an hour, so my food doesn't get cold?"

"I'll call you back in forty five minutes so you'll have a chance to get back to the apartment."

I pushed the END button on the cell phone just as I pulled into the parking garage. The black SUV was not parked across the street, but a dark green van with two men seated inside occupied the curbside a few spots down. The new situation confused me.

I pulled into my parking spot impressed at how I was able to lease a $50,000 car in such a short time and at how I gave my stalkers the slip for a second time.

Karen called as planned and I managed to keep it very businesslike. I gave her the information on our next client and told her that I would call the client the next day.

"Everything all right?" Karen asked as if she knew more but would not say.

"Sure, everything is going great. We are making money and what could be better?" I answered with as much enthusiasm as I could generate until I came up with another plan.

"Just checking. We want to make sure that we do not get sloppy and make mistakes. Anything else I should know about?"

"That's all I have for now. Call me tomorrow after 3:00 pm and I'll have the details for the client meeting."

As I hung up the phone, I began thinking about the trouble that I had with the Department of Health and Human Services web site, and something about it troubled me. I decided to do some investigation on the logon ID and password that I was using to access the site.

Checking repeatedly, I successfully entered the ID and password of the organ recipient site on every attempt. Backtracking the method that I acquired the ID and password, I recalled my visit with Christine at the Beaufort doctor's office. I could visualize her waiting for me at the Sand Dollar bar, promising that she would never allow herself to be stood up again. I searched for recent information about Dr. Lyons that would change his eligibility for the donor program.

Dr. Lyons and I were members of the Beaufort Country Club, which for me was a justifiable perk from the company I served for 25 years. Dr. Lyons and I played 18 holes every Thursday morning, if I was not away on a business trip. Opening my wallet, I retrieved the business card from the country club with the phone number where I would call for tee time reservations. The assistant professional at the club seemed to change each year, so I was confident that the one answering the phone would not remember me.

"Beaufort Country Club. This is Carl," came the response on the other end of the line. I did not remember Carl, but the club always seemed to hire the same type for this position.

"Hey Carl. How y'all doing today? Hey, I was supposed to meet Dr. Lyons out there for some golf tomorrow and I forgot that tee time. I am having a hard time getting a hold of him and he'll surely give me a hard time if he knew I lost the information. Can you help me out?"

There was a silence on the other end of the line for a few seconds.

"Hell, it's no wonder why you are having a hard time getting a hold of him," Carl chuckled.

"Yea, why's that?" I continued to pry information that Carl apparently was more than obliged to supply.

"Because he's dead."

"Dead! You're kidding," I'm sure that I sounded shocked because I couldn't believe what I was hearing.

"No sir. Died right here on the ninth green. Very convenient for us. Kinda dented the green though when he fell."

"Whoa!"

"I'm surprised you didn't know that. The funeral was Monday. Very big deal around here. They closed the course for the afternoon. Haven't done that since Bobby Jones died."

"Had he been sick?" I asked.

"I doubt it," Carl said, "he was playing golf with a woman half his age. A real looker. Probably couldn't keep up with her and died trying."

"Who was the woman?"

"Don't know. Never saw her before. She was gone by the time Doc Lyons made it to the ninth green."

I quickly hung up the phone as too many things rushed through my head at that moment and I could not keep up with the charade with good-ol-boy Carl.

The news about Dr. Lyons puzzled me. His death would certainly explain why I could not get into the Organ Donor web site with his ID and password, but why was I able to get in later. I am sure that a federal department such as the Department of Health and Human Services would not make mistakes that serious. Should I continue to use the site with Dr. Lyon's ID and password or should I find another?

Gathering a little more information about the next client and some potential organ donors, I searched for data to put closure on our last client in Florida.

I reviewed the Naples Daily News web site. Of the three top stories, one was on the heart transplant of Stephanie Swanson. The article contained quotes from her father Richard Swanson, interviewed at the Cardiac Surgery waiting room from the Sarasota Memorial Hospital. "Stephanie has been on the heart recipient list for a long time now and I guess that she reached the top of the list. We are so fortunate to receive the gift of life from a gentleman in Jacksonville. As I understand it, this person passed away yesterday afternoon and his heart was flown here to Sarasota last night. We found out at about midnight last night that Stephanie would be scheduled for the surgery this morning."

The article went on to list all of Stephanie's accomplishments, both in business and in community support. Preliminary reports from her heart surgeon were that she was in good condition with no complications regarding the transplanted organ.

Switching over to the Orlando Sentinel, I traced my trip across Florida from a few days earlier. The obituaries from the previous day listed Roger Merrill as "passed away in his sleep in Orlando after a yearlong battle with heart disease". The paragraph also listed his 23 years of service as a high-school chemistry teacher and his mother as the only surviving relative.

My final stop on this search was at the Florida Times Union where I searched for information on our latest heart donor, Harold Nelson. The article for Mr. Nelson's death was a little more interesting and significantly more damaging to my future wellbeing.

"Possible Homicide in Gas Station Attendant Death" was the column headline on page two. "The ambulance call was phoned in from an unidentified man while inside the gas station. This unidentified man then fled the scene in a white mid-sized car," reported a Good Samaritan who helped Harold Nelson until the ambulance arrived. Police are now looking for information on this unidentified potential killer and they are reviewing the tapes from the video cameras installed at the gas station.

Jesus Christ, video tapes? This was the most damning evidence. I had not thought about a video camera. I was certainly doomed. I became nauseous. It was just a matter of time before my face was plastered all over the TV and I would have police pushing past Charlie in the lobby and then knocking down my apartment door.

Forget about the fact that I had nothing to do with the murder of Harold Nelson; I was an accomplice in the murder and I witnessed the murder. I could not approach the police and tell them what I knew because they would ask me what I was doing in Jacksonville in the first place. Eventually, they would implicate me right along with Karen in the murder of many innocent people.

How could I possibly escape this latest dilemma? I would have already told Karen I was quitting if I was not afraid of what she and her associates might do to me. Needing more time to gain some control of the situation, I had to maintain the illusion that nothing was wrong.

twenty

Pounding on the apartment door woke me from a restless sleep. Throwing on a pair of sweats and a tee shirt, I silently tiptoed to the door. As I squinted through the peephole in the door, my expectations were of the police or the FBI. If it were Karen, she would somehow have let herself in the apartment without anyone knowing it.

As soon as my eye could focus, I realized that it was Charlie from the lobby. I opened the door.

"Good morning, Mr. White. I am sorry to bother you this early in the morning. A courier service brought this package over to you this morning and I signed for it."

"Thanks Charlie."

"Just for your information, Mr. White, I don't see any surveillance teams parked out front today."

"Really? Maybe they lost interest in watching me," I made up an explanation to help justify Charlie's findings.

"Thanks again for bringing this up."

Locking the door, I laid the package on the kitchen table while I headed for the shower. When I returned from the bathroom, I inspected the package but found nothing unusual. As I searched the knife drawer for a pointed knife, my cell phone rang.

"Ben? This is Karen. What's new?"

"Not much. I thought that you were going to call after three," I answered quickly.

"I will, but . . ."

"But what?"

"Did you get my present?"

"Present? Oh, you mean this package. I wondered who it came from. I haven't opened it yet." With all that had happened over the past week, my stomach ached and I had a difficult time trying to act happy.

"Well open it. I'll wait for you," Karen said, much more jubilant than I.

"All right, it's open. What is it?"

"It's a PDA."

"A what?"

"A PDA. A personal digital assistant."

"Oh! Why do I need this?"

"You can take this wherever you go and can access the Internet any time and anywhere. You can read and send e-mails. It is really cool. Read up on it and take it with you like your cell phone. Of course, you'll probably want to take your cell phone as well."

"Thanks," I answered more confused than ever.

"Anticipate any problems with this client?"

"Not really, very similar to the others. I have done some more background work and nothing jumps out at me to worry about. I'll fill you in after the call this afternoon."

"Sounds good. I'll call you then."

"Karen?"

"Yes?"

"Thanks for the present." I wanted to say more but was afraid to stir things up yet.

"No problem, now just make sure you take it with you wherever you go."

"I'll talk to you later." She must have sensed my declining attitude.

Holding the new electronic device in my hands, I studied the screen and controls. I positioned the instruction book in front of me on the desk and began to configure the device for myself while continuing to utter the last words from Karen, "make sure to take it with you wherever your go". I repeated it several times to myself, mocking her words each time.

Although I did not understand how exactly I would use this toy, I concluded that Karen never said or did anything that was not well thought out. I did not punish myself about it but knew something would come to me later.

I prepared for my call with a prominent oil executive that was in need of new kidneys. Karen was against clients that lived in Houston, but this one seemed to be a slam-dunk. Almost too easy. All of the information was there for the taking; solid financials, medium visibility, mid-life, and only second on the recipient list. There was also the added benefit of being able to witness, without traveling to another city, exactly what Karen was doing with the client and with the others that unfortunately happened to be higher on the list.

Sensing that Karen wanted all of her actions to be out of sight, I anticipated a negative response on this client. With my surveillance gone, I would be free to check out Karen's actions at the client's location and finally confirm all of my suspicions.

Number one on the list was an older Hispanic woman living in San Antonio. This would be very convenient for Karen; she could visit our oil executive client in Houston and then make the three-hour drive to San Antonio to "eliminate" number one on the list. Moreover, if I could arrange for a donor than was also close, Karen could handle all three transactions easily in one night.

At 2:00 pm, I called our client at his home. Returning from his dialysis treatment at the Texas Medical Center, the 52 year-old executive was more than happy to drop the $10,000 I was asking for the information Karen would provide the next evening. It probably was not his money anyhow, but that of the oil company. He even suggested to me that he would be willing to pay more to get these kidneys so that he could get back to work.

Puzzled about the ease at which I sold the information and at the cost compared to the value that I was to provide, I searched for five donors in the area with the correct blood type match, one of which was the Mayor of a Houston suburb.

Karen called at 3:05 pm and I provided all of the information that she would need including names, addresses, phone numbers, companies, and bank account balances.

"We'll do this one, but next time skip over the possible Houston clients; too many possibilities for error. I want to make sure that you are far away from the money transactions in case law enforcement gets involved."

In an effort to test the new electronic gizmo that Karen had given me, using my laptop computer, I made a list of groceries that I needed from the store and stored it in an e-mail to myself. Grabbing my PDA and cell phone, I rode the elevator down to the parking garage level. The new BMW started effortlessly and I circled my way down to the street level.

Just as Charlie had indicated, I could not spot a surveillance car parked on the street. After parking the car in the grocery store parking lot, I grabbed a shopping cart and turned on my new PDA. Using the stylus supplied with the unit, I selected e-mail and then the e-mail that I had sent a few minutes earlier. The grocery list popped up immediately and I began filling the shopping cart.

Other applications for this device quickly filled my head while I went from aisle to aisle, when the unit beeped at me and an e-mail appeared on the display. "Just wanted to see if you were using your PDA. If you are receiving this, please send me a quick response" was the e-mail from Karen.

I brought up the keyboard window and with the stylus typed in a simple response. "This thing works great! I am thinking of many more applications. Thanks a lot." It was a coincidence that I happened to be out with the PDA turned on so that I could receive and respond that quickly. I made sure that I turned it on each time I left the apartment.

On the way home from the store I attempted to again detect whether I was still being followed, just as Karen had showed me. I had not been. Upon my return to the apartment, still no surveillance car parked on the street in front. I was again puzzled. I was unsure who followed me and then abruptly disappeared. I started to feel a little more at ease.

With a little time on my hands before I needed to map out my movements for the next day, I decided to revisit the Omaha Police Database on the Internet and see if there was more information on the file.

A new file now appeared in the folder "092500-Armstrong". Inside the new file identified as "1987 Ford Bronco – Brake Pedal Linkage", were a report, picture, and x-ray identifying the probability that the linkage that connects the brake pedal to the master cylinder had been cut 90% through. Three counts of homicide replaced the cause of the accident previously listed as accidental.

Switching to the Omaha newspaper web site, I stumbled on a picture of Detective Carter holding the failed brake linkage assembly. "We now have the evidence proving homicide, and we continue to check out leads to probable suspects," Detective Neil Carter explained.

Although I had no evidence, I knew that Karen was somehow responsible for these deaths as well. Just to be on the safe side, I would avoid Omaha and Detective Carter for any future clients.

Our new client lived just outside the 610-loop in downtown Houston in an old area of gated communities that housed many of the oil and medical executives from the Houston area. George Billings was the CFO of the largest oil & gas company in the United States. Both of his parents were deceased but Margaret, his current wife, still had both parents alive and living in Houston.

George's father-in-law was the CEO of the same company several years' back and had a great interest in the well being of his successful son-in-law. The whole family was oozing money and this was our chance to get some of it.

Rachael Sanchez, a 75 year-old Hispanic woman, lived by herself in the poorer section of San Antonio in a run-down 5-room house. Her husband of 45 years had passed away a few years earlier. Rachael's two boys had moved back to their previous home in a small town in Mexico to avoid the draft and fighting for the United States during the Vietnam War.

Mrs. Sanchez suffered from kidney disease for the previous five years and had been on dialysis for the last three. Since dialysis was no longer as effective, the doctors placed her on the waiting list for new kidneys. Too bad, she would never know that she had made it to the top of the list.

I located both of the addresses using my map software, familiarized myself with the streets in Houston and San Antonio, and convinced myself that I could get positioned appropriately out of sight before Karen made it to each neighborhood. Switching to the Texas site for organ donors, I sorted by Houston and the surrounding 200 miles, so it would include San Antonio and Austin.

Identifying many donors that matched George Billings' blood type, I started to eliminate the ones that were not convenient to the elimination of Rachael Sanchez in San Antonio. Understanding why Karen wanted five names and addresses, I then could help select and organize them.

My top name with same blood type, Clarence Robb, was a black bus driver for the San Antonio School District. Clarence lived by himself, never married, and no obvious family. Fortunately for Karen, Clarence lived only a few blocks away from Rachael Sanchez. I hoped that the proximity of the two possible deaths occurring within minutes of each other would not cause reason for suspicion.

Karen called back later that evening for information on the five donors. Feeling slightly paranoid on giving her Clarence Robb's name, I questioned whether the close location to the number one recipient might disclose my knowledge of her plans. In any case, the other four names listed included donors who were two to three hundred miles away from San Antonio. Her only logical choice was Mr. Robb.

Assessing the continued surveillance of the apartment, I cautiously strolled out onto the balcony. Surprised after several weeks of continuous stakeout, I could not spot anyone down on the street. I scanned the nearby buildings but came up empty. Switching on the TV, I checked the national news to see if there was any coverage on the death of Harold Nelson in Jacksonville. Finding nothing, I searched the net for newspaper coverage.

There was another article in the newspaper that further detailed the evidence that the Jacksonville police had in their possession on the case. "Both video tapes had been removed from the machines prior to our arrival. The manager of the gas station reports that the tape players were in good working condition and that there were tapes in the machines when he left the station earlier that day. The witness on the scene reported no removal of the tapes while he was waiting for the ambulance and police to arrive. The police are still checking for fingerprints."

The damning evidence that would have implicated Karen and me was not evidence at all, but the property of someone else. If I did not remove the tapes and Karen did not take them, who could it have been? Maybe someone saw Karen or me and decided to blackmail us. Either way, I still could not let Karen know about it because then she would know that I was following her. Later that same evening, if I was lucky enough to get a close vantage point, I could gather the final evidence against Karen.

Although extremely tired, I struggled in drifting off to sleep. With all of the thoughts of murder swirling in my head, I acknowledged that what I had gotten myself into was wrong, very wrong. I understood the difference between right and wrong. Although exceedingly in over my head, I wrestled with a plan to extricate myself from the situation. Witnessing first hand, what Karen was capable of; I was terrified of the potential outcome.

Yet, there was another side of the situation that was exciting. I had transitioned from a humdrum, relatively successful, predictable life, through a scary time without a job, and thrust into an unwanted separation from a wife of 26 years. Then all of the sudden, I am traveling to Venezuela and Europe and I have money in the bank and I am driving a new BMW. I do not punch a clock and I am my own boss. Well, kind of. Most men would die for this situation. I sincerely hoped I would not.

Collecting my names, addresses, and maps for my evening's jaunt around South Texas, I donned black pants and a lightweight black turtleneck shirt similar to what I had seen Karen in on my previous stakeout. Scheduling Karen's meeting with George Billings for 8:00 PM that evening, I had the advantage of diminished light.

At 7:00 PM, I grabbed my cell phone and new PDA, drove the BMW through the garage to the gate and peered out in both directions. I carefully executed a zigzag course towards Mr. Billings' house, eluding any potential followers. With an estimated travel time of less than ten minutes, I carefully inspected the rearview mirror for any tails.

Entering the correct neighborhood, I marveled at the expensive brick homes shielded by six-foot brick fences and adorned with the most elaborate landscaping that I had ever witnessed. As I approached Mr. Billings' place, I again spotted a gate with a control box just past the sidewalk. Passing by three times, I searched for a convenient place to park the car and to find suitable hiding while waiting for Karen to arrive.

As soon as I settled in an inconspicuous parking spot, I turned off the engine and arranged my documentation for a quick get-away. As I opened the door to make the two-block walk back to Mr. Billings' residence, my cell phone rang. Startled, I did not know whether to answer it or let my voice mail pick it up. If it was Karen and there had been a change of plans, I needed to know it. I composed myself and then answered.

"Ben. This is Karen again. What is going on?"

"Not much. Any problems?"

"Not really. Just was double-checking on things. What are you doing right now?" Karen asked as if she already knew the answer.

"Nothing actually." If she only knew that I parked two blocks away from our client's house and that I was prepared to watch the transaction go down, she definitely would have walked away from the meeting.

"I wonder if you can look in the file you showed me before and tell me the name of the client that we had in New Jersey?"

"Why?" I asked, knowing there was no way I could pull out a file that was back at the apartment.

"I thought I read something about the guy," Karen explained.

"Actually, I'm sitting on the throne," I lied, hoping that she would buy into the excuse. "Let me call you back in a few minutes."

"No, I'll call back right before tonight's appointment."

"Great."

I settled back into the driver's seat upset that I would have to drive back to the apartment to answer a stupid question for Karen. It was almost as if she had known that I was there at Mr. Billings' house. However, how could she know? Careful to ensure no one followed me back to the apartment, I pursued a complex non-direct route.

The interruption bothered me increasingly as I started home. I wondered if I had enough time to get to the apartment and then back to our client's house. As I stopped at a traffic light, I glanced down at my cell phone on the seat. The light from the PDA cast a blue green glow on everything in the front seat.

Then it occurred to me. It must be the PDA. What if Karen placed a tracking device inside the PDA and she could track me wherever I went. She could have had the device altered and then sent it over using a courier service. She did make a big deal out of me taking it with me whenever I left the apartment. It all made sense.

Racing across town, I parked in front of the apartment building. Riding the elevator to the apartment, I placed the PDA on the kitchen table and left it turned on. Just for safety's sake, I grabbed the file folder that Karen had referenced so I could answer her questions while I was on the road. If my suppositions were correct and she knew that I was back at the apartment, she would not be calling back anyhow.

I was back into the BMW driving towards George Billings' residence for the second time that evening. It was 7:45 PM. Since Karen would be somewhere around the house checking things out, I sought out my parking spot carefully, approaching from another direction. My previous parking spot was taken, forcing me to find another one a block farther away.

Finally reaching the house on foot, I witnessed Karen backing into the driveway blocking the gate open as she had previously. I slid in through the gate next to the black station wagon rental. Karen strode up the brick walk to the ten-foot wooden doors on the porch of the executive's home.

Without a convenient place to hide on the grounds in front of this house, I viewed from a distance. I witnessed Karen and George Billings walk past the front window and into a room that was out of my view. Recognizing my logistical limitations, I concluded that the money transaction with the client was not what I really came to look at anyhow.

Escaping through the gate, I quickly slipped back to my BMW. After a few turns to get out of the neighborhood and with a confidence that the deal would go down as planned, I was on I-10 heading for San Antonio. If I was wrong about Karen's involvement in the crimes, I was about to take a three to four hour waste of my time. Convinced though that I was right, I still needed evidence providing ammunition if our partnership went south.

Arriving in San Antonio a little after midnight, I was convinced that I arrived before Karen. Easily finding Rachael Sanchez' house, within ten minutes and after passing the house three times, I settled into a parking spot two blocks away in the parking lot of an abandoned Laundromat. I pulled a dark blue cap onto my head to cover my gray hair and then worked my way between parked cars into Ms. Sanchez' back yard.

On the east side of the house, a live oak provided limbs well within my reach, allowing me to climb to about twenty feet. From this location, I could see the street and witness movement around most of the house. I relaxed for a few minutes and tried to adjust to the darkness. Once adjusted to my visual limitations, I was surprised how well I could see the things that were going on around me.

A warm breeze rustled the leaves in the tree and disguised any noise that I might have generated. The half-moon in a crisp sky cast charcoal shadows on the dry grass lawn. After 25 minutes, I spotted headlights turn onto the street in front of me and my heart began to race. The car slowed as it approached the house and then went past. The identical process repeated several times and then the car disappeared around a corner out of my view.

I heard or saw no movement for ten minutes until I noticed a movement of shadows out the corner of my eye near the back of the lot. Without making a sound, I rotated my head in the direction of the action and saw a silhouette crouched beside a bush. With very shallow nose breaths, I remained muted until the shadow began to edge forward. The faint sound of a window fan was the only discernable sound.

As the shadow moved from the darkness into the light, I was convinced Karen was on the job. With the graceful movements of a dancer, Karen slipped something between the door and jam and instantly slid inside Ms. Sanchez' house. Leaving the door slightly ajar, she eased herself deeper into the house.

As I began my dissent down through the branches, I caught sight of another pair of headlights turning onto the street. I remained stoic hoping the intruder would pass by quickly so I could gather the evidence I had come for. The car slowed in front of the house as if searching for an address, then continued down to the curve in the road, stopped, and turned the lights off.

Climbing back up to my original spot in the tree, I observed for a few more minutes, as the driver exited the car and stumbled in through the front door of the neighbor's house. Obviously, returning from a long night out at the bar, the man posed no apparent threat to the execution of my plans.

Cautiously descending the branches of the tree, I noticed through the nearest window, the flickering glow from a flashlight sweeping the bedroom walls. Motionless again, I studied the rehearsed motions of a master, removing a syringe from the black backpack, drawing the liquid into the syringe, and administering the apparently lethal dosage of some undetectable chemical.

Since the curtain that hung across the lower window camouflaged the bed, I was unable to watch the insertion of the needle into Rachael Sanchez. Some things you just do not need to witness to know they happened. Karen waited at the victim's bedside for a few minutes, then re-packed the backpack, slung it over her arms and retreated through the back door.

Remaining immobile, I surveyed Karen's flight from the crime scene, back into the shadows where she spent most of her adult life. After hearing the engine start, I concluded my descent; the massive trunk shielding my body until Karen's car motored past.

Scanning the map for Clarence Robb's street, I decided a short dash for a few blocks would be better than taking a chance on using the car. Recognizing Karen's station wagon hidden behind some overgrown oleanders near the end of Mr. Robb's street, I slipped past abandoned cars and insignificant rundown homes towards the victim's residence.

Mr. Robb's house was the typical ranch style single floor structure duplicated many times in the neighborhood. The trees were mature and the grass was spotty, absent of any moisture. The lot sizes in the neighborhood were generous with dilapidated swing

sets and abandoned cars parked everywhere. Man-made lighting
was poor.

Two shirts hung from clotheslines draped loosely between two T-
shaped wooden poles in the back yard. As a thick cloud uncovered
the glow from the moon, the shadow of a clothesline poles cast
symmetrically on the side of Mr. Robb's house in the shape of a
Christian cross. I briefly remembered the many Sundays staring
at the cross on the altar at the church where we were members; my
mind wandering as the pastor delivered the sermon. We attended
every Sunday while the children were growing up. I missed the
other members and wondered what had happened to them. In
addition, I wondered what had happened to me.

Crouching behind a stout shrub at a neighbor's house, my
unobstructed view of the back door and windows on the rear of the
house was ideal. Karen ignored the back door of the house, opting
for one of the three windows across the back of the house. Karen
inspected the three windows, choosing the one closest to me.

With a retractable knife, she made a small slit in the corner of the
screen, unlatched and removed it, then pulled herself up and through
the window without a sound. Olympic gymnasts could not have
performed any better. Neighborhood dogs broke the silence, their
barking far off in the distance.

Quietly tiptoeing across the yard to the house, I peered through
the corner of a window in an attempt to witness Karen's elimination
of one of San Antonio's potential organ donors. Obviously
choosing the wrong window, I located a dark room filled with boxes
stacked five feet high. I moved to another window and spotted
Karen dialing the nightstand telephone. I was unable to hear the
words she spoke into the receiver. Instead of placing the handset
back on the phone cradle, she placed it in the hand of the body that
lay motionless beside her. She then placed a bracelet on Mr. Robb's
right wrist.

Karen exited the house via the rear door as I eased back behind
the trunk of a tree in the side yard. She pulled a can of something
from her backpack, with the attached brush applied it to the screen,
and then placed the screen back into the window. Moments later,
Karen slipped into the shadows, then out of my sight.

As soon as I was confident Karen had left the scene, I retraced my steps walking instead of running back to the BMW. As I pulled the car door shut, I faintly heard a siren in the distance. Lowering my car window, the siren's break of early morning quiet got louder. I waited and watched as an ambulance approached with red lights flashing. The van speeded past and then turned on the street where Clarence Robb's house was located. It must have been 911 that Karen called from Mr. Robb's bedroom telephone. Since Clarence was the prospective donor for Mr. Billings, he would need to be at the hospital either when he died or soon afterwards. That had to have been the explanation for Karen's telephone call.

Somewhat disappointed, I drove back to Houston with much time to reassess my feelings toward Karen and my future business with her. I was confident that when I checked my news sources over the next few days that George Billings would get his new kidneys, he would drop off the organ recipient list, and I would read obituaries for Rachael Sanchez and Clarence Robb. I wondered who would care about them.

Would anyone in law enforcement be able to figure out what was going on? If I could draw the correct conclusion, I was sure they could as well. How long would it take before they would catch us? I again envisioned the shadow of the cross on the side of the victim's house and decided to call it quits.

twenty-one

A gain, the cell phone woke me from an intermittent sleep. It was Karen of course. She reported her success from the night before, a deposit in my Swiss account effective that day, and a request for information on the next client. She also tried to engage in small talk in which I had no interest.

After a shower, I poured myself a glass of juice and stared at the PDA lying on the kitchen table. I retrieved a screwdriver from the drawer and pried off the back cover. A piece of black electrical tape was stretched across the printed circuit board and another small circuit board was taped on top. Red and black wires protruded from the somewhere inside the electronic sandwich and into the device. It was definitely not the same configuration that came off the assembly line. If I had not trusted Karen before, based on the altered PDA that she had sent, I certainly could not trust her in the future.

Why would she want to keep such tabs on me? She could not have seen me as a threat, as she was much more sophisticated than I at the business we were now engaged in. She was the mentor and I the student. After the previous night, I knew that Karen was aware of my surveillance. Perhaps she was aware of how much I really knew about all of her victims.

Lounging around the apartment all day, I felt sorry for myself regarding the situation I was in. Sitting in front of the computer several times during the day, I could not get excited about doing anything. Managing to jot down some possible names for another client, I struggled with what to do with them. I knew that I had to quit. But how?

After deciding to go out for dinner and a few drinks that evening, I purposely left the PDA at the apartment knowing that I could always be able to claim forgetfulness as an excuse. Since I had money in the bank and there was a strong possibility I may lose it all someday soon, I decided on an expensive four-star restaurant a few miles from the apartment.

Without reservations, and no history with that restaurant, the matre'd asked me to take a seat at the bar until they could make a table available. I was not disappointed as I had the whole night to myself and had decided to enjoy it. I ordered my first Heineken as my cell phone rang.

"Hi Ben. How was your day?" It was Karen again.

"Fine how about you?"

"Did you get my e-mail?"

"Well, not really. Actually, I'm at a restaurant."

"Where is your PDA that I got for you? Don't you like it?"

"I must have forgotten it," at last, I was able to use my excuse.

"Shame on you. What restaurant are you at?"

"Vaughn's Steakhouse on Main Street. I'm still at the bar until they find a table for me."

"Nice place?"

"Very nice. I figured that I deserved it."

"You do. You've been working hard and doing a great job."

"I try," I replied, trying to keep up with her small talk in spite of the fact that I was losing interest quickly.

"Well, Ben, when you get back you can read my e-mail and get me some information. It can wait until tomorrow though. Have a good time tonight."

"I'm going to try."

"Talk to you tomorrow sometime." Karen hung up and I switched the phone off.

There were several executives seated at the bar, most of who were there for drinks and conversation alone. After fifteen more minutes, a well-dressed brunette took the stool next to mine.

"This seat taken?" she asked.

"No. It's yours."

"Thanks. Christine," she said, extending her hand towards me as if this were the appropriate protocol.

"Ben. Ben White," I reciprocated, not knowing if last names were appropriate.

"What do you do, Ben?" Christine nodded to the bartender for service.

If she only knew about the organ list manipulation, undoubtedly she would be shocked. Anyone would be shocked. Sequencing through possible answers to the question, I settled on the one that I could support the best, "I'm a recruiter. A head-hunter." I turned towards her with the answer and for the first time got a good look at her face.

A strikingly beautiful woman, Christine possessed distinct facial features perfectly accented with a minimum of makeup. Her eyes were deep green and they appeared to be expressly interested in what I had to say.

"That's an interesting profession. You work out of Houston?"

"Yes I do currently."

"Where is your office?"

"Actually, I've just started my company and I am working out of the apartment until I can bring up my client list, then I'll hire another associate and establish an office."

"Where is home?"

"Beaufort, South Carolina"

"I bet that's pretty."

"It is pretty," I admitted, remembering for a moment my favorite view across the tidal marsh at high tide.

The conversation became quiet for a few minutes while the bartender brought her drink and exchanged a few words with her. Christine was obviously a local, frequenting that restaurant and bar many times.

"I see that you don't wear a wedding ring. Are you married?" she turned towards me again. Christine wore several rings however none on the ring finger of the left hand. I could only assume she was not married either. Based on her suit, I had her pegged for a director or vice-president of a company.

"Divorced."

"I'm sorry."

"Don't be. It was my fault. I guess I became quite unreasonable."

"You?" she asked smiling.

"Hard to believe?"

"You seem so laid back," Christine admitted.

"More like laid off, if you want to know the truth. After 25 years with the same company, they laid me off. I couldn't find anything for eight months until I decided on this next adventure."

"You poor man," she laid her hand on my shoulder sensing my depressed attitude. Her touch invoked more of my interest.

"Yea right."

"Well, you must be here for dinner. Are you meeting someone?"

"Nope, just me."

"Then let's have dinner together. There is no use in both of us sitting by ourselves."

"I'd be honored," I said, anticipating the opportunity of sitting across the table from a beautiful woman.

On the way to the table, one of the waiters stopped to say a few words to Christine and I waited a few steps away. He gave her the thumbs up as she came to join me at the table. I did not understand the gesture but did not question it. Once seated at our table, I took the opportunity of finding out more information about my attractive dinner date.

"So, Christine, what about you? You married?"

"No, never married. But I would rather talk about you some more."

"Why is that?"

"I guess that I just feel more comfortable talking about someone else."

Christine ordered another cosmopolitan and I another Heineken. The menus lay in front of us still unopened. I sensed that she was enjoying the conversation although, other than both being single, we had very little else in common. The attention I received from Christine was easily the high point of my week. I desperately wanted to share my experiences about Karen and the business and all of the research that I had worked on in the past few months.

The conversation moved onto the personal computer, the Internet, and the methods of research on the computer. Starting to share some possibly damaging information, I gracefully diverted to areas that were less evidentiary. Christine shared some expertise in researching basic information on names, addresses, telephone numbers and place of employment. She followed with experiences that she had when telephoning employers about employees, which could be beneficial when working as a recruiter.

"I know that you said you don't want to talk about yourself, but based on your expertise, just exactly what do you do? I have you pegged for a vice president of a company in one of these high-rise buildings down here."

"Huh, that would be nice," she laughed, "but thanks for the compliment." A few uncomfortable moments elapsed.

"So . . . then . . . what do you do?" I repeated.

"Actually, I'm self employed," she answered quickly as if she stumbled onto the answer.

I waited for a more definitive answer, but none came. "Self employed, doing what exactly?"

"Oh, lots of things really."

"Like what?"

"I'm really in the service sector."

"What kind of service?"

"Entertainment, actually," she admitted reluctantly while sporting an embarrassing smile.

"You know, Christine, I am getting the sense that you really don't want me to know something because you are being awfully vague. I do not want to pry. I'm just interested."

"Ben. I am an escort," she blurted out. "I accompany men and sometimes women and sometimes both to dinner, or events, or just back to their hotel rooms."

"I'm sorry that I forced you to say that," I said after the surprise wore off.

"No, it's all right. I just didn't want you to think that I hustled you and conned you into becoming a client."

"I don't think that, although even if you had, it's not all that bad of an idea," my mind started to process the possibilities of such a situation and a vision of Christine without clothes excited me.

"Why don't we order and then we can talk about that after dinner. What else can we talk about now?"

"Let's talk about travel. Have you been on any interesting vacations?"

We continued to talk through dinner about vacations, travel, politics, education, and family. When the check arrived, I insisted on paying. Although, it was my idea to meet at my apartment, Christine was more than willing. She parked on the street in front and met me at the lobby door.

"Nice apartment. Looks like this business of yours is quite lucrative," Christine muttered as we entered my place.

"It's all right, I suppose."

"No, I'm really impressed. Most single men would live like slobs, but your place is spotless."

"Would you like a drink? A glass of wine?"

"Yea, a glass of wine would be great. Hey, what's this thing?" Christine picked up the PDA on the kitchen table.

"That's a PDA. A Personal Digital Assistant."

"Yea, what does it do?"

"You can pick up e-mails, access the Internet, that kind of stuff."

"What do you use it for?"

"E-mails mostly. I just got it a few days ago."

Christine wandered through the apartment looking at the furniture and out the window at the street below. "Great view!"

"Yes it is nice," I handed her the glass of wine and noticed a slight trembling in her hand that I had not seen earlier.

"Let's drink to happiness," she raised her glass and clinked it against my Heineken bottle.

"So how does this thing work between you and I?" I was becoming quite anxious.

"Well, Ben. Just exactly what do you want to do?"

"I want it all."

"How long would you like me to stay?" We moved to the couch and she put her hand on my leg and started stroking it.

"I'm sure that I would like you to stay a lot longer than I can afford. How about three hours?"

"I believe that I could accommodate. Why don't you get comfortable?"

"Do you mean I should get undressed?"

"If you'd like."

Christine left for the bathroom and I methodically removed my clothes folding them neatly on the chair. Hesitating slightly when I got to the briefs, I was unsure of the protocol with a hooker. I was well aware of the practice when you brought a woman home from the bar, both parties drunk, ripping their clothes from each other without regard for the garments or the feelings of the other partner.

Christine returned wearing a revealing low cut bra and thong, sat beside me on the couch and again started stroking my thigh. "Eight hundred."

"I beg your pardon?"

"My fee for the evening will be eight hundred."

"No problem. Do you want that now?"

"If you'd like. You might want to put it over there by my purse."

"Oh . . . okay. I need to visit the bathroom anyhow. Don't you go anywhere."

"I'll be right here waiting for you. Hurry up."

Retrieving the wallet from my pants pocket, I removed the eight bills, stacked them neatly on the table, and headed for the bathroom. It had been a long time since I had carried hundred dollar bills in my wallet.

The bathroom was located across a short hallway off the living room. Since I only departed to sprinkle on some cologne and use the mouthwash, I did not close the door all of the way. Noticing movement in the living room as I peered between the door and the casing, I witnessed Christine tiptoeing over to the table, placing the bills in her purse.

She then retrieved a small object from her purse, peeled a piece of paper from it and then stuck the object up under the table. For the first time that evening, I realized that she was in my apartment for a reason besides the delivery of sex. My brain tingled as it does when I am struck by a situation that I don't understand. I decided to let the evening play out before I questioned her about her actions.

Returning to the living room, Christine removed her underclothes and lay on the couch waiting for me. As I lay on the couch on top of her, I remembered the movies where the girl had hidden a gun under the cushion, ready for the perfect moment to grab it with deliberate surprise. I felt for lumps in the cushion but could not find any. Just to be safe, I suggested that we move to the bedroom where I closed the door behind me.

After an hour of rolling around together positioning ourselves in many different ways, searching out the otherwise forbidden zones of pleasure, we managed to mutually reach a peak that demanded a break in the action. As I lay on top of Christine, clearly in a position of strength, I contemplated whether to acknowledge what I had seen while peering through the bathroom door an hour earlier.

I surprised myself as to how subjective I could be at a time of exhaustive passion. Maybe I was reaching my age of wisdom. It seemed obvious to me that Christine had placed a listening device under the table where I could not see it and where someone could eavesdrop on all of my conversations. It also seemed obvious, that Christine was working for someone else because her obvious profession was in the adult entertainment field. I weighed my alternatives.

If I did not tell her, then whomever she was working for would think that they were successful in placing the bug and if I knew it, I could use that to my benefit. However, I would not be free to talk freely in my own apartment. If I did acknowledge that I saw her placing the bug, then whoever hired her would know that I was on to them.

I just could not figure out who was behind the added surveillance. It was possible that Karen could have hired this girl so that Karen would know what I might have otherwise been keeping from her. It was also possible that the FBI hired Christine so that they could build a case against me. Thirdly, the FBI could still be following Karen and using my connection with her to find out where she was.

"I need to go use the bathroom," Christine whispered into my ear.

"Just a minute." I stretched my arms out to meet her hands and then we interlocked fingers.

"What do you mean just a minute?" her voice started to tremble as she tugged against my grip.

"Who are you working for?" I made the decision to attempt to find out my enemies.

"What do you mean? I told you, I am an independent escort. I work for myself."

"Christine. I saw you place a bug under that table in the living room."

"Let me up," she demanded immediately, struggling under my weight and restraining grasp.

"Not until you tell me who you are working for."

"I don't know what you are talking about."

"Look, I paid for another two hours. We can wait right here until you get your memory back."

She slowly closed her eyes knowing that she would not be able to escape the situation. "I knew I shouldn't have taken this job."

"Look, I won't get you in trouble. Tell me who hired you and you can be on your way. You can always tell them that you placed the bug successfully and I found it later and dismantled it."

"Either way, I'm history," she admitted.

"Just exactly who are these guys?"

"I don't know."

"What do you mean, you don't know?"

"These two men in suits approached me about a week ago and flashed a badge in front of me. I thought they were going to bust me. They ask me to follow you, get invited back to your apartment, and stick this device under a coffee table somewhere near the middle of the living room. I guess that I assumed that they would protect me from arrest on prostitution charges if I agreed. I couldn't say no."

"Were these local cops?"

"I doubt it. Local cops don't dress that nice. And local cops don't look like Marines like these guys did."

"Are you supposed to meet them after you leave here?"

"I'm sure that they will find me."

"I'll leave the device there for a few days and then short out the battery. Tell them that you accomplished your mission. Don't tell them that I know about it."

"Can I get up now?"

I rolled off and Christine walked to the bathroom, her head hung in the shame of capture.

"You want your money back?" Christine returned after dressing.

"No, that's all right. I guess you have earned it. Now we have a deal, right?"

"I'll tell them that I got it planted correctly," she answered.

"Great! Other than that, I had a great time."

We walked back out to the living room and I gestured to Christine about the listening device.

"I had a great time. Thanks," I repeated for the benefit of my listening friends.

After Christine exited, I returned to the end table to get a better view of the bug that she had placed there. I lay on my back and used my feet to push myself under the table. There was a black lipstick sized cylinder with small holes in the end pointing down towards the floor. I studied the device for a few seconds admiring the small size and the technology that would allow a microphone, transmitter, and battery in such a tiny package.

As I prepared to scoot out from under the table, I noticed another previously unseen object inside the fold of the lampshade of the table lamp located near the center of the table. As I got closer to the object, it appeared to be another listening device, this one somewhat smaller than the device under the table and dark gray as opposed to black, obviously a different brand.

This discovery further confused the situation. Had Christine placed two bugs in the apartment while I was in the bathroom or did someone else place this bug? Who else had access to the apartment? The only other persons who had been inside the apartment were the FBI agents when accompanied by the apartment manager, and Karen, when she visited me after moving in.

Could this be Karen's doing? As I continued to look at the device, it made sense that Karen would use a device that was smaller and looked more professional. In addition, it made sense that I did not witness her placing the device in the apartment as I had with Christine. In addition, this meant that Karen did not hire Christine. It was not really Karen's style. Anyway, Karen could probably get into the apartment unnoticed anytime she wanted to, even if I were there.

Sliding the security chain across the door, I moved to my laptop and checked for e-mails. Knowing Karen would expect some information on the next client by the next day, I started to bring up the organ recipient web site. I questioned how much longer I could handle the enormous weight the situation placed on my value system. I struggled with the conflict of doing what was right versus doing what would keep me alive.

twenty-two

Although I left the previous day with many uncertainties and significant anxiety, a good night's sleep somehow shed a different perspective on my future. Knowing I was so involved in the crimes that were taking place around me, law enforcement would find out soon what was going on, they would find me, and I would spend the rest of my life in jail. Moreover, the fact that I lived in Texas, the capital punishment state, I would inevitably be put to death for these crimes.

That morning, it was clear to me that I needed to admit my guilt, identify the others involved, and demand immunity from prosecution. I assumed that if the authorities heard my story, they would realize the others were doing the "dirty work" without my knowledge and they would be much easier to convict based on my testimony. My only dilemma was to determine whom in law enforcement I could trust.

If I got a commitment from the FBI for immunity, once they heard my story, they could arrest the guilty, gather the evidence, and then put me on trial with Karen. The FBI was so big, I was uncertain if they could swing such a deal. I needed to find someone else who had an interest in the case and would be willing to compromise in order to get to the truth and punish the guilty party.

Sitting again in front of my laptop, I debated whether I should turn it on or just run away. Even if I ran, eventually, they would catch me. Though I had some money in the bank, it too would run out some day. No, I knew I had more work to do. I opened the drawer to my desk and retrieved the file I developed on the organ recipient list.

I glanced down the list of names with the word client or deceased written next to them. When I got down to the name Jackie Armstrong, my thoughts quickly switched to her brother, Detective Neil Carter from the Omaha Police Department. Immediately I conceded that the most advantageous course of action was to confide in Detective Carter and convince him to guarantee immunity for my testimony and conviction of the real murderer. Based on my research on Carter, he had the moxie to make this happen.

I searched the Internet for the telephone number for the Omaha Police Department, wrote it down on the back of an FBI business card, and stuffed it in my wallet. Since I was already aware of the bugging of my apartment, I decided to leave and make the call on the cell phone. With significantly more paranoia than the previous day, I drove down to the grocery store that I frequented at least once a week. If it was that easy to place a bug in my apartment, I had to assume that there might also be one in my car, so I left the car to place the call to Detective Carter.

Being early in the day, the store was almost empty except for the few workers stocking shelves. I retrieved a cart, put a few items in it and then placed my call while in the produce department.

"Omaha Police Department. How may I direct your call?"

"Detective Carter, please."

"I'll ring his desk."

"Carter."

"Detective Neil Carter?" I asked.

"Speaking."

"Detective Carter, I have some information for you in regards to the Jackie Armstrong case. Are you interested?"

"What makes you think that we are still investigating that case?"

"Let's just say that I have a hunch," I said.

"Whom am I speaking with?"

"First things first, Detective. Are you interested in hearing the information?"

"What kind of information?"

"Information on how the accident occurred and who is responsible."

There was a several second pause on the telephone.

"Are you still there, Detective?"

"Yes, and yes I am interested. Please tell me."

"I would like to meet with you and tell you in person."

"Great, how about right now?"

"I can't meet with you right now."

"Why not?" the Detective asked abruptly.

"How about tonight?" I asked.

"You're not here in Omaha, are you?"

"No."

"Where do you want to meet?" he asked.

"There is a coffee shop on Fletcher Road about a block away from the accident scene. I'll meet you there at 7:00 pm tonight."

"I know the place. What do you look like so I'll know it is you?"

"I know what you look like, I'll find you. And come by yourself."

"This had better be worth it, you are on my time at 7:00pm at night."

After pushing the end button on the cell phone, I drove back to the apartment, and then immediately booked a flight from Houston to Omaha. I selected a flight that arrived in Omaha at 5:10pm and the return flight returned to Houston at 11:00pm. Reserving a rental car at the airport, I quickly printed out some maps of Omaha so I could get to the coffee shop quickly. Since I knew that the living room was still bugged, I had to make the phone calls in the bathroom with the water running, out of hearing range for the listening devices.

In addition to the maps, I printed information that would convince Detective Carter that there were crimes committed and my limited involvement in them might warrant immunity. I also researched the concept of immunity from prosecution on the Internet and cited some real life examples as ammunition for the Detective. I placed all of the documentation in the leather briefcase given to me as a gift for twenty years of service for my previous company.

Opening the briefcase reminded me of the many business trips that I carried the briefcase to the airports, through the security x-ray machines, and under the seat in front of me on the planes. I reminisced on how I measured success during those years. I certainly never got in as much trouble as I did in the last several months working with Karen.

Confident that the PDA was my tracking device for Karen, I left it on the kitchen table, grabbed my laptop, and escaped in my car to a mall located about a mile from the airport. I called a taxi to pick me up in the mall parking lot and take me to the airport.

There was a cold rain falling in Omaha, painfully reminding me of the comfortable warm fall evenings back in South Carolina. With a 45-minute delay in the flight to Omaha, I was finally picking up my rental car at 6:15pm, with plenty of time to get across town to the coffee shop. As I cruised through the center of town, I recognized the Omaha Police Department building as illustrated on the web site that I had visited several times over the previous few months.

I turned onto Fletcher Road and started to look for the address of the coffee shop. About a mile after turning onto the road, I found myself driving down a steep hill. It finally occurred to me that I was coming up on the scene of the accident that killed Jackie Armstrong and her two sons. At the bottom of the hill, to the right, maybe ten feet off of the road, a large oak tree with the bark removed and black burn marks about ten feet up the trunk remained as a memorial for past accidents. It must have been horrible for this woman, trapped in a burning SUV, watching her sons die.

I slowed at the bottom of the hill, continued up another small rise and then past the coffee shop where I was to meet Detective Carter. It was 6:45pm and I could not spot the Detective through the windows. After all I had done to convince myself it was the right decision to trust this cop and all of the traveling that I had done that evening, I only hoped that he would not blow it off and not show up.

Turning around in a parking lot, I waited a few minutes, and then headed back towards the restaurant. As I passed the coffee shop parking lot, I spotted Detective Carter getting out of his dark blue Ford and moving towards the door to the coffee shop, looking left and right for anything out of the ordinary. Slowly passing by, I continued down to the next road, turned around and headed back a third time.

Confident that Detective Carter was unaccompanied, I pulled into the parking lot. Slinging the briefcase under my arm, I bolstered my confidence as I approached the man who I hoped would possess the power and compassion to save my life.

The rain diminished somewhat and the day swiftly slipped into evening. Dodging the puddles in the gravel parking lot, a chill traveled up my back and I shuddered as I reached for the door to the restaurant. I was extremely nervous.

Detective Carter, seated alone at a booth at the front of the restaurant, stared outside for my arrival. A teenage couple in another booth across the room and an older retirement-aged man seated at the counter were the only other customers.

"Carter?" I asked when I knew he was looking at me.

"That's me."

"May I sit down?"

"Of course."

"Are you going to give me your name now?"

"Not quite yet."

"All right. What have you got?" he agreed sighing.

"Let me start with some facts. Stop me if you do not agree with what I am saying. Jackie Armstrong was married with two children. All three died in a fiery crash not far from this coffee shop. She drove the same route down the Fletcher Road hill everyday because she took both of her boys to school each day and then picked them up in the late afternoon.

The Ford Bronco that she owned had many miles on it but had an excellent service record and had the brakes checked recently. The collision and subsequent fire, beyond the possibility for solid investigative procedures, damaged the remains of the wrecked vehicle.

And, Jackie Armstrong just happened to be your sister," I concluded as a waiter approached the table to take my order.

"Well, you have summed this case up quite well," Carter said "but you haven't told me anything that I don't already know, and that almost anyone could find out with a little reading and investigating. I sure hope that you have something more than this, or you have just wasted my evening."

I continued, "Jackie was suffering from kidney problems which originated from a previous car accident. Her damaged kidneys were deteriorating and her name first appeared on the list for double kidney transplant eight months before her death. She was number two on the recipient list at the time of her death. A Samuel Johnson from Dallas was number one on the kidney recipient list and he passed away on the same day as Jackie.

Mike Ellerton is a disk jockey in Tulsa, Oklahoma. He was number three on the kidney recipient list at the time of Jackie's death. With the death of Samuel Johnson and your younger sister, Mr. Ellerton became number one on the list and received the donated kidneys from another accident victim in Tulsa. I hope that this is a little more than a waste of your evening," I finished smugly.

"Where did you get all of this information about organ recipients?"

"Now we need to start talking about immunity," I insisted.

"Immunity?" the detective was surprised.

"Yes, immunity. Because I have some information and I am indirectly involved, I need to have some guarantee. As I'm sure that you can probably imagine, your sister's death is just the tip of the iceberg."

"Well, I . . . don't know. Immunity is difficult to justify," Detective Carter explained.

"That is exactly why I copied off these recent immunity cases here for you to look at." I pulled a small stack of papers from my briefcase.

Detective Carter spent a few minutes scanning the documents. "I don't know if these are relevant to this type of case."

"Fine, I'll find someone else," I yanked the papers from his hand, grabbed my briefcase, and stood up.

"Now, wait a minute. Sit down. Tell me a little more about your involvement. I can't guarantee immunity unless I know that the information you have will lead to a conviction and I need to know that you haven't committed a serious crime."

"I can give you the murderer of your sister and at least nine other victims. I knew nothing of the murders until a week ago. I only provided information to clients, but I have been paid for more than just the information."

"What evidence do you have?"

"I am an eyewitness to the murders and I have my bank statements."

"An eyewitness to the murders?" Carter was again surprised at what I had said.

"Well some of them. And although I was there, I didn't actually see the murder, but I was close."

"Don't you see, without hard evidence, we can't get a conviction. So, why did you come to me? Are you looking for revenge against the murderer, or are you looking for the best way out of a bad situation?"

"The latter."

"Sounds like with or without immunity, you can't win. But, at least with immunity, you might live a little longer," Detective Carter admitted.

"So is there anything that you can do for me?"

"Maybe. Stick around until tomorrow and I will get back to you. Have you got a cell phone number I can reach you at?"

"No, I'll call you in your office tomorrow at noon." I stood, shoved the papers back in my briefcase and headed for the door.

"You gonna stay in Omaha?"

"Yes."

"Do you feel as if you are in any danger?"

"Some."

"Just watch your backside until tomorrow."

I did just that. Passing a small hotel on my trip from the airport, I decided to check in for the night. I zigzagged back and forth on side streets to make sure no one followed me.

Paying by cash at the hotel, I registered under a fictitious name. I called the airline to reschedule my return trip as will advise. When settled, I checked my cell phone voice mail and discovered four messages left by Karen. She also left two e-mail messages. The last e-mail message was logged at 8:00pm and read as follows:

Dear Ben,

Where are you? I haven't lost you have I? I have been calling all day and you have not responded. I checked with your cell phone company and they said that you have your cell phone turned off. I

thought that you might have your PDA with you, but when I came to
see you at your apartment, I saw it lying on the kitchen table.

What is wrong? Are you all right? Please call me immediately
when you get this message.

Love,

Karen

All of the voice mails and e-mails worked up to this frantic e-mail sent by Karen. I found it interesting that she considered my well being important enough to come visit me at my apartment. I wondered if she made the trip in person or if she sent another one of her workers. I also questioned if the next time I saw her I would be looking at her from the witness chair, spilling my guts on how I got involved in these violent crimes.

As I rehearsed my testimony in my head, I was always sure to tell the jury that the same company loyally employed me for 25 years and then, in the twilight of my career, laid me off, sending me out to the wolves where it was difficult to survive. The ability to apply research and supply information for money is something that I developed on my own, as a direct response to not finding any other work.

I also questioned if I would ever be able to go back to the apartment in Houston. With so many uncertainties, it was difficult for me to function. I focused on my immediate actions, running them back and forth in my mind before committing to them. Surely, Detective Carter had run across other victims like me, good moral character, unintentionally caught up in some serious crimes.

Speculating that Carter was involved in this case on a personal level, he would want revenge against the person or persons responsible for his sister's death. I felt confident that he, more than anyone else, would be able to help me out so that he could get his conviction and I would get my freedom.

Checking out of the hotel at 10:00am the next day, I stopped at a restaurant for breakfast. At noon, I called Detective Carter at the Omaha Police Department.

"Carter," he barked out in the same tone as the day before.

"It's B . . . me," I said, remembering that I still had not given him my name.

"I'm glad you called. I have talked to some people and I think that we can make a deal."

"Great."

"Why don't you come down here to the station and I'll lay out for you what we've got."

"Hmm. I do not know that we are quite ready for that. Let's meet somewhere else. I will meet you in the Public Library downtown at 1:00pm."

"All right, but sooner or later you are going to have to meet with someone besides me."

"I trust you. At least for the time being."

"All right, I'll see you at 1:00."

At 1:05pm I spotted Detective Carter's car pass by and turn in the parking lot. After he entered the front door by himself, I followed behind him and caught up with him by the reference desk.

"Let's go in one of the rooms in the back," I pointed past the rows of tables and shelves of periodicals.

We closed the door behind us and sat across from each other at the only table in the small windowed room. Carter pulled out a handheld tape recorder and switched it on. "I have to do it this way," a serious look crept across his face.

"Fine, I guess. What have you got?"

"Here is the agreement. For your help in getting a first-degree murder conviction in the case involving the death of Jackie Armstrong, the Omaha Police Department will extend immunity from prosecution for the same charge. In addition, we will hold you immune from other related charges, such as any lesser murder charges."

"What about the collection and sales of information?"

"If there is a law that you have broken in regards to that, I can't help you there. Perhaps a good attorney could help with that. I need to caution you though, if you don't cooperate fully with the investigation and subsequent conviction, OPD can go after you and seek conviction on any of the charges I have previously told you about."

"All right, I guess this is my best shot. Let's talk." I signed both copies of the single sheet official-looking document, on Omaha Police Department letterhead and then stuffed one copy into my briefcase.

Starting in the beginning, which for me began back in Beaufort at the Sand Dollar, I revealed all of the exchanges with Karen, those in person, telephone calls and e-mails. As I was not clear, Detective Carter would ask the questions that would make it clear. As I explained to him about the idea of selling this type of information, I had to go back to Venezuela, at the bar on the roof of the hotel.

When I explained about Warren Smithson, Carter jerked his head up to look at me as if I had struck a nerve. I remembered the notation that he made about Smithson on the case notes for the Jackie Armstrong case that I found on OPD's database, but I did not tell him about it.

I shared the list of our clients and the list of the recipients that accidentally passed away 1 to 48 hours after we visited our clients with the information that they desired. I also presented the list of donors that I had selected for Karen each time she visited our client. I crossed off all of them that had passed away and donated organs to our clients.

Carter dismissed most of the evidence as circumstantial. "I need something more solid to get a conviction", he would say repeatedly. "I can place Karen at the sight of 4 murders at or about the time of death, isn't that good enough," I would say. "I need more", he repeated.

"I know that you expect Karen, or her associates are watching you. Do you know who else is watching you?" Detective Carter asked.

I explained what Karen had told me about the people that were following her. Then I told him the story about the alleged FBI agents that visited me in Beaufort. The visit made by the two men with FBI credentials at my apartment when I was not there led me to believe that it was in fact the FBI looking for Karen and not me.

"How did you get access to the data bases if they were password protected?"

I began to explain the login ID and password from Dr. Carl Lyons that the nurse in Beaufort put right in front of my eyes. I purposely did not reveal the hacking software that Karen had provided me, just in case I would need to use it again.

I also described the incident of losing access to the login ID and password for a few hours and then getting it back again. I further explained that based on this, I checked on Dr. Lyons only to find out that he had passed away. I am sure that his passing would have triggered the removal of his login ID and password, but it had not.

The interrogation lasted a total of three hours, with Detective Carter replacing the tape four times to get all of the information.

"Sounds like we have got a case here, but I need that evidence that will allow us to find Karen and to put her away for a long time. I need you to set up one more client. Do your investigation on a potential client and subsequent victims. We will put someone in place as the victim and catch Karen in the act. It will be all of the evidence that we need to convict."

"You're kidding, right?" I asked.

"No, I'm dead serious."

"I may have already jeopardized my chances. I haven't responded to Karen and she knows that I am not at the apartment."

"Call her. Tell her you went on a small vacation. Use the listening devices in the apartment to let everyone know that things are back to normal. Just make sure that you handle your arrangements for the next client outside of the apartment. We don't know who else is listening in."

"Now I'm getting scared. I'm not sure I can do this."

"You have to do this, or you don't receive immunity."

"What?"

"You signed the agreement. It said that you will do anything that is required to get the conviction."

"My God, what have I got myself into?" My head dropped into my hands, I shut my eyes hoping to wake up, and this would all be a dream.

"Now get back home and start your research. Give Karen a call on the way and let her know that you are heading back to get to work. In addition, give me a call tomorrow morning after you have something setup. Keep it here in the Midwest if you can. Make it believable. Call me if you think anything has gone awry. I'll have the Houston Police there in an instant."

I could not remember if I had told Carter that I was living in Houston. It was not that I was trying to keep it from him, but I just could not remember divulging that information.

Carter left with his signed agreement and my life hanging in the balance. Now, whichever way I moved, I could get hurt. I sat in the library trying to assess my next move. I headed for the airport.

twenty-three

The taxi from the Houston Intercontinental Airport delivered me to the BMW parked alone in the mall parking lot. I scoped out the lot for other occupied vehicles before getting in, including a quick look under the car. The light from the parking lot lamps reflected off the still wet puddled asphalt. I certainly would not recognize a car bomb if I saw one, and it troubled me to consider that I was actually looking for one.

Charlie had already left his post in the apartment lobby leaving the lights turned down and the door locked. I waited to call Karen until I was comfortably safe in my apartment, where I thought I could control things better.

"Where have you been?" Karen barked out excitedly when I dialed the cell phone number that she left on my e-mail.

"Sorry, I took a mini-vacation for a couple days."

"Why didn't you tell me? I thought that something might have happened to you."

Of course, she was lying and her only concern was that I might go to the police, which actually is what I did. I kept cool though, believing she was not able to track me to Omaha.

"I was just feeling a little penned in. Now I am back to work. I should have some more information for you by noon tomorrow, if you would like to call me back."

"You sure everything is all right?"

"Yea, sure. I'm rested and ready to work again," I said.

"Anything else bothering you?" she asked, trying to pry some sort of confession out of me.

"No, I'm fine. Let's get to work."

"Okay, I'll call you tomorrow, but if there is a problem, call and let me know," she hung up without waiting for another response from me.

I quickly recalled my responses on the phone to ensure I did not say too much in the presence of the listening devices that were still active in the living room.

I punched away at the computer keyboard for a couple hours. Still no problem using Dr. Lyons ID and password. Switching to the liver recipient list to search for another potential client, I hoped that it would be my last. The situation turned out to be ideal.

Number one on the list, a man from St. Louis who previously received a donated liver, after two years, began to reject it. His health was failing as he finally reached the top of the list. The extensive cost for surgery from the first transplant and significant doctor's fees afterward depleted all of his savings and because he could not work, he could not replace it. With no other source of income, he became a prime prospect for elimination to make way for the number two on the list.

Number two on the list, our new client was a recently appointed trial judge from Chicago in his middle forties. His years as attorney allowed for significant alcohol abuse causing irreparable damage to his liver. With money stashed away, he fit the profile of those that would pay to live a few years longer. Finally meeting his life long goal of judgeship and without the liver transplant, his body would not allow him to enjoy it.

I became somewhat concerned with the fact that our client was a judge. However, after doing a little more research, I discovered some pretty shady dealings in his past. Convinced he would pay for my information, I was not quite as sure that he would pay to eliminate the number one candidate on the liver recipient list.

Copying addresses, telephone numbers and the financials that Karen would be interested in; I also included relevant financial information on the remainder of the families. I now had three calls to make, the normal one to Karen, the second to Detective Carter and then the call to the client.

Most of the telephone calls from Karen were extremely structured and controlled, but that morning was different. She seemed hurried and it sounded, at one point, like she dropped the cell phone onto the floor. It took her several seconds to retrieve it and during the interval, I could faintly hear what sounded like an announcement over a loud speaker. "Next stop, federal center, 3rd & D" is what the words sounded like.

Before I could take the time to acknowledge, Karen was back on talking a mile a minute not leaving any opportunity to ask where she was and what had happened. I jotted the words "federal center, 3rd & D" on the notepad in front of me to remind myself to check it out later. We ended our call and agreed that she would call back after I had a chance to speak with our new client.

Carter anxiously awaited my call and agreed that the situation that presented itself seemed ideal. He assured me that they would not only witness Karen in the act of attempted murder, but also would save the victims from certain death.

As I hung up the phone with Detective Carter, it occurred to me that control shifted over to me for once. If I performed as planned, the police would witness Karen in the act of attempted murder. On the other hand, if I injected too much uncertainty, Karen would walk away from the transaction. I felt confident that she trusted me, but trusted her own instincts more.

The telephone call with our new Chicago client delayed while I waited for the judge to return home from his doctor's appointment. His father, also an attorney, took the call reluctant to let me speak to his son. With some coaxing, I convinced him.

The bad news from his doctor's visit was somewhat troubling for the judge but was a benefit for my sales pitch. We agreed on a price of $4,000 for information of his position on the list for a liver transplant, however he was unable to meet with Karen that evening because of a commitment. Karen did not like it when the clients had too much time to think about spending their money on information only. They might become too self-righteous and decide to blow the whistle on our arrangement. Unfortunately, pressured into this transaction, I accepted the appointment for the following evening.

Leaning back in my black leather chair, I hoped that I adequately covered all of my bases. Glancing down at the paper where I had written "federal center, 3rd & D", I tried to make sense of those words, apparently an announcement over a loud speaker. Although I did not have much experience riding a train, it sounded as if the announcement came from a train or subway, which would have put Karen inside.

Maybe the car became crowded and that was why Karen dropped the cell phone. New York, Chicago, Toronto, and maybe Boston were the only places I remembered that had subways. Unsure if Los Angeles had one, I ruled it out. Researching the subways in New York, Chicago, and Boston, I could not find a connection to any stop designated as "federal center, 3rd & D".

If it is federal, I reasoned, maybe we are talking about Washington DC. I checked the website for the Metro Line in Washington DC. Sure enough, on the Blue Line and the Orange Line, there was a stop designated as the "Federal Center" and it was located near the mall in Washington DC close to the intersection of 3rd and D Streets.

What was Karen doing in Washington DC? I could not remember any of our clients from there. Then I remembered what she had said about her past. She spent quite some time in the Washington DC area. Maybe she was visiting.

I pulled up a map of the area to see what might be around that area of the capitol. The Capitol Building was a few blocks away, as was the National Air & Space Museum. There was a NASA Building close, as was the Department of Education. Within one block from the Metro stop was a three building complex for the Department of Health & Human Services. I had visited that web site almost every day for the past several months and verified the address on the web site.

How could there be a connection between Karen and the Department of Health & Human Services? It did not make sense. There must have been another reason that she was on that subway. Maybe she was not getting off at that stop. There could have been a number of reasons. Moreover, I am sure that she lied a lot. After what I had seen her do, why should I believe anything she told me about her past?

The apartment telephone rang and my emotion immediately switched to paranoia.

"Yes."

"Mr. White?"

"Yes"

"This is Charles, down in the lobby."

"Good afternoon Charles."

"Mr. White, I just wanted to let you know that there has been a black van parked across the street all morning. Two men dressed in dark suits are inside. They have been looking in this direction for the past couple of hours."

"Thanks Charles, but I'm sure that it's nothing."

"Maybe not, but they are getting out of the van right now and they are walking this way. Mr. White, there is a freight elevator down the hall from your apartment. It comes out on the first floor right next to the back door. I'll try to hold these guys off as long as I can, but I will have to bring them up sooner or later," Charles explained as if he had been through this before.

"Thank you," I said hurriedly as I grabbed my cell phone, laptop, and ran down the hall to the passenger elevator.

Pressing the button to summon the elevator to the 15th floor, I waited for what seemed like ten minutes and then witnessed the elevator returning to the first floor. I quickly darted from the passenger elevator to the freight elevator and pushed the down button. The freight elevator located on the first floor seemed to take forever to reach the fifteenth.

I searched for an escape route if the cops reached the hallway before the elevator got there, but there wasn't one. The elevator started to move, past five, then ten, then fourteen. From down the hall, I heard the bell ring as the door opened on the passenger elevator. Finally, the freight elevator bell rang and the door opened. I jumped in and immediately pushed the button to close the door just as I saw the suits pass the corner of the hallway.

Not wasting any time, I stepped out of the freight elevator, through the back door and out into the back parking lot. At the side street, I turned away from the front of the building and never looked back. Quickly reaching Main Street, I took the bus to a cheap hotel a few miles away. I carefully assessed each individual as they entered the bus. Confident no one followed me, I relaxed slightly.

Once settled at the hotel, my first call was to Charles in the apartment building lobby.

"Charles, this is Ben White. I want to thank you for the help that you have given me. Are they gone yet?"

"Yes, Mr. White, they just left. When they found that you weren't in the apartment, they provided a search warrant and told me to either unlock the door or they would break it down."

"What did you do?"

"Well, I unlocked it of course. About that time, the apartment manager showed up, reviewed the search warrant and escorted them through the apartment. They carried about two file boxes of papers and your computer out of the apartment and then left me a business card to call if you returned."

"I'm sorry that I have caused so many problems for you Charles."

"Not a problem Mr. White. It has made it quite interesting around here over the last month or so."

"Did the search warrant identify why they wanted me or my possessions?"

"In the block identified by CRIME the warrant read FRAUD, MURDER, CONSPIRACY TO COMMIT MURDER."

"Who were these guys?"

"The business card says FBI."

"I don't know how to thank you again Charles. I appreciate your dedication in trying to protect me."

"Will you be back sir?"

"It's hard to say right now. I need to get some things straightened out before I dare come back."

Late in the afternoon, Karen called back on my cell phone for an update on our new client. Explaining how the call went, I tried to reassure her that although we had to handle an additional day, it appeared as if the transaction would come off without a hitch.

"Where are you?" I asked innocently.

"Oh, out and about. Just jetting all over the country. Taking care of this and that. You know I am not going to tell you anyhow. Unseen, unsuspected, inconspicuous is the secret for my success. Except for you Ben. You know where I am sometimes. But as I told you before, I trust you."

Panic overcame me as I considered the content of her answer and the memory of the misunderstood trust thing I naively agreed to earlier. I debated on whether to share with her the alleged FBI visit that I recently experienced. Questioning whether I should share the same information with Detective Carter, I finally decided that as long as I was still alive and not looking down the barrel of a gun, I would keep the information to myself.

Unable to revisit the apartment without apprehension, I contemplated decisions on exactly where I should be staying. I could stay in Houston and remain lost for a while, I could travel back to Omaha where I would be accessible for Detective Carter, or I could travel up to St. Louis and witness the capture of my partner in crime.

None of the options I identified was too appealing to me. I honestly would rather return to my old job, struggling daily to make the company successful. How I once regretted the monotonous repetitive nature of the manufacturing business world. It now seemed more appealing to me.

Placing a call to the Banque Privat, I transferred all but one hundred dollars from my savings account that Karen knew about into my private account. I also instructed them to prepare a wire transfer of $5,000 to the bank in Houston where I previously made the special arrangement. Calling a car rental agency, I had them drop off a car to the hotel where I was staying. It was normal for the rental agency to transact in this way however they had never made the drop at such a sleazy hotel.

As soon as the car arrived, I left the hotel with the door key on the dresser and drove to the bank where the wire transfer was ready for me to sign. Stopping at the nearby mall, I bought a couple pair of casual pants, two shirts, and some underwear. All of the clothing I bought was black. I was sure that my mother would think I was some kind of hood, which is what she would have called someone who was always in trouble with the law.

I thought about giving my mother a call, but decided to wait until some of my problems went away, if that would actually ever happen. She worried about me when my calls were too infrequent.

Reluctantly, I stopped at a restaurant for lunch before starting the long drive to St. Louis. Houston was a big city, so I was not as worried about my safety, especially while traveling in a rental car. St. Louis was also quite large and because I traveled there many times while working for the company, I knew how to get around.

The waitress delivered the sandwich that I ordered and then seemingly out of nowhere, a man dressed in jeans and a faded t-shirt took the seat on the other side of my table. My heart again began to race. I certainly did not know this man and I'm sure the expression on my face telegraphed my fear and confusion. I scooted my body across the seat preparing for an escape when a second man moved in and nudged me back as he took the space next to me.

"Mr. White," the man with the full head of slightly greased hair spoke as if he knew me well.

"Who are you?" I asked.

"Hopefully a future business partner."

"What do you want?" I tried to keep it short.

"We've been watching you, physically and on the Internet. We know what you are doing. We don't know how you are doing it, but we will find out."

"I don't know what you are talking about," I said.

"Is that the way we are going to play this, Ben? Please don't insult my intelligence."

"What do you want?"

"I want to establish a business relationship with you. You seem to have access to a list of clients who are waiting for organ transplants. Some of these clients are quite lucrative and are anxious. I already have a business where I supply young healthy organs to those individuals who can afford them. I need you Ben to supply a customer list. We will make the sales call and deliver the goods and you will get twenty-five percent of the take just for supplying the client information. Your hands will be squeaky clean. What do you think?"

"What makes you think I won't go to the cops?" I asked.

"Come on Ben. I think that you are well passed that. You wouldn't risk your own life just to put me away, would you?" the man asked.

Two uniformed city cops strolled into the restaurant, exchanged pleasantries with the cashier and the waitress and then took the booth right next to mine. I exchanged a defiant stare with the man sitting across from me. He raised his eyebrows, tilted his head, and without speaking, transmitted a message to my brain, "go ahead punk, make my day". I felt the pressure of a cylindrical shaft against my side and was afraid to look down to see the object. I took my breaths in short spurts.

"I'll have to get back to you," I finally said, hoping that they would not want to continue with the conversation.

"We'll see you again soon, Mr. White, and we can chat some more."

As the two men left the restaurant, I tried to time my restaurant departure with that of the two officers. I thought that I had been discreet with my actions, but while I was researching other people, someone was researching me. I desperately needed to get lost somewhere.

As I reached the cashier to pay the check, I noticed the news program shown on the TV on the wall across from the cashier's chair. With the TV volume turned down, the caption below the interviewee read "Warren Smithson". I recognized him as the same man I had seen in the hotel in Venezuela, and the one on the Health and Human Services web site that I visited every day. He stood in front of a podium with many microphones stuck in front of his face.

And then, the absolute worst thing that had ever happened to me in my 48 years, all of the sudden was broadcast to millions of people all over the United States. My picture. I could not believe it. I wanted to cover up the TV screen so no one could see. It was a picture of me taken a week or so earlier when I was in the apartment lobby talking with Charles. There was no use in speculating when I might get caught. I was caught. But why didn't they show Karen's picture? My mother would see that picture and I was not only scared but also extremely angry. Angry with Karen, but more than that, angry with myself for letting this arrangement go as far as it did.

I scurried out of the restaurant without waiting for the change. For a few minutes, I forgot about the two men that confronted me at the restaurant. Stopping at a drug store a block away, I bought dark brown hair coloring to change the gray color that was an obvious feature in the photograph, and I purchased a shaver to remove the small beard and mustache.

Driving to a nearby gas station, I performed the makeover in the men's restroom. Following the most direct route to the highway, I sped out of town. Glancing periodically at myself in the mirror, I questioned who was the man that looked back at me. Changed physically, I regretfully acknowledged my changed character.

Following I-45 to Dallas, I turned onto I-35 until reaching Oklahoma City. Quitting for the day at a small hotel between Oklahoma City and Tulsa, I picked up some fast food and returned to the hotel room. I did not witness anyone following me. I immediately turned on the 24-hour news station to see if I could see and hear the whole news story about the fugitive from Houston Texas. Waiting until the start of the hour, the story finally aired.

Warren Smithson, dressed in a dark blue suit, called a press conference earlier that morning, about an hour after I raced out of the apartment building and the FBI raided my apartment.

"We have evidence that someone has 'hacked' our organ recipient web site and database. This database is an extremely important database that I developed for all patients needing a new organ in order to survive their illnesses. Our investigation has led us to a suspect who currently resides in Houston. His name is Ben White and this is a recent picture. The FBI is currently looking for White.

"I cannot tell you how damaging it would be to have patient information leak out to the public. The patients are likely to suffer more that they already have. It would be devastating."

Actually, I had not "hacked" into the web site. Someone gave me an ID and password so that I could get into the database whenever I wanted. In addition, I would be willing to bet that Smithson had no idea what actually happened to his patients.

The story only lasted about one minute and buried itself in the other more important news of the day. While questioning how this information would effect the transaction that we had scheduled for the next day, the cell phone rang. "Ben. You all right?" Karen's compassionate voice was apparent.

"You saw it?"

"Of course I did."

"I guess that I wasn't as careful as I thought I was. Have you got any idea what they've got on me?"

"Don't know, maybe they are fishing."

"Well, I don't like being a fish," I said

"Where are you?"

"Oh, out and about. Just jetting all over the country. Taking care of this and that. You know I am not going to tell you anyhow. Unseen, unsuspected, inconspicuous is the secret for my success," I answered sarcastically.

"Touché."

"In any case, this fish does not like being in a fishbowl."

"I know the feeling," Karen assured me.

"Do you think this news will screw up our chances with our client tomorrow night?"

"It's hard to say, but it wasn't a very big story. I will check things out during the day tomorrow, and if things don't look good, I'll walk."

"Let's give it a try cause we might have to go underground for a while," I tried to be convincing, knowing that this might be my last chance to supply the needed evidence to Detective Carter affording my immunity from prosecution.

"I'm always underground," Karen answered.

I waited until the next morning to call Detective Carter. After driving for an hour on I-44 towards St. Louis, I stopped for a bathroom break and to call Carter.

"I was wondering when you might find the time to call," he said sarcastically.

"I've been driving."

"Where are you?"

"I'm around."

"Do you need to come in for protection?"

"No, not yet. I'm sure that no one knows where I am."

"Do you think that we are still on for tonight?"

"Well, I talked to Karen last night, and I think that I have convinced her to try. Hopefully the guy in Chicago and the guy in St. Louis didn't see the news report."

"Actually, we only have to worry about your client in Chicago. We have already arranged to put someone in the place of the victim in St. Louis. If Karen is successful with your client in Chicago, we will expect to see her in St. Louis a few hours later. We'll get her."

"Have you talked to the FBI yet?" I asked.

"No! This is my arrest. It is my deal. I'll let them know after it has gone down," Carter answered affirmatively.

"You got any idea what they have on me?"

"No, but I can find out. In the mean time, why don't you head for Omaha? Tomorrow morning we'll talk about placing you somewhere while waiting for the trial."

"Yea. I'll be there."

"The city has a couple places where we have housed witnesses before while they are waiting for the court system to get it all together. We just don't want you to get lost somewhere."

"You mean, you don't want to lose my testimony."

"Right. If you need to call me you can call the station and they will contact me immediately."

Once I returned to the highway, the trip to St. Louis went quickly. Second-guessing whether I really wanted to witness Karen's arrest in St. Louis, I recognized it was the only way to know for sure that they had arrested her and that I would be safe from her retaliation.

I pulled into the West Side of St. Louis, past the I-270 loop and into the downtown area. I turned off the highway into a gas station to fill the tank and to check the address of the current number one on the organ recipient list. I inserted the map CD into the CD ROM drive and waited while it whizzed and whirred. Clicking on "Find an Address", I typed in the exact address. Within a few seconds, the map appeared on the screen with a star identifying the address I selected. It was not far from the gas station.

The map did not indicate that the residence was a house on a busy downtown street, with no places to hide and absolutely no place to park. The houses in the neighborhood were mostly two-story, built in the early 1900's. The houses on the next street over shared an alley that ran along the back of the properties. The traffic prevented me from slowing and the streets did not lend themselves to easily turning around.

Driving down two additional blocks, I parked at a neighborhood convenience store and wandered back past the house on the opposite side of the street. I observed the surroundings as I walked, trying not to appear as if I was. At the victim's house, a sidewalk ran next to the street and one led up to a porch covered in screens. A middle-aged man worked in the front yard two doors down from our victim's house. Another man talked on the pay phone at the end of the street. Both men continually scanned the neighborhood while giving the appearance that they were supposed to be there. They both acknowledged my presence as I entered and exited their fields of view.

Turning back north around the block, I strolled down the alleyway behind the house. In the upstairs window on the back of the house, I spotted a woman staring out towards the alley. When she saw me walking, she moved back away from the window out of view. Another man on the other side of the alley appeared to be working on the engine of a rusted out Chevy.

It was obvious that Detective Carter had the place well staked out. I certainly did not know what Carter had in mind for the nighttime hours, but maybe there were less obvious places to hide at night. If I could spot these officers, I could just imagine how easy it would be for Karen. I hoped she had already been by there to check it out before Carter's team arrived. Continuing through the alley, appearing as if I had no mission, I eventually made it back to the rental car.

Obvious that I would have limited success in watching this arrest go down, I tried to envision what might happen that night. Karen would enter the house, probably from the alley, into the back of the house. The first floor windows were high off the ground, so she probably would enter the house through one of the smaller basement windows. She would ease her way to the bedroom, probably anesthetize the victim first and then inject him with a special undetectable chemical. And then, as she was leaving, the undercover cops would jump out, put the cuffs on her, and ten cop cars would come to a screeching halt in front of the house with lights flashing but sirens turned off.

So, if I knew that was going to happen, why did I even need to be there? I guess, because I thought Karen was good and would elude capture. She was a pro; in a much higher league that Carter and his team of amateurs.

While observing the neighborhood, I searched for possible surveillance opportunities, noticing an old hotel about a block away and at least five stories in height. As I drove into the small parking lot of the hotel, I determined that the top floor rooms might be an excellent location to view the front of the victim's house.

I confidently strolled through the lobby and directly over to the elevators as if I already were a guest of the hotel. The hotel clerk, busily shuffling papers, did not notice my entrance. Once in the elevator, I noticed that the building actually had six floors. I punched the button for the fifth floor. As I walked down the hall past the rooms, I stopped next to the maid's cart parked outside one of the rooms on the East Side of the building.

Through the open door and then through the hotel room's window, I quickly viewed the victim's house, partially obscured by the roof from the house across the street. Also hidden from view was the front door of the victim's house. Realizing I needed to be on the sixth floor in order to achieve the best view, I took the stairs back down to the first floor and then exited the hotel through a side door. I walked around the building and re-entered the lobby through the front door.

"I would like a room for the night," I handed the hotel clerk a credit card that I had previously acquired under another name.

"One night only?"

"Yes. In addition, I would like the room on the sixth floor. On the opposite side of the hotel."

The clerk looked up, amazed that I would have such a specific request.

"I like to sleep in and don't want the sun to wake me up at sunrise."

"Hey, no problem. If we've got the room, you've got it."

"Smoking or non-smoking?"

"Either."

"Room 613. Up the elevator and then turn left. Check out time is noon, so don't sleep in too late," she added.

The window in room 613 extended across the width of the room. Through the trees and over the roofs, I could see the victim's house, part of the street in front, the front door, and a narrow strip between houses where a bit of the alley was visible.

With help from the hotel clerk, I located a discount department store where I purchased a hundred-dollar pair of binoculars. Returning to the hotel, I checked out my new purchase and was pleasantly pleased with the results. Hoping that the results would be equally as impressive after the sun set, I placed the binoculars aside.

Dragging the side chair over to the window, I opened a beer, and positioned the fried chicken I bought out on the table. I scanned my field of view with the binoculars. The man working in his yard two houses down was still there, on his hands and knees, apparently pulling the same weeds over and over again. The other man at the corner was still using the public telephone, appearing uncomfortable for standing so long.

The transaction in Chicago, scheduled for 7:00pm, should have already gone down. If it had been successful, Karen would undoubtedly be on her way to St. Louis. The flight would take less than an hour. Securing and rental car and the ride from the airport would project her arrival at the victim's house by midnight. The earliest she could possibly make it would be 10:30pm.

I lied on the bed and set the alarm for 10:00pm.

twenty-four

Drifting in and out of sleep for a couple hours, I repeatedly cracked my eyes just enough to view the hotel alarm clock on the nightstand. At ten, I rose and shuffled over to the window. Darkness filled my field of view however the lights from the street lit the front of the victim's house. Only the first floor front room on the left side had a light on. I scanned the street but could no longer locate the man doing the gardening or the man on the corner at the public phone.

It was still early, so I took a shower in order to be fully awake when the arrest went down. I still did not expect Karen until a couple hours later.

Eleven o-clock came and then midnight. Still no Karen. Patiently waiting, I remained at the window with my glasses focused primarily on the front door and second on the alley behind the house. The traffic on the road in front diminished to one or two cars per minute. The otherwise busy street was now absent of any police cars or emergency vehicles.

At two o'clock, I began to doubt that Karen would show up. Curiosity overcame me. Knowing that Carter was somewhere in the area, I dialed the number for the Omaha Police Department and asked them to get a message to Carter as soon as possible. I gave out the number of the hotel, not wishing to relinquish my cell phone number. Ten minutes went by and I received a call from Carter.

"This is Carter."

"Karen hasn't shown up has she?" I asked with obvious anger in my voice.

"No, not yet."

"Do you know if she made the connection in Chicago?"

"Yea. She showed up and then she gave us the slip. I don't know if she made it to the airport or if she is driving."

"She won't drive it."

"How do you know?"

"I know Karen. She probably showed up in St. Louis, saw your undercover guys and decided to walk."

"You came here to St. Louis?" Carter asked after a few seconds where he obviously whispered something to one of his staff members.

"Yes, and it was rather obvious that you had the place staked out."

"She may still show up. In any case, I need to see you right away," Carter said.

"Why?"

"Because I just got word from the boss to bring you in. You know, for your protection."

Detecting a distinctive tone in Carter's voice, it occurred to me that once they had the hotel telephone number, they could quickly identify where I was staying. Laying the phone on the bed while Carter continued to talk, I immediately snatched my belongings and dashed quickly to the stairs and then out the side door to the hotel. Speeding out the back of the parking lot, I witnessed a police car race up to the front lobby. I did not look back.

The objective of my trip to St. Louis went unfulfilled. Taking to the side streets that eventually linked up to the expressway, I navigated myself out of town. This new situation forced me to run. Run from Karen, run from the FBI and after the failed homicide setup, run from the Omaha Police Department as well.

With the apparent advantage that no one knew what I was driving or where I was going, I rationalized that this advantage too would soon be short-lived. The situation that started out well controlled by me, suddenly spun out of control. With significant limitations on returning to Omaha, Houston, or Beaufort, I needed to find a safe place. I decided to take I-55 South, driving until I was satisfied I was not being followed.

Since I had no connection with Memphis, I believed that no one would be looking for me there. I was convinced that once the police interrogated the hotel clerk, they would know that I had shaved the beard and colored my hair. It would not be long before all law enforcement agencies had a computer-enhanced picture of my face.

I checked into a low class downtown hotel that probably rented more often by the hour instead of the night. Somehow, feeling safer at that hotel than I did anywhere else, I used my time to catch up on my research.

Viewing an update on the previous story about me, I failed to identify anything high key. After receiving several calls on my cell phone and not answering them, I decided to switch it off. I ordered food and had it delivered to the hotel for a couple days until the "cooped-up" feeling overcame me. Whether it was safer to stay at the hotel or leave, I knew that I had to get out.

The Omaha Police Department web site had my name mentioned under a list for arrest warrants. The crime listed was witness flight and conspiracy to commit murder. I still could not find anything about me at all on the FBI site.

Following the Mississippi River down to I-10, the logistics forced me into a decision that I was not yet prepared to make. Should I turn left to go back to Beaufort and the East coast, or should I turn right and go back towards Houston. I really saw no future in either location, so I was at a loss of where to go. I pulled the rental car into a rest area, parked it and let my head fall back against the headrest. I tried to use logic to help me decide. Finally, I thought about what Karen might do in this same situation.

Deciding to turn right; I recognized the West as a vast area to get lost, far away from Karen, the police, the FBI and the Health & Human Services Division of the federal government.

For the first time, I contemplated leaving the country for a while, wondering whether it would be safer any place else. I considered Venezuela, based on my short visit, wondering if I could easily escape there. Somehow, reinforced by negative news reports, Venezuela did not sound very safe either. It was too close to

Colombia. The next thing that came to mind was the old American standard from the movies. Mexico!

As soon as Mexico came to mind, I remembered what Karen had said. "In case anything happens, don't try to contact me. Just meet me at Rancho Hidalgo. It is safe there and no one will bother us." It took me several miles to remember the name of the town that Karen's Mexican getaway was close to, and several more miles to reconstruct the route that she told me to take. Something had definitely "happened" so I wondered if it was worth a shot. This situation might be exactly what Karen had in mind.

My only reservation with Karen's place was that she might have discovered that I had the goods on her and had contacted the police. But how could she? I had been careful. But, was I careful enough? Detective Carter's team was easy for me to detect. Did Karen associate their presence with me? If I went to Rancho Hidalgo, would she find me there and kill me? I had no other alternative. Maybe I could drive down and check it out before I actually committed myself.

As I approached Houston that evening, I considered the possibility of retrieving my car from the apartment parking garage. Knowing that the rental car agencies forbid people to take their cars across the border, it may raise a flag if I tried such a stunt. It was ten minutes to six, so I quickly called Charles at the apartment building hoping he had not already gone home.

"Charles, this is Ben White."

"Yes Mr. White. How are you?"

"I've been better. Has there been any more surveillance cars across the street?"

"Yes sir. There is one there now and has been ever since you left."

"Too bad, I wanted to try and get my car."

"I wouldn't try it sir."

"No, I guess not," I said.

"Mr. White?"

"Yes Charles."

"I want you to know that I don't believe the things that people are saying about you."

"Well thank you Charles. I appreciate your support."

"And Mr. White?"

"Yes."

"If you had another set of car keys in your apartment, I could let myself in and then drive your car someplace for you to pick up."

"You would do that?"

"Of course, Sir."

"I've just passed the beltway on I-10 going west. Why don't I meet you at the horse track parking lot and then you can drive my rental car back to the apartment and just leave it somewhere. The keys to the BMW are on the nightstand in the bedroom."

"I'll be there in about 20 minutes. And, I will take care of the rental car. Don't worry," Charles reported proudly.

"Charles, you have been a real friend."

The horse track parking lot was filling up for the evening's races and if Charles had arrived first, I hoped he would find a conspicuous spot close to the entrance. Charles was waiting for me when I turned into the parking lot. We made the exchange in an empty section of the parking lot and without him knowing it, I slipped a couple hundred-dollar bills into his pocket.

"And another thing, Mr. White."

"Yes."

"Something is up with Ms. Brooks."

"The apartment manager?"

"Yes sir."

"Why do you say that?" I asked.

"Two days ago, she met a lady in the lobby and the two of them went back to her office. I saw the elevator stop on the third floor."

"Why is that so unusual?"

"Fifteen minutes after the lady left the building, Ms. Brooks started grilling me about you, Mr. White."

"What did this lady look like?"

"She was about 5 feet 9 inches, short reddish hair, very fit, dressed in black pants and black sweater, and quite attractive."

"What did you tell Ms. Brooks?"

"I told her about the visits from the FBI and that I didn't know anything else."

With the added information supplied by Charles, I assumed that Karen must have been looking for me as well. She had to be quite desperate to allow another potential witness see her face. Undoubtedly, Ms. Brooks was highly paid for the information she provided.

I felt a little more reassured, surrounded by the luxury, quietness, and power of the BMW. The tinted side windows would not allow others to see inside the car. Charles sped off in the rental out of the parking lot heading east. I went west. I witnessed his departure in the rearview mirror and nodded my head in appreciation of his extraordinary customer service.

Within five minutes after my farewell to Charles, I again noticed a black SUV traveling in my lane, several car lengths back. Unsure of the driver's intentions, I decided to find out. I slowed to 55 and waited for the car behind me to pass. After passing, I changed lanes and accelerated past two cars in front of me. I concentrated on the rearview mirror waiting to see the next move from the driver of the black SUV.

Within a few seconds, I witnessed the black SUV changing lanes and passing the same cars that I had moments before. I slowed again and moved over into the right lane. The SUV slowed and moved over to the right as well allowing one car between us. As I tapped the brakes further, the buffer car between my car and the SUV decided to pull out and pass me.

The black SUV followed suit and before long, there was another car between our two vehicles. With one last test, I moved to the left lane, sped up to 80 miles per hour and remained at that speed for a couple miles. Once I was clear of all of the other slow moving traffic, I noticed the SUV approaching at a high rate of speed, rather obvious that I was on to his surveillance.

I realized that I needed to lose this guy before I reached San Antonio and made the turn towards the border. I passed a highway sign indicating an exit for another highway in two miles. The highway changed from two to three lanes. An eighteen-wheeler carrying steel rods strained at 70 miles per hour a few cars ahead of me.

I sped up to 75 miles per hour, passed the car in front of me and then pulled up alongside the truck in the middle lane. The black SUV made a similar move but several car lengths behind me. Another exit sign went by indicating one mile to the exit. I increased my speed to 80 and moved in front of the truck, out of view of the SUV. The black SUV moved up in the center lane, however still behind the 18-wheeler.

With the exit clearly in view, I slowed down to 55 miles per hour and almost immediately, the truck switched on his left turn signal. This forced the black SUV to switch to the far left lane. I gauged my speed to coincide with the truck, and then slipped off onto the exit while the black SUV passed the truck on his left. As the exit descended towards the underpass, my BMW was completely obscured by the 18-wheeler and the bridge structure. I witnessed the bright red glow of the SUV's brake lights as he passed the truck and moved over to the right lane.

I pulled off onto the other highway, parked my car behind a gas station, and waited. About ten minutes later, I witnessed the same black SUV driving back and forth around the intersection of the two highways obviously looking for my BMW. I waited for a few more minutes after the surveillance vehicle continued north then returned to I-10 and my trip to the border.

With at least six hours of driving before arriving at the Mexican border, I remembered that Karen instructed me to arrive at shift change in the morning, avoiding problems at the crossing. Driving until midnight, I stopped just north of McAllen Texas to catch a few hours of much needed sleep. Every thought that crept into my head that evening supported my decision to get out of the country.

Back on the road at 5:00am the next morning, I found a 24-hour grocery store. I stocked up on bottled water and groceries that I did not need to cook, anticipating the unexpected in an unknown Mexican location. Turning onto highway 83 heading West toward Rio Grande City, I scanned the road signs for Bridge Street. Bridge Street was the main street that crossed the Rio Grande into Mexico and I was amazed that it was merely an inconspicuous two-lane road.

Not seeing the Rio Grande before, except of course in movies, I expected to see an expansive river cutting deep into the countryside almost impossible to cross. Instead, the mighty Rio Grande existed, almost unnoticeable. In the middle of nowhere a couple of small buildings scattered about, with one connected to a bridge that crossed the 100-foot expanse of slow moving Rio Grande.

In the distance, across the bridge and down the road, another building maybe half a mile away, obviously housed the Mexican authorities. A dilapidated sign in the foreground identified the Camargo Bridge. I stopped at the only gas station outside the border crossing with the main guard building and the gate in plain view.

No vehicles traveled across the bridge to the United States and none lined up to leave. The sun was low in the east sky and by the looks of their uniforms, two guards had been there all night and the other two were just starting their shift. From the gas station, I heard the laughter from their conversations.

Not as worried about the Mexican guards, I had concern that either Detective Carter or the FBI would have all of the border stations on the American side notified that I might cross into Mexico. The gas tank now full and after a few more minutes of witnessing the behavior of the guards, I decided to make my move.

As I pulled up into the single lane with multiple signs and painted instructions, two guards broke away from their conversation and approached the car. I rolled down the window.

"Could I see your passport?" spoke the taller guard with the nametag "Anderson" pinned to his pocket.

"Sure."

"Where are you heading today?"

"La Coma."

"Been there before?"

"No sir."

"Business or pleasure?"

"Vacation," I answered.

"How long will you be there?"

"A week."

"Could you pop the trunk?" the guard asked as he started to inspect the contents of the front and back seats through my open window.

"Nice car. Can you lower the window in the back?"

"Sure. Thanks."

"Where do you live?"

"Houston now. I'm actually from South Carolina."

"What brings you out to Texas?"

"Work."

"What kind of work do you do, Mr. White?"

"I'm a recruiter. A head-hunter." Having used this answer so many times before, I almost believed it to be true. I was convinced that my delivery portrayed confidence.

"You don't have many things with you for a week's vacation."

"I plan to buy some clothes in La Coma."

"Wait here."

Through the building window, I observed the guard as he walked back into the office. Another guard picked up a piece of paper and pointed at it. Then they both looked up at me. Anderson shook his head no and returned to the car. A shrill started at my lower back and traveled to my shoulders as I anticipated my demise.

"Have a good time. Just don't recruit any illegal immigrants and try to bring them back with you," he laughed as he handed the passport back to me.

The gate lifted and I drove slowly across the bridge towards the Mexican guard building on the other side wondering when or if I would ever return to my home. I watched as the guard named Anderson walked back into the building and picked up the phone. Everything those days made me paranoid.

"Good Morning, Senor," was the greeting. "Welcome to Meheco."

The Mexican guard went through the same ritual with identical questions that I managed to answer without a hitch. Had I made it? Was this all there was to it? Did this mean that I would not be arrested and tried for all of the murders? Wouldn't someone come looking for me in Mexico? Well, at least it would be a new adventure and although I had not admitted it to myself, I reveled in each accomplishment.

A few hundred feet past the Mexican guard building the road teed into another two-lane road. The sign at the junction read Matamoras with an arrow to the left and Piedras Negras to the right. I turned left and followed the road as it snaked its way next to the Rio Grande for twenty or thirty miles.

Surprisingly, Mexico looked a lot like Texas, except that there were more people walking instead of riding. The number of trees diminished the farther I traveled away from the river. Scrub brush and short bushes dotted the sandy fields.

I turned right at the sign for San Fernando and concluded that La Coma must be too small to warrant any road signs. I abided by the highway signs for "97" as they led south through small villages and over moderate hills. Having set my trip odometer at zero while I was waiting at the border, I continued to check it while it slowly grew to 147 miles, exactly how I had memorized the directions from Karen.

I braked as I entered a small sleepy settlement with no more than ten to twenty buildings. The fading blue paint on a concrete block shop spelling out the town's name became my only indication that I had arrived in La Coma. A family of local Mexicans loaded into the back of an old pickup truck passed me as I reset the trip set on my dashboard. An old man with a wide brim straw hat sat motionless in a chair outside the door of what appeared to be a small diner. His eyes followed me as my BMW, now brushed with the dust of the Mexican plains, slowly integrated his hometown.

The trip out of town closely resembled the trip in. As the village of La Coma disappeared in the rear view mirror, the odometer turned over two miles and a small dirt road heading back east began to appear in front of me. The terrain rose from the flat by highway 97 to a gradual slope up a small mountain towards the East. The dirt road gradually rose up the incline until it became too steep and reverted to switchbacks. A cloud of dust trailed the BMW for several hundred feet until it settled back to the road.

Three quarters of the way up the mountain, a freshly painted small block guard shack barricaded the driveway. A wooden sign hung suspended between posts above the driveway displaying the name "Rancho Hidalgo". An air conditioner buzzed as drops of condensation fell precipitously to the ground. A shiny barbwire topped ten-foot fence traversed in each direction from the guard shack and a video camera was perched on a pole several feet above the fence. The BMW came to a stop in front of a tall guard dressed in pressed khakis. He appeared to be American.

He alternately glanced between the picture that he held in his hand and me in the car. He repeated this action several times and finally strolled over to my window. I started to speak but the guard interrupted me.

"We've been expecting you, Mr. White."

"You have?"

"Yes of course. Mr. White, if you would kindly continue up this road to the main house, Leslie will meet you there."

"O . . . kay. Thanks."

This was not at all what I had expected. Why the guard, the fence and the barbwire? Were they trying to keep people out or trying to keep people in? If Karen had all of these people on staff, she must have made a lot of money. At that point, with no place else to go and no one else to trust, I could not turn back. Maybe it would be all right. At least they were expecting me and I was being treated like a guest.

A few hundred yards further up the paved driveway, a house appeared. With red-tiled roof and adobe looking exterior, this large single story structure sat at the very crest of the mountain with excellent views in all directions. An attractive woman waited cheerfully for me at the front door.

As I exited the car, I glanced back down the mountain and spotted the guard shack, the dirt road and highway 97 as it intersected the village of La Coma. Several trees, no more than 20 feet in height surrounded the house giving me the feeling that this house had not been there for more than a couple years.

"Buenos Diaz, Senor White," the woman replied laughing at her poor pronunciation.

"Good morning."

"We have been expecting you," the middle-aged, also American looking, woman explained.

"I'm surprised," I admitted as we entered the finely detailed foyer.

"Welcome to Rancho Hidalgo. Come in and relax. Would you like a drink? A beer? A soda? Lemonade?" I recognized a Midwest accent.

"Yea, a beer would be great."

"Heineken, is that right?" Leslie asked.

Was this place too good to be true?

"Let me show you around."

The gathering room, located in the center of the house, decorated with colorful leather furniture, opened up through large glass doors to a large swimming pool. The panoramic view from the living room and pool area was breathtaking. Off to the sides of the gathering area in each direction were individual wings with large bedrooms, all with terrific views across the countryside. The oversized kitchen contained professional stainless steel appliances as well as pots and pans large enough for feeding many guests.

"This is your room," Leslie explained, strolling down one of the wings. "Feel free to take a nap, go for a swim, do what you want. Just don't leave the area."

I am sure I must have appeared as if I just woke up after my first night in jail and she sensed my uneasiness.

"You know, it might not be safe out there," she explained. "We're just thinking about your safety. Actually, we have everything here that you might need or want. And if we don't have it, we can get it."

"I'm sure you are right."

Maybe this place would be okay for a while. I continued to carefully inspect the premises, half anticipating Karen to step out and greet me at any moment. I remembered what she had said about there being time for us later. Was this the later that she talked about? In spite of all that had gone down in the past several weeks, I hoped it was.

"I'll be around if you need me," Leslie walked back towards the living area.

Admiring the view through the glass door down the mountain to the Gulf of Mexico, I decided to retrieve some items from my car. Returning through the foyer, I noticed Leslie in the kitchen.

"Do you have any snacks to munch on?" I asked.

"I think so."

Leslie opened one cupboard door where dishes behind it filled the shelves. She then opened another where the glasses were. Finally, in the pantry cupboard she found some peanuts. It seemed rather unusual she did not seem to know the location of the food in the kitchen. Did they have someone else who came in and cooked the food? Was Leslie new to the house? My mind was busy processing all of my many questions.

In a dresser drawer in the bedroom, I found a pair of swimming trunks and a towel, so I ventured outside to try the pool. The Gulf of Mexico spread as far as the eye could see past the pool to the

East. The mountain trailed off much steeper on the East Side. A small building on the water's edge appeared minuscule from the mountain's summit.

Leslie called me in for dinner at about 6:00pm, serving tamales, rice and beans. I invited her to stay and eat with me, but she insisted on retiring to her room. Clearing the dishes from the table, I loaded the dishwasher. Surprised when I did not find any dirty pots and pans, I concluded that Leslie brought in the dinner from town. After a long and stressful day and with the sun already set in the western sky, I decided to go to my room.

With the house wired with data ports for connecting a PC, I tried one of the jacks in the bedroom. One last time, I checked the organ recipient list for liver transplants. Much to my continued amazement, the judge, our latest client from Chicago became number one on the kidney list. Was Karen able to get to the victim in St. Louis after Detective Carter pulled his group out? Or did she actually get to the victim before Carter got to St. Louis? Had I blown my one and only chance to get out from under involvement with the murders? Disgusted with my success in implicating Karen, I decided to shut down the laptop and go to bed.

The extremely quiet house seemed void of any of the normal creaks and groans. Unable to adjust to the peace and quiet, I opened the bedroom door. Shortly after returning to bed, I fell asleep.

Apparently, a heavy thud woke me from an immersed sleep. Squinting at the clock on the nightstand, I made out 3:15am. Donning my shorts and a tee shirt, I quietly tiptoed out into the hall and down to the gathering area, which was dark except for a light above the kitchen sink. I recognized more muffled sounds seemingly from the hall where Leslie retired to after dinner. All of the doors to the bedrooms were open and the rooms were empty. The tousled blanket in the bedroom at the end of the hall led me to believe it was Leslie's room. The bathroom off Leslie's room was also empty.

I switched on the hall light. The locked door just off the living area further spurred my curiosity. A security panel and small keyboard next to the doorknob indicated importance. Placing my ear against the door, I could distinguish more muffled sounds some distance away. I checked the doorknob again but it would not turn.

Examining the keypad, I thought about combinations, passwords, and of course Karen. It occurred to me that maybe I could figure out the combination of keystrokes to get the door open. However, this being Karen's place, she would not make it obvious. Unaware of the number of keys to push, I tried to reason the answer.

Walking away a couple times, I came back each time and stared ponderously at the keypad. Remembering what Karen had told me about web developers who used spouse's names or numbers for passwords, I realized that I did not know that much about Karen. She never mentioned a husband. She talked about her parents, but not much.

Nine keys, one through nine. I tried to remember everything that Karen told me but nothing jumped out as being significant enough. Walking to the phone in the kitchen, I studied the pushbuttons. Eight of the 12 buttons had letters printed on them as well. I tried to consider a combination that contained numbers and/or letters. I remembered that the combination on my garage door opener from my old house contained four numbers and it was a nine-button keypad, so I further focused on four characters.

When I considered the fact that the combination could contain both numbers and letters, an overwhelming possibility entered my head. Starwars. In a possibly weak moment, Karen told me that she loved the Starwars movies. I thought about the two droid characters named R2D2 and C3PO from the original movie. Returning to the telephone to work out the combination, I reconciled R2D2 would be 7232. I punched the numbers into the keypad and checked the doorknob. Still locked. My self-esteem began to falter.

I walked back to the telephone. C3PO becomes 2376. I punched the numbers into the keypad. I heard a discernable click. Pulling cautiously on the handle, the door swung free of the lock and the plunger made a loud click. Amazed at the skills I had developed over the previous several months, I continued my pursuit, cognizant of the potential danger I might find behind a locked door with a combination lock.

A short landing directly in front of me led to steps that went down into a lighted room. In my bare feet, I walked quietly without creating any noise. Slowly, vigilantly descending the steps, I checked my available field of view continuously as I went.

At the bottom of the steps, a long hallway extended far beyond the footprint of the house above. Doors and windows along the hallway allowed an easy inspection of the contents of the rooms. Sneaking silently down the corridor, I peered through the first window identifying electronic consoles covering the length of the room. Red and green lights flickered while the television monitors displayed several nighttime scenes around the perimeter of the grounds, including the guard shack and the road leading up the mountain.

Across the hall, a room filled with armaments including rifles, pistols, and what looked like miniature missile launchers, occupied the shelves on one side of the room while the other side contained shelves of chemicals in jars and bottles. A solitary table with two folding chairs in yet another room reminded me of the interrogation rooms in some of the old movies I had seen.

At the end of the hallway, the light faded away into black and as I crept closer to distinguish what I could, I spotted a small four passenger vehicle mounted on rails that disappeared into a darkened tunnel. The ten-foot diameter tunnel was fashioned from a corrugated steel tube. After I acclimated myself to the general direction of the basement and tunnel, I realized that the tunnel went off to the East, down the mountain in the direction of the Gulf of Mexico.

As I reached for the switch on the electrical box located on the wall near the tunnel, I heard a shuffling noise behind me. As I turned my head in response, a hand grasping a washcloth pressed tightly over my mouth, nose and eyes, the arm shielding my view of the assailant. My struggles to fight the invasion steadily weakened and within seconds, I lost consciousness.

twenty-five

Rejoining the conscious world, I experienced severe pain. My throbbing head dwarfed the intense pain in my arms, hands, and chest. Opening my eyes slowly, one at a time, I avoided the harsh bright light and additional pain to the head. It took several seconds for my eyes to re-focus on the surroundings.

My eyes scanned the room and my position in it. I was in the middle of the room with only a table and two chairs that I had passed earlier. Attempting to move, the tightly wrapped gray duct tape around my arms and the back of the chair kept me immobile. My hands, pulled tight around the back of the chair, also secured by duct tape caused significant pain on my stretched skin. Tape also covered my mouth. The less I moved, the less painful for me.

Slowly turning my head to the right, I acknowledged the guard and Leslie from the previous day, conscious, but taped to two other chairs. They also had their mouths taped shut. The unsettling fear in their eyes as they watched me awaken made me even more uneasy.

I should have been more afraid than I was. Maybe my brain wouldn't allow pain and worry at the same time. What bothered me more than anything else was the lack of control. I had run out of options. I guessed that my decision to escape to Rancho Hidalgo had been the wrong one. I tried to stretch my arms without success.

Karen entered the room from the hallway, which took me by surprise and telegraphed my anxiety. "Glad to see you are still with us. I was a little worried about you for a while. I bet you are glad you shaved the beard and mustache now aren't you?" Karen tugged slightly at one end of the tape across my mouth and then ripped it off in one quick motion.

I winced in pain further aggravating my throbbing head, "what's going on here, Karen?" my throat and lungs burned with my first words, yet I was surprisingly calm. I feared for my life but I did not reveal it.

Karen noticed my pain in speaking, "I guess I was a little aggressive in the application of the sulfuric ether. I didn't want to kill you, just put you out until I could gain some control."

Karen looked at me as if it were just another day in her life. She was not excited or sympathetic or angry or pleased.

"Who are these guys, Ben?" she nodded in the direction of the other two prisoners.

"I thought they belonged to you. They were here when I got here."

"No, my staff are all Mexicans. You don't happen to know where they might be, do you? Oh, by the way, you can be sure these two aren't talking. At least not yet."

"Why am I all taped up here?"

"Well Ben, I think it is time that I am completely honest with you."

"You've been lying?" I asked naively, obviously knowing the answer.

"Just business Ben," she said in a soft peaceful tone. "Nevertheless, I do want to thank you for your help. You have followed my directions exactly, and with the exception of being a little too inquisitive about my actions, you have been very predictable."

"So, what's going to happen now?"

"Oh, just sit back Ben. Relax. I'm going to tell you everything. You still have a major role to play in this project."

"Could I get some water?"

"Sure, I'll be right back. Don't go anywhere."

"Right," I said sarcastically. I turned towards Leslie and the guard who were wide-eyed and listening intently to every word. "You guys cops?" I whispered in their direction, trying to fit the pieces of the puzzle together. They both nodded in the affirmative.

"I don't suppose that you have a plan?" They both shook their heads indicating not.

I allowed the water that Karen provided to linger as long as possible in my throat to sooth the irritation and deaden some of the pain, and waited for Karen's explanation.

"I watched you for about a month before I first met you at the bar in Beaufort. I was looking for someone who was out of work and would be desperate for money. I needed someone who had some skills: computer, people, salesmanship, and negotiation. Your previous company trained you well on these skills.

"I also knew that your weakness is women, so I played on that as much as I could. Getting the ideas put into your head about the organ lists was quite innovative, if I do say so myself. I needed to place many individuals in your path along the way. I also needed to convince a couple of AP writers to publish articles about organ donation.

"Getting you into the same bar in Venezuela with the Director of the organ program was probably the most difficult. Thankfully you enjoy going to the bar. However, at first, I needed to get Angelo to take a vacation, and then I needed an excuse to get you there. It is surprising that once you add girls into the equation, you men are very predictable. I also knew that I needed to get you out of Beaufort, where you were comfortably too conservative.

"Then, there was the guy in the alley in New Orleans."

I sat perplexed until I remembered about the strange occurrence with the man in the alley. "He worked for you?"

"Yea. It probably was not worth the money that I spent to place him there. Based on his feedback, you were pretty drunk. Then, there was the man that you met at the bar in Germany. I didn't know how much convincing it would take to get you to go along with the program. I guess some of it was overkill."

"I can't believe that all of that was going on without me knowing it. You didn't mention the escort in Houston."

"What escort?"

"You didn't send an escort to spy on me?"

"No."

"Sounds like we've both been duped," I said.

"I think that you're testing me. There was no escort," Karen commanded with slight uncertainty.

"Whatever you say Karen. What now?"

"Well Ben, the rest is just money in the bank as they say."

"You killed all of those people. Didn't you?" I asked, redirecting her testimony, wanting her to finally admit to me that she murdered for money.

"Ben, it's a job. It's what I was trained to do."

"What about Jackie Armstrong from Omaha?"

"Just a name on a list, Ben. Your list, by the way."

"What about the twin twelve-year-old boys that also burned to death in that car?"

"You should have picked a different victim," Karen explained as if she was void of any compassion. "Just collateral damage."

"How can you be so callous? I asked.

"Practice, I'm afraid."

"How did you kill that man in St. Louis?"

"Actually, he was the first victim that I eliminated before I collected the money from our client in Chicago. The police were nice enough to get him out of the house and into a hotel where it was easier to kill him. Why?"

"Just curious, I knew it was a little risky."

"What happened to the video tapes in the gas station in Jacksonville where you killed Harold Nelson?"

"I could have made a mistake there. Again, getting a little sloppy. When I got to the airport, I replayed the scene from the gas station in my head and remembered the cameras above the counter and the door in the gas station. I called a colleague to go in and remove the tapes from the machine before the ambulance got there. You would have got caught as well, you know."

"How did you know that I was there?" I asked, disappointed that she caught me without my knowing it.

"Sometimes I have someone tail me to see if I am followed. I hired a private detective in Naples and he spotted you a few miles out of Naples," Karen admitted. "He called me before I got to Tampa, I located your rental car behind me."

"Why didn't you try to lose me?"

"You had to find out sometime. It was all part of the plan."

"So, how does the rest of the plan play out for me?" I asked, disguising my failed attempts at freeing my hands from the tape.

"The FBI is looking for you for the murder of several people. We have placed some evidence, including some items with your fingerprints, at each of the murder sites. All of the evidence points to you, Ben. We have produced a suicide note on your behalf for your laptop which will be found next to your body back in Houston." Karen removed a floppy disk from her pocket and waved it at me.

"And just exactly how will I commit suicide?" the longer I kept talking, the longer I would live, I thought.

"You will first inject yourself with Versed, a nice little sedative. Then you will inject a lethal solution of potassium chloride with a muscle relaxant. Within two minutes, you will look a lot like the other victims did. The police will find you, the suicide note, and the two empty syringes at your side, all with your fingerprints on them, of course. Actually, it will be another Karen assisted suicide. However, the FBI will have their suspect. Case closed. Unfortunately you won't be able to donate your organs because they won't find you in time." Karen moved her hand, hidden behind her back, revealing a syringe filled with a clear liquid.

I pulled with all my might against the tape but could not move enough to make a difference. Karen had a serious look on her face and for the first time, the situation made me sick to my stomach. I rocked back in the chair until it tipped backward, slamming my head onto the concrete floor, twisting my wrists behind me.

"Don't fight this one Ben, it's the good drug."

Before I could right myself, I felt the piercing sting of a needle in the meat of my shoulder. Karen tipped the chair back up while my attempts to fight back slowed. She placed the piece of duct tape back across my mouth.

Waiting helplessly, I anticipated the feel of the chemical in my body. Before my surgery a few years earlier, the anesthesiologist used Versed before the anesthesia. I remembered the feeling of slowly losing consciousness and then nothing until I awoke in recovery. Surprisingly, I did not get the same feeling with Karen's injection. I closed my eyes, dropped my chin to my chest, and waited.

"Morning Karen," came a new voice, one that I vaguely recognized. I cracked my eyes slightly to see Warren Smithson entering the room behind Karen. She jerked her head around towards him. I closed my eyes quickly before Smithson or Karen had a chance to witness my actions.

"Warren! What the hell are you doing here?" Karen exclaimed, surprised at first, then disgusted.

"Just wanted to make sure that you are taking care of business."

"Haven't I taken care of all of your dirty business?" I could sense significant distrust and hatred in the dialogue between the two of them. I continued to listen without moving.

"Everything going per the plan?"

"I'm just about to give Ben the second dose."

"Did you get the money?" Smithson asked.

"What money?"

"The money that was supposed to be in the Swiss bank account. It's not there."

"What are you talking about? I just checked it last week," Karen said.

"Well, it is not there now. Are you sure you didn't take it?"

"What the hell do I want with money?"

"I guess it is a little late to ask old Ben here about it now. That's okay, I'll get it somehow. Now, don't let me stop you. We have to get the body back to Houston by midnight," he said.

I tried to put the pieces together in my head. How was Warren Smithson involved with Karen? And, how did he know about Rancho Hidalgo? I started to link Karen's Washington trip to Smithson, the Department of Health and Human Services and then put together a possible connection between the two of them. I continued to listen intently, wondering when I would begin to feel the effects of the drug.

Karen snapped back, "I'll take care of my end. You take care of yours. In addition, the next time you want people killed, don't call me. I don't like you. If it were not for General Gates, I would have never taken this assignment. I can't believe that he would think of you as a friend."

"It is not always the friendship thing, Karen. Sometimes we do favors so we get favors," Smithson commented in obvious control of the situation.

As I remained stoic in the chair, I again felt the sting of a needle and the infusion of liquid building under my skin and the feel of Karen's hand squeezing my arm. Waiting helplessly for some indication that my body would methodically shut down, my head started to spin.

In the minute that followed, my mind took me on a journey through my past that was so vivid and sharp. I raced through my childhood years, my early relationships with girls, and my college days. The journey slowed as I began to consider my work life and the 25 years I spent working for the company. It occurred to me that I would not be sitting taped to a chair waiting for chemicals to stop my heart, if it had not been for the company abandoning me after so many years of service. It had been the only life that I knew, and without it, I was lost.

I was so lost, I could not believe I took the path that I finally ended up taking. Karen was right. It was my list that she acted upon when she murdered those people. I was responsible. How did I ever get to this point in my life? I really deserved to die.

However, as I waited and listened to the conversation, nothing physically happened to me. I still felt the throbbing headache from the ether, the pain from the duct tape as it stretched the hair on my arms and chest, but I was still alive. It had to have been more than the two minutes that Karen described. I could still hear Warren Smithson and Karen arguing about whom of the two was smarter. I eased my eyelids open just far enough to test my senses.

"Who are these other guys?" Warren gestured to the other two taped to the chairs watching the drama unfold.

"I still don't know. I will get them to talk before I leave. Or, I'll probably just kill them." I heard the scuffing of chairs on the concrete floor as Leslie and the guard apparently tried to free themselves from the tape.

"We might as well take care of all of the loose ends," Warren explained confidently as he unholstered a black 9 mm pistol from behind his back and pointed it directly at Karen. The slide mechanism rolled back with a click as a bullet entered the chamber.

My heart started to race. I was horrified of guns. You do not stand a chance with guns. It is easy to make a mistake and then someone is dead. You cannot wish the bullet back into the gun.

"This wasn't part of the plan, Warren. If you do this, you know General Gates is not going to let you live. I am a professional. I executed your plan exactly as you laid it out. I helped you set up this guy to take the fall, and then I eliminated him. This is not a money issue, and you know that I cannot talk to anybody about it. Why would you consider taking this action?"

"Because I have a plan to continue with the program. There is much more money to be made. And, you are not in my plan. I am working with someone else now. They are going to take my lists and eliminate the ones that can't pay."

"You know Gates is relentless. He won't stop until he kills you," Karen explained with a little vulnerability in her voice.

I expected Karen to again gain control of the situation. Maybe she was waiting for just the right moment. Instead, shielded from Smithson's view, she reached into her front pants pocket and retrieved a small capsule which she slipped into her mouth.

Smithson spoke first, "Gates is dead. I took care of that problem yesterday. You are the remaining loose end. Now tell me again Karen, who did you say is going to kill me?"

"Maybe I will," a different, deeper voice entered the room coming from the doorway. I again cracked my eyes slightly as Karen and Warren looked up in total surprise. Detective Carter slid through the door and placed a pistol to the head of Warren Smithson. My head again started spinning. How did Carter know about Mexico? I was sure that I never told him. I remained quiet, keeping my eyelids barely open and then closing them periodically to avoid attention.

"Who the hell are you?" Smithson tensed slightly with the feel of cold steel against his neck.

"Detective Neil Carter, Omaha Police Department."

"You are a little out of your jurisdiction, aren't you Detective?"

"Maybe. You're under arrest Director Smithson. I would strongly suggest that you hand over the weapon, before I scatter your brains over these walls."

"Do you know who you are dealing with?"

"As a matter of fact, I do. And so will many others. I have recorded everything you have said and done since you both have been here. In fact, I used your equipment. Karen, will you reach over there and pull that tape off Ben? That has got to be uncomfortable."

"But, he's dead."

"No he's not. He is just resting. I replaced the potassium chloride and the Versed with saline before you got here. I also installed some microphones and the video camera over there, so I could record all of the helpful information that I will need to prosecute both of you. By the way Karen, you're also under arrest."

I raised my eyelids slightly. Karen slowly reached down toward her right calf. An echoing gunshot went off and Karen fell to the floor holding her right leg around the ankle. A small pistol caromed across the floor against the wall. I must have jumped an inch in my chair.

"Jesus!" Karen cried out in pain, blood soaking the black pants.

"The tape," Carter repeated.

Smithson released his grip on the pistol and Carter quickly snatched it from him. As soon as I felt the tugging on the tape, I allowed my body to awaken, releasing myself from the chair. As soon as I was free, slowly regaining my equilibrium, I drudged over to free the other two prisoners.

"These guys work for you, Carter?" I asked, hoping I finally understood what was going on.

"Sure do."

Smithson chimed in, "you know, you are in Mexico. How are you going to get us back to the States to put us in jail?"

"Actually, the same way that you got here. We are going to take this rail car down through the mountain and then get onto your boat. In fact, your boat captain has already been taken into custody."

Once Leslie and the guard were free, they quickly retrieved the cuffs from Carter, rolled the new prisoners arms behind them and tightened the cuffs on them. Leslie retrieved the small pistol and pointed it at their captives.

Behind Detective Carter, a well-dressed Mexican police officer entered the room and everyone froze. At least three other police officers stood in the hallway, pistols drawn. Karen and Smithson turned to witness the latest arrivals.

"You see Carter, we own the police down here in this town," Smithson claimed confidently. "Who are you?" Smithson nodded to the uniformed officer with apparent control of the situation.

"Subcommandante Pedro Hernandez. I serve the town of LaComa," he announced in broken English.

My hopes for survival from a few moments earlier were again in jeopardy. I watched old movies about the Mexican Police easily influenced by the American dollar. Although free from the restraints and out of medical danger, I again feared for my life. And now, there were more guns.

"Pedro, you arrived just in time. Get these cuffs off of me and arrest these guys," Smithson motioned towards Carter.

Carter kept his pistol pressed against Smithson's neck, "you may have paid these guys off, but I doubt that you own them. You see, when I told Subcommandante Hernandez about the Rachael Sanchez murder in San Antonio, he advised me that he knows the Sanchez family and he became extremely upset. He was more than willing to cooperate and give us all the help we need to get you back to the United States," Carter explained confident of the pending arrest. "And another thing. You assholes killed my sister. I would have chased you for the rest of my life. It will be my pleasure to watch both of you fry or rot in prison waiting to die. It's what you deserve."

Smithson's head and shoulders hung with the realization that his opportunities for escape had vanished. Karen's expression remained emotionless.

As Carter, his team, and the Mexican police started to escort the two new prisoners toward the hallway, Karen looked back at me in disgust, consequently with the same piercing stare delivered in the Sand Dollar Bar in Beaufort. She rolled a capsule forward in her mouth, holding it in her teeth and biting down until it exploded into her mouth.

"I underestimated you, Ben."

"This the end of the line for you, Karen?" I asked, with the confidence that knowledge made available.

"Maybe so. Just remember, I have made some good friends along the way, not just enemies. We'll see what happens."

"It sounds like one of those good friends is now dead and another is on his way to prison," I added appropriately and she nodded in acknowledgement.

"One more piece of advice?" Karen asked as she reached the hallway.

"Sure, what's that?"

"If I were you, I'd find another way to make a living," she laughed and left the room almost as violently as when we first met.

"Just remember, Karen, this was your party, not mine," I yelled out the door as she left the room. I found it odd that in spite of all that had happened, I still felt sorry for Karen and tried to envision a set of circumstances where we could be together, however not in prison.

I watched as Carter pushed and shoved Karen and Warren Smithson into the rail car. Subcommandante Hernandez buckled the two of them in and then he and another policeman sat across from them with their pistols drawn and pointed at the two prisoners.

Karen cast one final glimpse back towards me, groaned in an obvious burst of pain, and bent over at the waist unable to hold herself upright.

"What the hell is going on now?" Carter complained.

"I think she took something," I said. "She had a capsule in her mouth."

"How long ago?" Carter asked.

"Only a few minutes."

Karen convulsed for the next several minutes until her body finally stopped twitching and fell silent. Carter stepped into the rail car, forced his finger into her mouth, and started to shove it as far down her throat as he could. It was too late. Carter placed two fingers on her neck, searching for a heartbeat, but could not find one.

"Shit," Carter said in disgust. "Get her the hell out of here."

The car descended out of sight.

Carter and his two associates returned to the interrogation room. "Let's tie up some loose ends," Carter said after a long sigh. "Are you all right?"

"I am now," I said. "Man, was I glad to see you. How did you know about Rancho Hidalgo?"

"Actually, it was something that Warren Smithson said when I interviewed him on the phone about a month ago."

"You knew about Warren Smithson?"

"Let's just say that there were too many unexplained deaths all related to the national organ donor program. Director Smithson tried to blow me off. He said that he was late for a flight to Mexico and we could talk more when he got back. When I asked him if it was business or pleasure, he said business.

"I couldn't understand what business he could possibly have in Mexico, so I had him followed. He flew to Houston and then took a boat. Docked right down the hill from us. We asked a lot of questions around here and finally hooked up with the Mexican Police. That's when we found out about a woman that matched Karen's descriptions. When you called me and puked out your story, I put it all together. As soon as you disappeared from St. Louis, I thought that you would probably end up here."

"Wow. Good work. What happens now?" I asked, finally accepting the fact that I would live.

"As soon as I saw Karen and Smithson show up, I contacted the FBI. They will be waiting for the boat at Corpus Christi and I guess now they will take Karen to the morgue and Smithson into custody there. They are sending a special escort for you. You are going to be the key federal witness on this case.

"Since we still don't know if there are any other government or non-government people involved in this conspiracy, the FBI wants to keep you under wraps, outside the country. At least for a few weeks."

"Where?"

"Actually, I think that it's probably your choice, at least within reason. It has to be a discreet location and not easily accessible."

"I think that I know just the place," I said, unable to wipe the grin off my face.

twenty-six

Aconstant twelve knot breeze only slightly cooled the near-equator sun five miles off the coast of Venezuela. Surrounded by palms and the beauty of several young half-clothed women, I relaxed, knowing that the horrors of jail time or death had eluded me.

My new bodyguard, FBI Special Agent Green, lay on a lounge chair no more than ten feet from me. The girls had surrounded him as well, however he was always in reach of his nine-millimeter pistol.

One of the hotel staff approached and whispered something to Agent Green. "I've got a phone call. I'll be right back," Agent Green said and threw his backpack over his shoulder.

When he returned a few minutes later, he sat on the end of my lounge chair.

"What's up?" I asked.

"It seems that the folks in Corpus Christi have lost Karen's body."

"What are you talking about?"

"I mean, she was stored in one of those stainless steel drawers in the morgue, and when they went to transfer her body to Washington, her body was not there."

"Oh my God!" I said, my mind racing with possibilities.

"What's the matter?" Agent Green asked.

"She's alive!"

"What?"

"Don't you see? She took a pill that made her seem like she was dead. Everyone just assumed that she killed herself because she didn't want to be taken alive. She was . . . is an expert in that chemical stuff."

"Oh shit. Don't worry, we'll catch her again."

"No you won't. She'll be so far underground, you'll never find her."

"She'll probably come looking for you," Green said, "and then we'll get her."

"No she won't. She doesn't care about me. She already tried to kill me because it was part of the plan. She's not a vengeful person."

The sun buried itself behind a thick puffy cloud and all I could think about was when I would see Karen again.

THE END

Printed in the United States
1472500005B/25-27

9 781593 300890